Dutch Threat
a murder mystery

Josh Pachter

Genius
Book Publishing

Milwaukee Wisconsin USA

This book is dedicated with love to my daughter,
Rebecca K. Jones.
She writes novels, too, and you should read them!
Start with her Goldie Award finalist, *Steadying the Ark*.

Author's Note

All of the characters and incidents described in this book are fictional, and any resemblance to actual people and events is purely coincidental.

The Begijnhof, however, is a real place, and its history and appearance as presented here are accurate. The next time you're in Amsterdam, you should definitely pay it a visit!

A Map of the Begijnhof

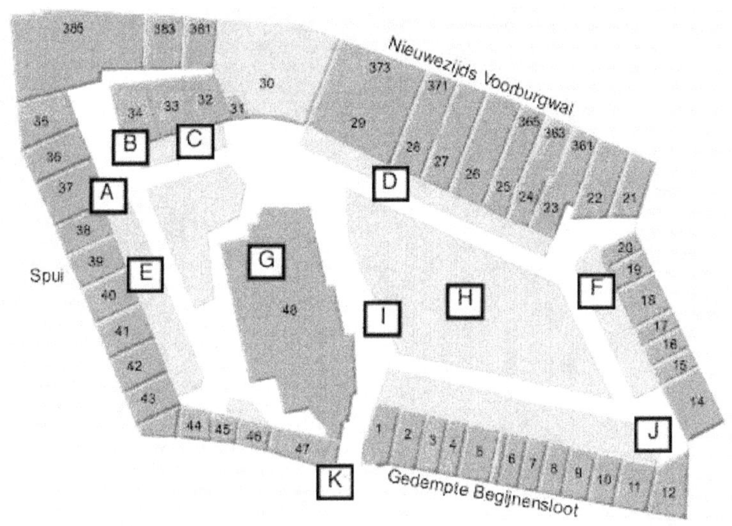

Key

A = the "time tunnel" entrance from the Spui

B = #34 ("het houten huys")

C = #33 (Ans Moen's house)

D = #28 (Ellen Antonie's house)

E = #40 (Rietje de Klerk's house)

F = #19 (Lien Boonstra's house)

G = the English Reformed Church

H = the bleaching green

I = Cornelia Arents' gravestone

J = the passageway to the Amsterdams Historisch Museum

K = the Begijnsteeg door

Dutch Threat

PROLOGUE

"I had to kill them," the murderer said. "Don't you see? I didn't have any choice. And now, I'm afraid, *you* have left me without a choice."

The knife was pointing right at my heart, as threatening as any gun would have been. The killer was maybe six feet away from me, but it would take only a second to cover that distance.

One second to close the gap between us, two seconds to raise the knife and plunge it into my chest, perhaps another half a minute for the blade to do its damage.

Which left me, I figured, with about thirty-three seconds left to live.

And that's when I saw her, standing in the hallway, her head cocked prettily to one side and a question shining in her eyes. What the hell, I wondered, was *she* doing there?

And, much more to the point, what the hell would she do next?

CHAPTER 1

While a pair of coeds I didn't recognize were passing out the test papers, I printed my name and "History 527: Absolutism and Democracy" and "Final Exam" on the cover of my University of Michigan blue book and flipped it open. The eager beavers in the front rows were already scribbling, but I was hidden away at the back of the lecture hall, by the doors, and it'd be a couple minutes yet before the girls worked their way up to my neck of the woods. So I just sat there, watching Prof Harriman give us the eye and trying to convince myself not to worry.

Most of the professors under whom I've had the always dubious pleasure of taking classes have brought in elite squads of jackbooted grad-student storm troopers to proctor their exams for them, so they can hang out in their offices and sip sherry while we proles sweat through the mental obstacle courses they dream up for us. But not old D.S. Harriman. No, he was there himself, in living blubber, all three hundred pounds of him. I think he really liked to watch us suffer.

He had on his usual size eighty-seven dingy-gray suit—he only took about an eighty-four, but he apparently subscribed to the "buy baggy" theory, so people would think he was busy losing weight—and, because it was final-exam day and a special occasion, his other tie, the one without the gravy stain. His bald head gleamed moistly under the fluorescent lighting of the hall, and his jowls quivered with delight as the first howls of anguish began to rise from the peanut gallery.

Rumor has it that the "D.S." in D.S. Harriman stands for something Biblical, something along the lines of David Samuel, but we history majors know better.

De Sade, that's the nasty old bastard's name. Has to be.

A pile of test booklets reached me from the right, and I took one and passed the rest on.

Here goes nothing, I thought, and, if I hadn't lapsed into fairly cynical agnosticism God knows how many moons ago, I'd've crossed myself and sent up a couple of Hail Marys, just to play it safe. As it was, I sighed out about six quarts of breath I hadn't noticed myself holding and turned hopefully to the first question:

Discuss democratic theory—as evidenced in the writings of Jean Boudin, the Vindiciae Contra Tyrannos and Doleman's Conference— to demonstrate that democracy is a justification for revolution.

"Mr. Farmer!" Harriman's bloated baritone boomed at me from his lair at the front of the room. "You are not, I trust, discussing this examination with your neighbor?"

"No, sir!" I winced at the accusation. "Just talking to myself, sir. Sorry."

This was practically the truth. I had not been chatting with the dweeb beside me when Prof Harriman's eagle eye had spotted my lips aflutter—perish the thought! But I hadn't really been talking to myself, either.

If the truth be told, I'd been petitioning my Maker, and what I'd been saying was, "Our Father Who art in Heaven, hallowed be Thy Name…."

♋

"Time, ladies and gentlemen."

I dropped my pen and looked up in shock. Was it two hours already? Must be: my hand felt like I'd had a hungry lab rat gnawing on it for about fifteen minutes longer than forever.

And there in the distance stood Harriman, fat and rumpled and grinning from ear to ear. You'd swear the university paid him a bonus for every one of us he flunked.

He wasn't flunking *this* boy, though, not this semester. The exam had been a mother, true, but I'd been ready for it. B- at the absolute worst, and, if the moon was in my seventh house and the Good Lord had been paying attention to my prayers, I might've even pulled myself an ace.

The damn thing was over with, at any rate, my final final of the term, so I was now officially on summer vacation, with nothing whatsoever scheduled until classes started up again in September—three lazy, hazy, crazy months in the future.

As they so aptly put it during the darkest days of the Reign of Terror: *Lassez les bon temps roulez!*

I tucked the test booklet inside my blue book, doubled-checked that my name was on the cover, and passed the package toward the aisle.

Stood up and flexed my fingers, hoping to work some circulation back into my traumatized hand.

Wished a happy summer to a couple people I knew and started moving in the direction of the doors.

When a deep voice bellowed: "Mr. Farmer!"

Curse!

I turned back and looked down at him, and he was standing there on the stage, thirty rows before and below me, crooking his Jimmy Dean sausage of a finger with a fat smile on his face and an evil glint in his beady little eyes.

Now what?

He couldn't think I'd really been asking someone for help, back at the beginning of the exam period, could he? No way: he didn't know me well, but he knew me better than that. Well, then, what did the lousy glitter-dome want?

One way to find out, eh?

I fought against the current of escapees, feeling like one of those sockeye salmon heading towards the happy spawning grounds—only they've gotta struggle upstream, don't they, and I (hopefully not metaphorically, hopefully not for the third time) was going down.

By the time I reached him, I'd scared myself half to death. He thought he'd seen me cheating, the blankety-blanked jerk, and he was going to rip up my paper and make me take an alternate exam—or worse.

"Professor Harriman," I said in a rush, as soon as I got within range, "I—"

But he wasn't sticking around for explanations. He turned away from me without a word and lumbered up the steps and out the back door of the lecture hall. I caught it as it was swinging shut behind him, and caught *him* as he was stuffing himself into the elevator.

We rode up to the fifth floor in silence; by then, I'd figured maybe I'd better keep my big mouth shut until I found out for sure what the old sleazeball was up to.

He waddled down the long corridor to his office, and from the looks of him you'd swear he'd completely forgotten about me.

But he did hold the door open with a corny show of Old World politeness, and as he shooed me on in ahead of him I wondered if I would ever again emerge to greet the light of day.

Harriman's "office" was actually just a miserable six-by-eight cubicle with a single grimy window overlooking the Quad and the other three walls lined floor-to-ceiling with bookshelves—except for the doorway, of course. There was a battered metal desk heaped high with books and papers, and a motheaten armchair with spots on it, and what had to be the original Underwood typewriter collecting dust on a wobbly stand placed at right angles to the desk. A faintly moldy smell hung in the air, and I wasn't sure if it came from the books or the furniture—or, at these close quarters, from good old D.S. Harriman himself.

He waved me to the armchair cordially enough, and planted himself in the wide swivel number behind his desk, selected a pipe from a rack of them and stuck it between his teeth without lighting it.

"Coffee?" he suggested.

I scanned the office curiously. There was no percolator, there were no cups. As far as I knew, the only machine in the building was back down on the ground floor, near the elevator we'd come up in.

"Ah, no, thanks," I said.

"Mmmm. So you're all through for the summer, then, is that correct, Mr. Farmer?" I could hear him straining to sound like a human being, and I'll tell you what: if that was his best shot, I was not impressed.

"Yes, sir," I said, holding up my end of the conversation.

"Do you have plans for your holiday?"

"Plans? Well, no, sir, not exactly. I'll go home, I guess, see the folks. Pick up a job, maybe, if I can find something where I don't have to say, 'Do you want fries with that?' forty times an hour."

He leaned forward and dumped his elbows on his desk and his chins on his palms. "And your young lady? Patricia, I believe her name is?"

How the hell did he know about Pat? She was an undergrad—in English, no less—and she wouldn't set foot in the history department if Hurricane Andrew came to town and Angell Hall had the only storm cellar on campus. Who *was* this guy, a latter-day J. Edgar Hoover?

"We, ah, we came to a parting of the ways about three weeks ago, sir. I guess your sources are a little late with the information."

Harriman lifted one eyebrow—a neat trick, I grant him that—and rumbled, real man-to-man-like, "Problems?"

I sighed. "No, well, not exactly *problems*, Professor. We tried living together for a while, only she didn't want to give up smoking and I didn't want to give up breathing, that's all, so we—"

"—came to a parting of the ways. I see."

"More or less, sir."

He sat there sucking on his unlit pipe, and one of those sickly silences fell upon us, like in "Casey at the Bat."

"Uh, Professor Harriman?" I said at last.

He straightened up, then, and put away the pipe. "I'm a nonsmoker myself, these days." He smiled ruefully, if the grotesque shape his lips twisted themselves into could be called a rueful smile. "Doctor's orders, I'm afraid. But I don't suppose you are particularly interested in the state of my heart and lungs. Let me tell you why I asked you up here this afternoon."

I waited for it.

"I am working on a book, Mr. Farmer—my *eighth* book, in point of fact. I have been fortunate enough to be able to conduct the lion's share of my research right here at our Graduate Library." (The U of M's Ann Arbor campus has three main libraries—the Graduate, the specialized Business Administration Library, and the

Undergraduate—generally referred to as the GLib, the BAd, and the UGLi. Bah-dump-bump.) "There is, however, some intensive work to be done on site. The project will take approximately two weeks, and I had originally planned to handle it myself, this summer. But another of my perhaps too-cautious doctor's orders prohibits me from undertaking the significant amount of travelling which would be required. I am therefore interested in contracting you, Mr. Farmer, to complete my research for me. I will pay all of your expenses, of course, plus a stipend of, shall we say, five hundred dollars per week? I would require you to leave immediately, if these terms are acceptable to you—or as quickly as is feasible, if there are arrangements you must make before departing. You will be back in a fortnight, having earned the sum of one thousand dollars, which I shall pay to you in cash, half in advance, and you will still have the bulk of the summer at your disposal."

I'd like to be able to report that I took this all in my stride, but the truth is that I may have goggled just a bit. (Okay, a *lot*, maybe.) It took me a minute or two to mull the thing over, and, when I had it fairly well mulled, the only reply I could think of was, "Why me, Professor? I mean, it's not like I'm the only one of your students with a head for research."

He smiled again—or at least that's what I think it was supposed to be. "Certainly not, my boy. Anatomically speaking, that is. But your head, I've noticed, has for my purposes the distinct advantage of housing a *brain* of sorts."

A compliment from D.S. Harriman! Would wonders ever cease?

"Does my proposal appeal to you, Mr. Farmer?"

"Uh, yeah, well, sure." I didn't much like agreeing with this overbearing doodah about *anything*, but, hey, he was talking a thousand American crabcakes here. "Only, well, where is it you want me to go?"

"To a place called the Begijnhof, in Amsterdam."

I swallowed. "Amsterdam? You mean like upstate New York, right? Near Schenectady?"

"Don't be absurd," he said impatiently. "You know perfectly well that my field is *European* history. I mean, like, the Netherlands, Mr. Farmer. Near Belgium."

Somehow he didn't seem quite as repulsive as usual when he said it.

CHAPTER 2

A lemon-drop sun was working its way up a pale-blue sky when my plane left Detroit Metro for New York at eleven the next Saturday morning. By the time I caught my connecting flight at JFK, it was midafternoon and still sunny.

When we touched down at Schiphol Airport, eight hours and a six-hour time difference later, it was Sunday, and, on that side of the Atlantic, slate-gray clouds threatened rain and the sun was having trouble clearing customs.

I haven't had occasion to do an awful lot of flying in my twenty-four years, so I haven't seen an awful lot of airports. Those I *have* seen have all been pretty interchangeably awful, and Schiphol was no exception. Newsstands, duty-free shops, hordes of faceless people lugging luggage and renting Hertzes and either joyously greeting or tearfully taking their leave of the hordes of faceless friends and relatives who were either joyeously picking them up or tearfully dropping them off. It wasn't until I'd collected my first entry stamp in my brand-new rush-job passport and rescued my backpack from the carousel and walked beneath the green "Nothing to Declare" sign and out of the terminal that it really sank in that I was in Holland, in Europe, on soil more foreign than Canada for the very first time in my life.

Prof Harriman—that dear old benevolent soul, towards whom I was now feeling positively chummy—had made all kinds of arrangements for me, and all I had to do was find my way into town and check into my hotel.

There were a half-dozen off-white taxis pulled up outside the terminal doors, and I tapped meekly on the driver's window of the first one in line.

The old-timer behind the wheel looked up from his newspaper and rolled down his window a couple inches. "*Ja?*"

"Ah, 'scuse me. Do you, ah, do you speak English?"

He made a face. "No, young man. I do not speak English," he said, in perfect English. "This is Holland. I'm a Dutchman. I speak Dutch."

I ducked my head, embarrassed. "Right, stupid question, sorry. Listen, I need a ride downtown. Are you…?"

He narrowed his eyes at my backpack. "You can better go with the KLM bus," he said. "It's only four Euro to the Central Station."

Ever the practically bankrupt college student, I came this close to asking him to point me to the bus stop—but then I remembered D.S. Harriman was picking up the tab. "Well, okay," I said doubtfully, "if you don't want the fare…."

He straightened up at that, tossed his paper on the passenger seat beside him and reached around to open the back door for me. "Of *course* I want the fare! You need a ride, I have a taxi. Jump in, young man, jump in!"

I shrugged out of my pack and swung it inside and climbed in after it.

"Where downtown?" the old guy said, as he dropped the cab into gear and pulled away from the curb.

The good professor had booked me a room at a place his travel agent had recommended, just a couple minutes' walk from where I was going to be doing his research for him. "The Nova Hotel," I said, "in the"—I dug a slip of paper with the address on it out of my wallet—"oh, God, in the Nee-you-weh—"

"Nieuwezijds Voorburgwal." The cabbie nodded his approval. "Very nice. Not the Hilton, but nice. If you can afford there, you can afford the twenty Euro for the ride."

Twenty Euros sounded like a hell of a lot, but I did a rough mental calculation and figured it came out to about seventeen bucks, less than I'd paid in New York for the transfer from LaGuardia to JFK.

"Does everybody here speak English?" I leaned forward and rested my elbows on the back of the driver's seat, so I could talk with the cabbie over the hum of his engine and the steady drone of highway noise.

He lifted his right hand from the wheel and made one of those *comme çi comme ça* gestures. "Now, *everybody*? Not really. The kids don't get it on school until they're a year of thirteen, and the farmers don't bother with it much, but city people know at least a little, sometimes a lot. We're a small country, only fourteen million of us. The rest of the world's not going to bother learning our little *kikker* language, so we have to learn everyone else's if we want to be able to communicate. English, French, German—we can overcharge you in *lots* of languages."

After maybe fifteen minutes of flat farmland, we hit the outskirts of town. The old guy pointed out an enormous white convention center—the RAI, he called it, as proudly as if he'd built it himself—and later on the twin brick-and-slate steeples of the ornate Victorian Rijksmuseum. Then we started twisting through a maze of one-way streets, past endless rows of narrow four- and five-story brick houses with oddly shaped gables, over stubby bridges spanning a confusion of intersecting green canals. "A thousand bridges," the cabbie told me, "a hundred kilometers of canals. Some people call Amsterdam the Venice of the North, but they're wrong. Actually, Venice is the Amsterdam of the South."

At last we pulled up in front of the hotel, across the street from the Scientology and Dianetics Center and next door to the Tingel Tangel Jazz Club. Half the signs in Amsterdam seemed to be in English, which was about half comforting and half disappointing. I paid off the driver with an orange banknote with a picture of a stone archway on one side and a Roman bridge on the other, so much nicer than our drab American greenbacks that I almost hated to part with it. He made change, and I tipped some of it back to him and asked for a receipt. He scribbled out something about as legible as my doctor's prescriptions, waved goodbye and tootled off, and I shouldered my pack and clambered down a couple stone steps to the Nova's semi-sunken glass front door.

They were expecting me, and the receptionist checked me in and sent me on up in the elevator to a small but cozy room on the third floor. It had a single bed with a decent mattress and a reading light clipped to the headboard. It had a sink and towels and a closet and a miniscule bathroom with a toilet that if I sat on it my knees pressed up against the beige tiled wall. It had a drain set into the bathroom floor and a showerhead at eye level, which I guess was what the girl at the desk must have meant when she assured me there was a *douche* in the room. It wasn't much, room 214—that "2" threw me for a minute, until I remembered reading somewhere that what we Americans call the first floor the Europeans call the ground floor, and what we call the second floor they call the first floor, and so on, so that my third-floor quarters were on the European second floor, whence 214—but it was clean and it was quiet and Professor Harriman was paying for it, so I'd be delighted to call it Home Sweet Home for the next two weeks.

I probably ought to have been jetlagged and groggy from all the travelling, but I was too excited about being in Amsterdam to sleep, so I unpacked my pack and cleaned up a little and caught the elevator back down to the lobby.

I'd read up on the city during the week it'd taken to push through my passport, and there was plenty I wanted to see, but I figured it wouldn't hurt to start out by getting my bearings, so I'd be ready to commence work in the morning.

The receptionist told me all I had to do was turn right and follow the tram tracks for a couple minutes, then make a left at the pianos, and I'd see a sign for the Begijnhof on the wall about twenty meters ahead on my left.

So I went out the door and up the steps and to my right, and followed the tram tracks past a cluster of little stamp shops on one side and the Amsterdams Historisch Museum on the other. One of the stamp shops, at the corner of Rosmarijnsteeg, was in a building that must have been close to collapse; it had been shored up with five thick logs with the bark still on them, bolted to a wooden platform eighteen inches out from the side of the building at ground level and clamped to the brick wall six feet above my head with rusted iron braces. A bass-ackwards way of doing things, I thought—and yet the results seemed sturdy enough, and a damn sight cheaper than ripping the whole building down and starting over again.

A long yellow streetcar rumbled past, blue sparks spitting from its overhead wires. It stopped briefly to discharge and pick up passengers, and, when it rattled off again, I spotted the piano shop on the corner behind it.

Swinging around the corner, I found myself in a big, bustling square with a street sign telling me it was the Spui—although how that was supposed to be pronounced was completely beyond me. Spwee? Spewie? Spoy?

Whatever it was called, it was a lively place. First thing that caught my eye was the sea of white tables shaded by colorful Cinzano umbrellas spilling out across the sidewalk from a cafe to the east. An assortment of bookstores and restaurants lined the southern and western sides of the square, dominated by a bulky gray Universiteit van Amsterdam building. The Spui's northern boundary, on my left, consisted of a row of ten brick houses, and the tallest of them—five stories of red brick with a dozen white-trimmed windows and a pointed gable—had a stone bas-relief of a tall woman in a flowing white gown above its arched doorway and, off to one side, a blue-and-white sign reading "Begijnhof" with an arrow pointing to the door.

Dis mus' be da place, I concluded. And decided that, as long as I was in the neighborhood, I might as well stop in and introduce myself, if anyone was to home. There was no doorbell, though, and no knocker, and I was debating the advisability of pounding on the tall wooden door with my fists when a sweet old lady wheeling a battered all-white bicycle down the sidewalk stopped just behind me.

"*Moet U d'rin?*" she asked, or at least that's what it sounded like.

"I'm sorry," I said, "I don't speak Dutch. Do you—?"

She flashed me an understanding smile and broke in on me in heavily accented English: "You want to go inside, yes?"

"Yes," I agreed, "but, uh, how do I—?"

"It isn't locked," she said, that last word coming out *lock-Ed*. "You can go ahead in."

"Ah, it isn't locked," I nodded. "But I—"

"No, it's good, don't worry. Go in, go in!"

I looked around the square, and no one was paying any attention to us. Shrugging, I tried the iron door handle. The old lady was right: it wasn't lock-Ed.

"Go in," she said again, pushing air away from her with gnarled white hands.

It didn't feel right, walking into somebody's house unannounced like that, but the old girl didn't seem especially senile, so I figured, *hey, maybe she's the cook or something, just do it.*

Had I But Known at that moment what would happen over the next couple days, would I have gone on in, I wonder—or would I have turned around and collected my pack and caught the next plane back to the land of the free and the home of the Whopper?

Doesn't matter, really. I *didn't* know what was waiting for me within the walls of the Begijnhof, so I pushed open the wooden door and set foot into Wonderland.

CHAPTER 3

I found myself in a dim-lit narrow hallway with a ceiling of intersecting Moorish domes of yellow brick and white stone trimmed with green. The walls were brick, the floor was stone inlaid with geometric mosaics. It was all straight out of the Arabian Nights, and if Ali Baba had popped out of a jar of olive oil and stolen my watch, I wouldn't have been the least bit surprised.

Behind me, the lady with the bicycle coughed meaningfully, and I excuse-me'd and stepped aside to let her pass. At the far end of the hall, maybe thirty feet from where I stood, she went down six stone steps and through a second doorway, wheeling her bike down a grooved wooden ramp which had obviously been set there for that purpose. I trooped along after her, down the steps and through the inner doorway and into the Seventeenth Century.

The street noise, the traffic, the rumble of the trams, the crowds—all gone. I was in a broad and peaceful courtyard, and I swear it was like that narrow hallway had carried me three centuries into the past. The old lady was pushing her bicycle along a dusty brick path lined with a dozen lovely two- and three- and four-story brick houses on the left, and open on the right for about fifty yards, at which point it curved right and lost itself behind a pretty country church with a tall brick bell tower capped with slate.

Dazed by the unexpected quiet, I started down the path. There was a bulky metal sculpture of a nun or something on my right, and up ahead I could see the dame with the bicycle turning in at a gate in the green picket fence which separated the tiny front yards of the houses from the path, and another old lady peered down at me suspiciously from the second-floor window of the second house on my left, but otherwise I seemed to have the entire place to myself.

Past the church, I could see that the path looped around a kite-shaped plot of grass, past more houses and the long blank north wall of the church and back to join up with itself again. In the center of the loop, the grassy area was raised slightly above ground level and set off by a low brick wall; the grass was sprinkled with clusters of white and purple narcissus and shaded by five tall chestnut trees.

So this, then, was the Begijnhof, this oasis of calm in the heart of the frantic city. This was where I'd be spending my working hours for the next couple weeks.

Not bad, m'lad!

I'd only planned on looking in for a minute and saying a quick hello, but now that I was here, I couldn't think of any particular reason for leaving. It was such a relaxing spot, such an idyllic place to be. Even the weather was cooperating: the clouds had lifted, and the sun was out at last. With what I'm sure must have been a sappy sort of grin on my face, I strolled around the perimeter of the central green, soaking up the atmosphere and the fresh scent of the summer flowers.

The houses were beautiful, each with its little garden and its gauzy white curtains behind white-trimmed windows. Most of them had their doors on the ground floor, but a couple had stone stairways with dark green railings leading up a flight to the main entrance, with a plainer door set into the side of the steps below. Bottom door for servants, I guessed, and top door for the family and its guests. Pretty fancy.

One of the houses wore an inscription carved into a thick granite lintel between its second- and third-floor windows: *INIVRIA VLCISENDA OBLIVIONE.* Latin, I conjectured, which was all Greek to me. Nearby, another house was dated: *Anno 1660.*

There was bird song in the air, and an occasional squawking and flap of wings. Pigeons waddled around with their beaks to the pathway, searching for lunch. If I listened carefully, I could just make out the passing of trams in the distance, but, except for that, it might as well have *been* Anno 1660.

Back in front of the church after my circuit of the green, I looked the joint over more closely—and discovered to my surprise that the ornate letters etched into the stone above its wooden double doors read *English Reformed Church, Anno 1607.*

Even in *here,* even the *church* was in English!

A bronze plaque to the left of the doors confirmed it: "This church is believed to have been built in 1392," it said, in English capitals. "In 1607 it was given to English-speaking Presbyterians living in Amsterdam. It was enlarged in 1665. An extensive restoration was completed in 1975. An international Christian community continues to worship here."

I tried the doors, and they were unlock-Ed. There was a wood-paneled vestibule, and then the church proper, one large white room with an arched ceiling and blue support beams. The walls, incongruously, were lined with flags; I recognized the Stars and Stripes, the Maple Leaf, and the Union Jack, but there were half a dozen others I didn't know. Above the altar and beneath a stained-glass window showing a group of Pilgrims praying around the mainmast of a ship at sea was painted, in English, the legend, "Create in me a clean heart, O God."

There were twenty rows of plain wooden pews flanking an aisle that stretched from where I stood up to the altar, and a man in a lightweight gray suit with a turned-around collar was sidling up and down the narrow spaces between the rows gathering prayerbooks. Sunday services must have let out not long ago.

I'm not usually much of a Boy Scout, so I guess it was the general tranquility of the place that inspired me to do my good deed for the day. The minister was working the right side of the center aisle, so I took the left side and pitched in.

He noticed me then, and flashed me a gracious smile. "That's very kind of you," he called across the wide room.

"My pleasure."

We met up back by the vestibule door, where there was a wooden rack for the prayerbooks. A thicket of organ pipes gleamed proudly from its perch above the doorway.

"The Reverend William Llewellyn Jones, L.L.B., B.D., M.A.," he introduced himself, wiping his right hand on his trousers and holding it out to me, "although most everyone in my 'flock,' such as it is, calls me Reverend Bill."

We shook hands. "I'm John Lewis Farmer," I said, "B.A. and trying to finish my M.A., A.S.A.P. And, back where I come from, most everyone calls me Jack."

"You're from America, then?" Reverend Bill's accent was veddy veddy British. He was in his late thirties, I'd venture, a little shorter than my own six-two, but thin where I'm, well, not thin and light-complected where I'm practically Mediterranean. He had clear brown eyes under fine eyebrows and a shock of sandy hair, a straight nose and a pleasant smile and a small black mole to the side of a weakish chin.

"Sure am," I admitted. "Battle Creek, Michigan, home of Kellogg's Corn Flakes and not a whole heck of a lot else. You're English, right?"

He wagged a chiding finger at me. "Welsh, if you please. There *is* a difference, you know, though not many of you Colonials seem to be aware of it. Is this your first visit to the Begijnhof?"

"Yeah, it is, actually. My first day in Amsterdam, too. First day in Europe, when you get right down to it."

"Your very first day on the Continent, and here you are!" He clapped his thin hands together at chest level and held them that way, beaming all over his pale face as if he'd just been elected Pope, or whatever it is Presbyterians get elected. "My, my. My, my, my! This *is* an honor. Are you on summer holidays, then? Just doing Holland, or is this one of those eleven-countries-in-eight-weeks Grand Tours you Americans seem to enjoy so much? If it's Sunday, this must be Amsterdam, that sort of thing?"

Anyone else and I'd probably have been offended, but Reverend Bill managed to come across as truly friendly, truly interested.

So I told him what I was here for, and he immediately took me by the elbow and steered me back out through the vestibule to the double doors. "If you're here for two weeks," he said, "we'll have buckets of time to chat, but right now I suggest you pop over to the Wooden House and make the acquaintance of Gerrit Rombach. He was here for our little service just now, so I'm quite sure you'll find him in. He's in charge of the archives, you know, and I expect he'll be delighted to meet you."

Gerrit Rombach, that was the man Professor Harriman had told me to see. I didn't much feel like bugging him on a Sunday, but with Reverend Bill so pleased to be able to bring us together I figured I'd at least drop by for a second and let him know I'd arrived.

So I promised the good Rev I'd look him up for a cuppa and ambled back toward the Wooden House. It was the only wooden structure in the Begijnhof—everything else was brick—and the first building I'd passed on my way in, right across from the statue of the nun that'd been one of the first things I'd noticed after emerging from the time tunnel.

What I noticed now was not the metal sculpture, but the flesh-and-blond female heading for the entrance of the place next door to the Wooden House, where the same old lady I'd spotted earlier was still at her post in the second-floor window, looking out at the scene below as if she didn't quite trust it.

The girl I had my eye on was no old lady. Far from it. She was my age, give or take, and about as pretty as a human being can get without the help of an airbrush. She had a soft oval face that didn't need makeup and wasn't wearing any, and sapphire eyes so blue I could feel their color from twenty feet away. Her long silken hair was tied back in a ponytail, and she wore a turquoise scarf salted with silver spangles around her neck and faded jeans over a black leotard which displayed curves that made my fingers tingle.

She saw me looking at her, and I guess she must have read mah mind, because I swear to God I saw her cheeks pinken as she passed through the green picket gateway of number 33 and let herself into the house. She turned around in the doorway and raised a hand and waved at me. Then, smiling, she closed the door behind her.

One flight up, the sainted old soul in the window was glaring at me with what I believe is called a moue of distaste. Actually, make that about a moue and a half. She must have been tuned in to the Farmer brainwaves, too, and I could see she didn't much care for the way I'd been eyeballing her granddaughter. I raised a hand and waved at her, and went next door to the Wooden House whistling "Dixie."

It was really an attractive building, four stories high with the ground floor dressed in white stone behind a shallow garden crowded with two massive rhododendron bushes, and, upstairs, weathered boards stained black and dotted with double tiers of white-framed windows at the second and third floors—I'm talking American here, if it's all the same to you—and a simple triangular gable. Just above the deep-green front door, the words "*het houten huys*" were painted in black Olde English letters, with the three initial lower-case haitches highlighted in red.

I knocked on the door and heard someone bustling around inside. A minute later, it swung open to reveal a middle-aged Munchkin in the doorway. He was a burly gentleman, though short, with deep-set black eyes and graying hair combed across the top of his head in a futile attempt to make it look like he wasn't a candidate for Minoxidil therapy. He was biting his lower lip as he stood there, and it was plain that he was upset about something. "It's Sunday," he said, in English. I felt like I was wearing a sandwich board with "American Tourist!" on it in screaming Day-Glo capitals. "I'm closed today. You'll have to come back another time."

"Mr. Rombach?" He'd been about to shut the door in my face, but he hesitated at the sound of his name. "I'm Jack Farmer, sir. Professor Harriman sent me? From the University of Michigan?"

His troubled face lit up. "Mr. Farmer! Mr. Farmer!" he cried, swinging the door wide and squeezing my hand like he was trying to get water out of it. "*Je komt als geroepen, jongen*! Come in!"

CHAPTER 4

Excitedly pumping my right hand, Rombach pulled me inside what turned out to be a combination office and information center, sat me down at a plain deal table piled with little booklets in a dozen languages, introduced me to his midnight-black cat Dropje with an explanation that the name was Dutch for Licorice, and didn't settle into a chair of his own until he'd brewed a big pot of tea and set a steaming cup in front of me.

"It's nice, isn't it?" he nodded encouragingly, before I'd even taken my first sip.

So I sipped, and it *was* pretty nice at that. Even the smell was nice, rich and fruity, and the taste was delicately sweet, although I hadn't added any sugar to the cup.

"Mango tea," Rombach said, pushing the plate of cookies at my elbow a silly millimeter closer.

I took the hint. The cookies were nice, too. Sort of gingerbready, although not quite. *Speculaas*, according to Rombach, who jumped up again to rummage through a messy old rolltop desk in the far corner of the room. "Dexter called me last week," he muttered, as he pulled out sheaves of papers and ruffled through them and shook his head at them and shoved them back again. "I wrote it down, I know I have it here somewhere."

Dexter?

The reference confused me, but then suddenly I got it.

Glitterdome Harriman was a *Dexter*?

I almost choked on my tea, and, for something to do instead of laughing, I found and opened the English-language version of the Begijnhof's information booklet. Dropje padded over and rubbed against my leg, and I flipped pages with one hand and stroked her deep soft fur with the other.

"The Beguines, or Sisters of St. Begga," I read, "came in 1346 from a village near Amsterdam to found a community in the city, and to be near the site of the Miracle of Amsterdam…."

"*Waar is die verdomte papiertje nou gebleven?*" Rombach huffed.

"The Begijnjof is a treasure-house of seventeenth- and eighteenth-century architecture, for all the well-known types of Amsterdam gables are to be found here: step-gables, neck-gables, clock-gables…."

Clock-gables? Well, frankly, my dear, I didn't give a—

"*Hebbes!*" Rombach announced triumphantly, and he came barreling back to the table with old Dexter Harriman's message clutched in his chunky hands. He laid the slip of paper before me and stabbed a forefinger at it. "Here, look, he said me you would be here on *donderdag*—sorry, on Sursday—but today is already Sunday!"

So that's what all the brouhaha was about. "Yeah, well, we thought at first I'd be coming in on Thursday," I explained, "but it took a few days longer than we expected to get my passport, so we had to change my ticket. I thought Professor Harriman called you to tell you about the delay, but—"

"Ah, I see. I see." He rubbed his chin thoughtfully. "But there has come up a problem, Mr. Farmer, an unexpected somesing. I have been asked to—how do you say it?—address, yes, I have been asked to address a conference at the university in Groningen, in the north of Holland. It's a four-day meeting, it starts tomorrow morning, so I must go there today. I won't be back in Amsterdam until Friday."

Ouch, that *was* a problem. I'd have to ring Dexter—Dexter!—and tell him it'd be most of a week before I'd be able to get started. Of course, if he was willing to spring for the extra expenses, that'd give me a couple days' vacation time before I had to settle down to work. Things could certainly be worse.

"The committee only called me on Tuesday," Rombach was saying. "They had first another speaker planned, but he became—how do you say it?—*hij is ziek geworden*. He became ill, yes, so they asked me to replace him. I sought you would be here on Sursday and we would have time to make arrangements, so I accepted, but then it came Sursday and Friday and Saturday and you didn't arrive, and it was too late for me to cancel from the conference, and—"

"Wait a minute, wait a minute!" I held up my hands. "What's all this got to do with *me?*"

The hassled lines of his face cleared up. "Yes, of course, you don't know it. I want you to come and stay in *het houten huys* while I'm away."

"Stay here? But—"

"I know, I know." He bobbed his head impatiently. "Dexter explained you it's only old ladies who are allowed to live in 't Begijnhof. Even *I* have to have a *woning* outside, in the town."

Actually, Dexter hadn't explained me any such thing. In fact, he hadn't explained me much of *anything*: in his inimitably pompous style, he'd told me he wanted me coming into the place without any preconceived ideas about it. Sounded sort of dopey to me, since I was only here to do historical research, but, hey, he who pays the piper calls the tune, right? As long as Harriman remembered to fork over the second half of my thousand clams, I didn't care *what* he told me or didn't tell me about the living conditions.

"But for five nights it's no problem," Rombach went on. "Upstairs is a little room with 'n bed, sometimes I take a nap in the afternoons if it's not so busy. You can sleep up there, and there's 'n *douche* and a little kitchen in the back. I'll leave all my keys with you, so you can do your work, and when I come again on Friday you can go back in your hotel."

"Well, that's very kind of you, Mr. Rombach," I stammered, "but—but you don't even *know* me."

"Mr. Farmer," he said, tapping the prof's message significantly, "I have known Dexter Harriman for more than twenty years. If he trusts you enough to send you here in his place, then I can trust you, too, I sink."

"Well, I—"

"And someone has to take care of Dropje," he added. "It's impossible to go away for so long and leave her here alone."

"Yeah, well, I—"

He played his trump card. "Dexter is paying your expenses, isn't he? So if you stay here, instead of in the hotel, you can put away the money you're saving in your pocket." He tossed me a conspiratorial wink. "If you don't tell Dexter, I won't."

The crafty little bastard!

"Mr. Rombach," I said, "you just bought yourself a catsitter."

ᙓ

It didn't take me long to repack my pack and check out of the Nova. They made me pay for a night's lodging, although I hadn't spent more than twenty minutes in the room altogether, but they agreed at least that I was entitled to drop by in the morning for breakfast.

I was back at the Wooden House by two thirty, and the first thing Gerrit Rombach wanted to do was run me next door and introduce me to the Wicked Witch of the West. "She's 'n—how do you say it?—an invalid, yes," he said. "She spends most of her time by the window, watching the people come and go. She'll worry if she sees you coming in *het houten huys* after business hours; it's better if we go there for just a few minutes and I explain her you'll be taking care of Dropje for me."

The second-floor window was empty when we knocked at the dark-green door of #33, though, and it was the blonde in the sexy leotard who opened up for us. She had a fat textbook in her hand and a studious frown on her face when she came to the door, but she brightened up some when she saw us. Maybe she had a thing for short, burly, balding gentlemen in their fifties, but I'd like to think it was me who brought the smile to her lips, not Rombach.

They exchanged a few sentences in Dutch, and, listening to her speak that unfamiliar language, I noticed for the first time how musical it could be.

"The sister says Mevrouw Moen is sleeping," mine host translated, "but she will tell her everysing when she wakes up."

So this was the old lady's sister, and not her granddaughter? No *way*, I thought, does that compute: there had to be fifty years' difference in their ages. And, anyway, Rombach had called her *the* sister. Was she supposed to be one of those St. Begga nuns, or what? She didn't look nunnish in that shapely leotard and those tight jeans, but what do I know about European nunsmanship, you know?

"If you'd like to come back later," she said, and the way she tilted her head and let her voice ride up on the penultimate syllable punctuated the sentence with a question mark and turned it into an invitation. Her English, I was happy to hear, was flawless.

"Sure, I'd love to come back later," I nodded. "See you later." I waggled my fingers at her, and she remembered and waggled back and eased the door shut with a sparkle in those luminous sapphire eyes.

"What is she, a nun?" I asked, latching the green picket gate behind us.

"A nun? No, no, she's a nurse, she takes care of Mevrouw Moen. Why do you—? *Ach, ja, natuurlijk!* You don't call them sisters in your country, do you?"

"Uh-uh. We don't let 'em dress like that, either."

He chuckled. "Yes, I've seen it on the American television programs. Your nurses always wear those awful white uniforms with too much *stijfsel*—how do you say it?—too much starch, yes, and those heavy white shoes and white stockings. Terrible, terrible."

Next door at the Wooden House, a stoop-shouldered old feller in worn but neatly mended work clothes was waiting by the front door. He seemed annoyed about something, and the second he saw us he pulled a battered pipe from beneath his bristly gray mustache and commenced to growling. I stood there like a bump on a log while they went at it, and, when Rombach finally had the old codger calmed down, he introduced him as Henk Kleijwegt, the Begijnhof's caretaker and general handyman.

Some tourists had apparently eaten a picnic breakfast smack in the middle of the central green that morning—the bleaching green, he called it—leaving a mess behind, and Kleijwegt was agitating for larger and more numerous "Keep off the Grass" signs in a greater variety of languages. Rombach promised to take care of it as soon as he got back from the north of Holland, and explained that I was going to be in residence for the rest of the week. Kleijwegt didn't seem any happier about that prospect than he'd been about the picnickers.

Back inside *het houten huys*, Rombach spent maybe ninety minutes familiarizing me with his archives, so I'd be able to locate the material I needed, and another quarter of an hour filling me in on Dropje's idiosyncrasies and showing me where her food was stashed. Once all that was taken care of, he handed over a ring of keys, wrote down the phone number of the hotel where he'd be staying, wished me luck, and was gone.

The cat mewled softly when he left us, and it was that sad sound more than anything else that brought home to me how very all-alone I suddenly was. I looked around the room at the masses of books and pamphlets that surrounded me, and it was sobering how empty the place felt without Gerrit Rombach fussing busily amidst the clutter.

Something brushed my leg, and I jumped about a third of a mile in the air—no, wait, make that a half a kilometer.

Dropje.

She miaowed, then arched her back and pressed up close again. A deep-throated purr rolled around inside her. I laid a hand on her side and felt her ribcage vibrate.

"You hungry, baby? Well, listen, it's you and me against the world, here, Licorice. C'mon, I'll fix you some dinner."

I gave her a bowl of munchables and some water, and she dug right in. Watching her gobble, I realized it was well past four and I hadn't had anything but tea and cookies all day, not since the yellow stuff they'd identified as scrambled eggs on the plane this morning. I was beginning to crumble—I mean, except for a couple hours' rack time in the air, I'd been up around the clock—but my stomach was letting me know that it was ready to have some attention paid to it.

What did people *eat* here in Holland, though? And where did they go to get some?

I fished a windbreaker out of my pack, locked up the Wooden House, and set off in search of my first European meal.

I got as far as the inside entrance to the time tunnel, then stopped and turned around and looked back.

Mrs. Moen had not yet returned to her duty station.

Hmm, I thought.

There was no answer when I knocked at #33, though, and I had the unhappy thought that maybe the sister had gone home for the day. But then at last I heard footsteps, and the door swung open and there she was. She'd taken her hair out of the ponytail, and it danced around her shoulders and framed her face in honey.

"Hi," I said. I've always been known as a rather scintillating conversationalist. Keep the girls back home in stitches, I do. "I was just wondering if—"

"Yes, of course, come in!" A mischievous smile played across her lips. "I told Mevrouw Moen you'd be back. She's awake now, and I'm sure she'll be very happy to meet you."

"No, well, you see, I—"

But I was stuttering at her back. I followed her down a hallway and up a narrow flight of stairs and back up the corresponding second-floor hallway to the bedroom at the front of the house.

"I came to see *you*," I whispered, as I edged past her into the room.

"I know," she whispered back, and, though she kept her face quite properly composed, there was laughter in her eyes.

I'd only anticipated finding *one* old woman lurking in the bedroom, but it turned out there were four of them: Mrs. Moen herself was in bed, propped up to a sitting position by about a half-dozen fat pillows, and the lady I'd seen earlier with the white bicycle and two others I didn't know were ranged around her in matching wooden chairs. It was just like the Queen of Hearts and her court, and, the way she was glaring at me, I expected Mrs. Moen to start yelling "Off with his head!" at any moment.

Behind me, my lovely guide murmured a few words of Dutch and withdrew, leaving me to face the music on my own.

CHAPTER 5

Some music.

"The Sounds of Silence," by Simon and Garfunkel and Garfunkel and Garfunkel.

All four of the ladies had delicate little china saucers on their laps, and delicate little china cups on their saucers, and delicate little expressions of distaste on their faces, like I was a particularly virulent strain of virus and they were scared to death they might catch me.

Well, three of them, anyway. The fourth one, the bicycle lady, was actually sort of sweet. She must have been somewhere in her late sixties or early seventies, but her skin was still smooth and youthful—except for her hands, which looked thirty years older than the rest of her. She had clear gray eyes and what I think they call a retroussé nose and high cheekbones; her hair was a fugue of blacks and grays, trimmed short and lightly waved. She wore a plain gray skirt and a white blouse with ruffles at the throat, and she for one seemed more curious about me than ready to call for the exterminator.

She had some English, too, I remembered, so when I finally broke the uncomfortable silence it was to her I spoke.

"Ah, my name's Jack Farmer," I said. "I come from America. You know, the United States? I'll be staying next door in the Wooden House for a couple days, while Mr. Rombach's away."

She gave me an encouraging smile and opened her mouth to reply, but, before she could get a word out, the crone in the bed jumped in.

"I am Mevrouw Moen, and this is my house," she said sourly. Her English was accented, but clear. Her voice was firmer than I'd expected, seeing as how she was supposed to be an invalid. I don't know what was wrong with her, but her temper and her tongue at least seemed to be in perfect working order. "The Begijnhof is for women. I do not approve of a man sleeping here. If Gerrit Rombach was concerned about his cat, he could have left it with me."

I could see why he hadn't, although the sister probably would have wound up doing the little work that was involved, anyway, if he had. I've never liked people who refer to babies and animals as "it."

"*Ja, nou, Ans,*" the bicycle lady said soothingly, "*het gaat maar om 'n paar dagjes.*" Then she remembered I couldn't understand her and gave me what must have been a translation: "It's only going for a few days."

That consolation didn't cheer Mrs. Moen up much, but whatever else she had to say about the matter she kept to herself. She was really an unattractive woman. Blowsy, sort of gone to seed, with rough features and deep frown lines and her thin lips set in a permanent scowl. Only her steel-gray hair and pale-green nightgown were carefully arranged, and I suspected the sister had been responsible for brushing and combing the former and washing and ironing the latter. The human race hadn't done Mrs. Moen many favors during her seven decades on the planet, and she had clearly devoted her declining years to evening up the score.

"I am Ellen Antonie," the bicycle lady introduced herself, and, indicating the other two women, she presented them as Mevrouw Boonstra and Mevrouw de Klerk. "Mevrouw Boonstra, *U spreekt geen Engels, as ik 't goed heb?*"

Mrs. Boonstra put the tips of her fingers to her lips and giggled. "*Geen woord,*" she said shyly. She was a tiny creature, with a network of fine lines that reminded me of fragile porcelain radiating from the corners of her mouth and eyes. Blue veins stood out along her legs and the sides of her neck and the backs of her slender hands, and even her hair had a blueish tinge to it. Her light-brown skirt and flowered blouse were lovingly cared for.

"Mevrouw Boonstra"—Ellen Antonie had to pause and search for the phrase she wanted—"she isn't speaking any English. No words."

I grinned sheepishly at the lady in question. "I don't speak any Dutch, either," I said, louder than I needed to. Why is it we treat people who don't happen to know our language as if they're either deaf or stupid? If they don't understand us at ten decibels, they're not going to understand us any better at sixty, are they? But for some mysterious reason, we automatically pump up the volume, anyway. "I'm sorry."

She giggled again, shook her head, and retreated behind the protection of her teacup.

That left Mrs. de Klerk, who was probably the oldest of the four, a tall, reedy woman in fawn slacks and a loose-fitting shirt under a perfect cap of snow-white hair, her watery brown eyes magnified behind thick bifocals. Her lipstick and rouge were badly applied, and managed to emphasize the mannishness of her features, rather than softening them. When she spoke, her deep tones didn't surprise me. "Rietje de Klerk," she admitted grudgingly. She seemed about as pleased to have me spending the week in the Begijnhof as that old debbil Moen.

So there we were, four Jills and a Jack, and I'll tell you what: it was not a festive occasion. There were only three chairs available, there were only four cups, so the ladies of the club sat there sipping tea and giving me the eye, and I shifted my weight from foot to foot uneasily, feeling more or less like a museum exhibit that's just turned out to be the work of a forger instead of an authentic Old Master.

Ellen Antonie made an effort to keep the conversation rolling, but she wasn't getting a lot of help from her friends. She had the house six doors down from Mrs. Moen, she said, #27, while Mrs. Boonstra was in #19 at the far end of the bleaching green and, if I looked out the window, I could see Mrs. de Klerk's place at #40, to the left of the time tunnel, with its back to the Spui. (I can't figure out how to spell it the way she pronounced it, but it came out sounding something like an Irishman saying "Spow" after biting into a lemon.)

Moen had lived in the Begijnhof the longest of the four, since the early seventies—although there were a number of women not included in the present company who'd been there even longer—and Boonstra was the new kid on the block, having arrived in 1981. The way Ellen Antonie explained it, when a resident died, her house reverted to a central organization, which quickly turned it over to whoever happened to be next on their waiting list of deserving local spinsters. What with Amsterdam's chronic and critical housing shortage, the Begijnhof's units were avidly coveted. Antonie herself had been on the list for eight years before she was offered #27, and she was one of the lucky ones: there were fewer than fifty houses in the complex, and at any moment there were literally hundreds of Golden Girls in third-floor walkups who would sell their souls for just a spot on the waiting list.

How come they didn't stick several women into each house, I wondered, doubling or tripling or even quadrupling the possible population? From what I'd seen of them, the buildings were plenty big enough—and too big for a single individual to rattle around in alone.

Nobody had an answer to that one, and even Ellen Antonie seemed to find the suggestion scandalous. The Begijnhof houses had been one-woman residences ever since they were built for the original Beguines, the Sisters of St. Begga, and no one was about to start messing with three centuries' worth of status quo.

I found all this pretty interesting, actually, and Ellen Antonie seemed to be enjoying the opportunity to practice her limited English—but Moen was getting huffier by the minute, and de Klerk was squirming uncomfortably in her chair, and poor Mrs. Boonstra just sat there with her empty cup on her lap, trying to pretend she wasn't completely mortified by her inability to make any sense whatsoever out of the gibberish we were talking. There was a decided chill in the warm summer air: half a degree colder, and somebody'd've had to scrape the frost off Mrs. de Klerk's glasses.

By the time I'd been there fifteen minutes, I had the distinct feeling I'd overstayed my welcome by about a quarter of an hour, so I lied about what a pleasure it'd been meeting them all and started making I'm-afraid-I-must-be-going noises.

Ellen Antonie invited me to drop by #27 sometime and visit; she was the only one of them it really *had* been a pleasure meeting, and I promised her I would. Mrs. Moen and Mrs. de Klerk made a point of not seconding the bicycle lady's hospitality, bless their imitation hearts, and of course Mrs. Boonstra didn't have any idea what was going on. When she saw me centimetering towards the door, though, she looked so relieved I was afraid she'd have a coronary right then and there.

I made my escape, and, at the bottom of the stairs, I found the sister waiting for me. She was trying to keep a straight face, but as soon as she saw me she collapsed in silent laughter. "You look like you've been in a war," she gasped. I did not return her smile, and she cupped her hands over her mouth and took in a breath and sighed it out again. When she dropped her hands, she was wearing a mask of exaggerated solemnity, but she was having trouble keeping it in place.

"I'm so sorry," she said. She was holding her breath, and the words came out half-strangled. "I just couldn't resist bringing you up there. Can you forgive me?"

How could I *not* forgive her? She was so damn cute I wanted to run away to Rio with her, and forgiving her seemed like an important first step in that direction.

So I nodded and sniffed out a half-hearted laugh of my own, which was all it took to set her off again. Chuckles erupted, tears spilled, and before long she was hugging herself tightly and groaning in real pain. My dignity was fairly well shot by then, so I gave up and got hysterical right along with her.

I guess it *was* pretty funny.

When the sound of wooden chairs scraping a wooden floor reached us from above, she grimaced and pointed at the ceiling and put a finger to her lips. I got the message: if we could hear them, chances were that they could hear us, too, so maybe we'd better cool it.

We cooled it, and when Antonie, Boonstra and de Klerk came tramping down the steps in alphabetical order, we were the picture of two sober young people having an earnest discussion about European unification, or whatever it is that sober young people discuss earnestly in these troubled and troubling times.

The ladies traded polite Dutch with the sister, but I might as well have been the Invisible Man for all the attention I got—except, of course, for Ellen Antonie, who switched over to English for long enough to remind me of my promise to visit her. And then they were gone.

"See that?" I said. "The party just wasn't any *fun* without me."

"I really *am* sorry," the sister murmured sympathetically. "Was it very awful?"

I made a face. "I would give it about a nine-point-nine on the scale of awfulness," I said. "Mrs. Antonie's pretty friendly, but the other three?" I blew out air and shook my head. "Tigers. And I hate to break it to you, but your boss is the worst of the bunch."

She pursed her lips. "I know. I have to live with her, remember?" A sudden smile lit up the hallway. "She's not *always* cranky, though. Only when she's awake."

That seemed as good a time as any to pop the question, so I screwed my courage to the sticking-place and went for it. "Uh, listen," I said, "I was wondering. Would you do me a favor?"

"A favor?" She tilted her head to one side, curious.

"Yeah, well, the thing is, why I came over here in the first place was to ask you—"

I hesitated, tongue-tied.

"To ask me what?"

"Well, I'm brand-new here in Amsterdam, see, and it's practically dinner time, and I haven't hardly had a bite to eat all day, so I was thinking—well, like, I thought maybe you could recommend a restaurant I could go to."

A pair of brilliant sapphires glittered at me. "Of course," she said, "I'd be glad to. That's not much of a favor, though, after what I put you through."

I swallowed and took the plunge. "I wasn't finished. See, I don't know my way around town at all, either, so I was hoping you could sort of show me how to get there. Have dinner *with* me, I mean. If you'd like to. If you can get away."

She leaned toward me and touched my arm. "I was afraid you weren't going to ask me," she said. "Look, I've got Mevrouw Moen's supper all ready for her. Let me bring it up and tell her I'm going out and get a sweater from my room, and I'll be down in five minutes."

CHAPTER 6

"So, listen, I can't keep calling you 'sister' if we're going out to dinner together, can I? Haven't you got like a *name* or something?"

We were just leaving the Spui behind us, following the tram tracks away from the direction of the Nova Hotel. The city must have been interesting, I guess, but who was interested? Not me. I was interested in the very pretty girl at my side, and, if you could see her, I know you'd understand.

"No, don't call me sister," she agreed. "My name's Yet. Yet Schilders."

"Yet?" I repeated.

"That's right."

"You mean like Y-e-t, Yet?"

Her smile turned surprised. "No, no. *Yay*-e-t."

This was rapidly getting beyond me. "Yay, E.T.? What's *that* supposed to be, three cheers for the aliens?"

It took her a second to get it, but she *did* get it, and groaned, then realized her original mistake and colored a bit. "Not yay," she said. "Djay."

"Oh, *J!* And in Dutch you pronounce it like a Y?"

She nodded. We were walking along a canal past some buildings, but don't ask me for details.

"My name's Jack," I said. "Jack Farmer. You're not going to call me Yack, are you?"

She giggled. "In Holland, a jack"—she pronounced it "yack" and fingered the cloth of my windbreaker—"is one of these, not a name for a person."

"A jacket, yeah. And in America, a jet"—I said it "jet" and pointed at the contrail a miniature airliner was drawing across the sky far above us—"is one of those, and not a—"

"—not a name for a person." She finished the sentence before I could, laughing. I was liking her a lot. "We call those *straaljagers.*" She shaded her eyes and watched the speck of plane pull its white smoke along behind it. "It's a nice word, I think. *Straal-jager.* It means 'sunbeam chaser.'"

"Sunbeam chaser. That *is* nice. So, listen, how about if I call you 'Yet' and you call me 'Jack'? Will that work?"

"That sounds fine. Hello, Jack." She touched my hand briefly—which, oddly enough, was exactly what I was hoping she'd do. Some people would call that a coincidence. I call it communication, and I double dare you to prove it isn't. "So, Jack," she said, "what kind of food do you want to eat?"

⌘

The waiter set a metal warming tray in the middle of our table and lit the pair of small round candles in its base, then went away and came back with enough food for a family of six. He was a dapper little Asian man in a spiffy tux, and he spread about twenty-five bowls filled with assorted colors of stuff I couldn't put names to in front of us like it was the most normal thing in the world. Maybe it is, in Holland. But I was impressed enough to tear my eyes away from Jet and let her tell me what was what.

The various bowls of brown stuff were different kinds of meat, most of them smothered in *pindasaus*—which translates into English as peanut sauce and tastes a lot better than it sounds. The yellow stuff was a spicy cole slaw, and the crispy tan stuff was a giant shrimp cracker called *kroepoek*, and the white stuff was shredded coconut, and the stuff that looked like chicken and shish kebab and peanuts was chicken and shish kebab and peanuts. Jet called the shish kebab *saté*, and it too turned out to be yummy drenched in *pindasaus*.

I'd told her I wanted to try a really typical Dutch meal, and she'd beamed and said that meant we had to go to a Chinese restaurant and order off the Indonesian menu. While I was working that out, she took my arm and led me out of the sunlight into a shaded neighborhood of narrow one-way streets lined with houses that seemed shabbier than any I'd seen so far. This was the famous red-light district, she informed me, and I was as freaked out by the scenery outside Kwong Ming's as I was by the pagodas and dragons and intricate fake-jade and fake-ivory carvings that decorated the inside.

I mean, I'd heard Amsterdam's night life was pretty hot, but the red-light district went beyond what I'd expected. Just about every other structure was a sex club, with big plastic signs out front showing silhouetted couples doing it in an assortment of positions that ranged from the merely bizarre to the anatomically impossible, under headlines like NONSTOP HARDCORE LIFE SHOW and REAL LIVE FUCKY FUCKY. Then there were the porno movies, and the shop windows crammed full of vibrators and leather goods and candles shaped like erect phalluses, dozens and dozens of magazines with interchangeable cover pictures and such titles (all in English) as *Split Beavers* and *High School Pussy* and *Deviate Thrills*, inflatable plastic teenage girls with wide-open hungry mouths, pills and creams and lotions and sprays that advertised themselves as "potency extenders," Ben Wa balls and French ticklers and a really astonishing range of dildoes in every conceivable length and longer. *Lots* longer.

I'd never actually *seen* a dildo before. I'd never seen *any* of this junk before. It's all available back where I come from, I'm sure, but they keep it hidden away behind painted-out windows so the kids don't have to look at it and it doesn't scare the horses. Here in Amsterdam, though, the governing philosophy seemed to be, "Thou shalt let it all hang out."

Speaking of which, the part that knocked me out the most was the meat markets. Everywhere we walked, scattered amongst the clubs and shops and movie houses and bars and Chinese restaurants were these big picture windows with honest-to-God red lights hanging above them and these teeny little roomlets behind them. Each room sported a sagging camp bed and a sink and a towel, and most of them held a bored female on a stool by the window, doing a crossword puzzle or knitting or reading a paperback novel. They came in all ages and shapes and sizes and colors and stages of undress, from emaciated girls of sixteen with glazed eyes and needle tracks on the insides of their elbows to big fat mammas in their forties who licked their lips and jiggled their massive breasts in a grotesque mockery of sexual enticement as we strolled by. By the time we'd passed our fiftieth red light, the phrase "window shopping" had taken on a whole new meaning for me.

Jet—who'd grown up in this city—took it all in her stride, but I kept going "Jesus, look at *that!*" every time we turned a corner.

It wasn't until we were settled in the restaurant with cold beers in front of us that I was able to get my mind out of the gutter, off the meaningless sex of the red-light district and back where it belonged: on the lovely blond nurse sitting across from me—and, okay, I admit it, on the deeply meaningful sex our surroundings had me dying to have with her.

"So what's a nice Dutch girl like you doing in a perverted place like Amsterdam?" I said. If I'd been around in the 1930s, I'd've probably been writing snappy dialogue for the movies instead of going into the history biz.

"You look good with a white mustache," Jet said. "Distinguished. Older."

"Older?" I set down my glass and wiped foam from my lip. "I'll bet I'm older than *you* are. How old are you?"

She hesitated a moment before admitting to twenty-four.

"Hmmm. Me, too. When are you going to be twenty-five?"

"In January."

"Ha, gotcha!" I pointed a thumb at my chest and smirked. "September 13th. I *am* older than you are."

"September?" She sipped beer. "That makes you a virgin, doesn't it?"

"A virgin?" I was about to defend my manhood when I got it. "Oh, a Virgo. Yeah, that's me." I put my elbows on the table and lowered my voice. "Don't say that other word in this part of town, though, okay? You could give a guy a bad reputation."

Then the waiter showed up with our warming tray and our food, and we ordered more beer and downshifted from talking into eating.

I don't know how we did it, but we polished off almost the entire *rijsttafel* between us. *Rijsttafel,* Jet told me, means "rice table," although she'd ordered ours with thick seasoned noodles called *bami* instead of rice. Once a month, she said, when she was in nursing school in Amstelveen, she'd come into one of Amsterdam's four hundred Chinese restaurants with the four other girls in her study group and split a rice table for three people five ways. We'd ordered the two-person meal, and left over less than they used to. I guess I really was hungry—and Jet packed away a pretty healthy share of cuisine herself.

Dessert was *pisang goreng*—halved bananas fried in a light batter and dusted with confectioner's sugar—and sliced apples and oranges in syrup and a big pot of jasmine tea. Delicious.

And when we were finally ready to leave, just after nine— we'd been in there for more than three hours!—the bill came to something like forty dollars, and Jet said that included sales tax and a tip! With prices that reasonable and Jet apparently enjoying my company as much as I was enjoying hers, I was having trouble coming up with one good reason not to spend the entire summer in The Netherlands.

She tried to pay half the check, but I wouldn't let her. When she insisted, I got sneaky and told her there was no way in the world that the *rijsttafel* wasn't going to be my treat, but I'd be happy to let her buy me dinner tomorrow night, if she wanted to.

She leaned back and folded her arms, which did very attractive things to the shape of her leotard. "I don't know how Mevrouw Moen would feel about my going out two nights in a row," she said seriously.

I poured the last of the tea into our cups. "She's a real slave driver, huh?"

Jet sighed. "Well, she is, really, but it's not that. I live there with her, so I'm on call twenty-four hours a day if she needs me— but her condition is stable, and I wind up with a lot of time to myself."

"What's wrong with her, anyway?"

She pulled back her hair with both hands and stretched. That, too, did things to her shape that would have made her a hit behind any window in town. "It's a combination of things. Her heart, mostly. Her legs. And *zuikerziekte*—what do you call that in English? Sugar sickness?"

"Diabetes?"

"Yes, that's it. Diabetes. She doesn't look too bad, for her age, but she's really quite ill."

"And you don't like to leave her alone," I concluded.

"No, no." She toyed with her cup. The tea was cold by now and not worth drinking. "I *like* to leave her alone. She's not an easy woman to get along with. She just sits in that window all day, minding everybody else's business and complaining."

"She has friends, though," I said, remembering the hen party that afternoon.

Jet frowned. "They're not really *friends*, Jack. Mevrouw Antonie is so sweet, she'd visit Attila the Hun if he was laid up in bed. And Mevrouw Boonstra only comes because Mevrouw Antonie does; they're very close. I don't know why Mevrouw de Klerk was there today. She's never been to the house before, that I know of. I don't think I've ever even *seen* her before; she's supposed to be a real hermit. But this afternoon she just showed up at the door—actually, I think Mevrouw Moen called her and asked her to come, but she didn't tell me why. Mevrouw Antonie and Mevrouw Boonstra got there ten minutes later, but I don't know what *they* were doing there, either. They usually come by during the week; I think today was the first time they've been there on a Sunday."

"Uh-huh." I had my chin on my hands, and I was watching her turn her cup around on its saucer. "So what about dinner tomorrow night?"

She looked up at me, then, and the overhead lighting set reflected diamonds in with the sapphires.

"I'd like to, Jack," she said. "It's just—oh, I don't know how to explain it. I just finished school last December, and this is my first case. I've only been there four months. I think it'd be easier if she treated me nicer, but, since she doesn't—"

I got the idea she wasn't going to finish the sentence, so I did it for her: "—you feel guilty about leaving her."

She nodded unhappily. "I know it's silly, but—"

"It's not silly. I understand. Listen, do you want to get back there?"

She pushed away her cup and saucer decisively. "No, I don't. I want to walk around with you and talk some more. I'm just not sure about tomorrow night, that's all. I'll have to think about it."

So we walked around and talked, and we hit a couple quiet, smoky bars and drank a couple more beers and talked some more. Jet herself was a nonsmoker, praise be, and I chalked up another point in her favor.

It was well after eleven by the time we got back to the Begijnhof, and I was really beginning to flag.

Still, I made it to the outer door of the time tunnel a step ahead of her and reached to open it for her with all the gallantry I could muster.

It wouldn't budge.

"I thought this door was supposed to be unlocked," I protested.

"Not at night. The ladies would have a fit. There's a caretaker who comes around at nine and locks it. Didn't Mr. Rombach give you a key?"

"Henk Kleijwegt," I remembered. "Yeah, I met him. He seemed about as friendly as your boss and Mrs. de Klerk." I dug Gerrit Rombach's keyring from my pocket, and Jet helped me find the one that fit the wooden door.

It was incredibly peaceful in the courtyard. Jet's house and most of the others were dark, and the only illumination came from the old-style street lamps, which'd been converted from gas to electric, and the gibbous moon that hung above the chestnuts.

The contrast between inside and outside—between the noise and bustle of a city that didn't seem to realize it was late Sunday night and the gentle serenity of a lazy country village—was overpowering. I liked what I'd seen of Amsterdam so far, but I liked it in here a lot better.

I walked Jet to #33, through the gate in the picket fence and up to her doorstep.

"It's been a lovely evening," she said, standing close to me in the moonlight. "Thank you."

"My pleasure," I said. "You're welcome. Thank *you*."

I held out my hand, and she took it in both of hers and went up on her tiptoes and kissed me. It was a short kiss, but a warm one, and so unexpected it left me dazed.

"I usually take a walk while Mevrouw Moen has her lunch," Jet said softly. "Would you like to go with me tomorrow?"

"Yeah," I said, "a walk sounds great."

"I'll come by and pick you up around noon, okay?"

"Around noon. Sure." She was still holding my hand. "I'll be looking forward to it."

"Me, too." She let go of me, then, and found her key. "I'd better go up and make sure she's sleeping comfortably. Goodnight, Jack."

"Goodnight," I said.

And then I was alone, gazing blankly at the dark-green door.

A week ago, I'd been back in Ann Arbor, cramming for final exams and wondering what to do with my summer—and now, one measly week later, here I was in Heaven, livin' right next door to an angel.

I might have stood there all night, if it hadn't been for the scream.

It was Jet who was screaming, and her shrill voice ripped the tranquil night to tatters.

The door was locked, but the knob rattled loosely in my hand, and one good shoulder-block was all it took to spring it. I pounded up the narrow stairs three at a time and found her in the old lady's bedroom, beside the bed.

The lights were out and the room was dim, but the moonlight that filtered in through the gauzy white curtains was enough to show me the kitchen knife clutched tightly in Jet's right hand. The blade and Mrs. Moen's pale nightgown were black with blood.

"Oh, shit," I breathed.

It was not, perhaps, quite as snappy as my usual patter, but it was all I could think of at the moment, so I said it again.

CHAPTER 7

Lieutenant Roelof Smit of the city's Murder Brigade was a blocky, broad-shouldered man in a rumpled business suit. His thinning blond hair had been hastily combed, his necktie was clumsily tied, and the puffiness beneath his pale-green eyes told me he'd been dragged out of bed against his will. His bushy walrus mustache made him look like a Keystone Kop, but the situation wasn't funny and the lieutenant was *not* smiling.

Nobody in the room was smiling. A grim photographer was taking pictures, his flashbulbs a frequent distraction. Two patrolmen in royal-blue uniforms were sniffing around for clues. Mrs. Moen was dead, and an assistant medical examiner was bent over her body, probing the black wound in her chest with a silvery instrument I couldn't put a name to.

Once he was satisfied that his minions were getting their jobs done, the lieutenant came back to us. Jet was sitting in one of the wooden chairs the ladies had occupied that morning, though I'd pulled it as far from the bed and the horror which lay there as I could get it. She'd done a lot of sobbing while I called the police and we waited out in the Spui to let them in, and she was still terribly upset. But for now, at least, the crying seemed to have passed. Her eyes were red with grief, she took rapid shallow breaths and held a tear-stained handkerchief tightly in her fists. Her knuckles were white with the desperate strength of her grip.

I stood behind her chair, my hands resting lightly on her shoulders. I could feel the warmth of her skin through the thin fabric of her sweater. When Smit and his team had arrived, a quarter of an hour earlier, he'd insisted that we show them up to the murder room and stick around until he was ready to question us. Jet was shaking violently as they set about their tasks, but the shakes had eventually subsided to a trembling I could only notice because I was touching her—and then that too had passed.

The trembling would return, I felt certain, and so would the tears—when the initial shock of Mrs. Moen's death wore off and left harsh, lingering reality in its place. For now, though, Jet had Lieutenant Smit to focus on, and I was grateful to him for the way he spoke to her. I couldn't understand a word of what he was saying, but the tone of his voice was gentle.

He seemed to be explaining something to her, not interrogating her. She listened carefully for a while, and then she reached up to touch my hand and whispered a few sentences which included my name. Smit argued with her, but she'd made up her mind about whatever it was, and eventually the lieutenant shrugged his shoulders and raised his eyebrows and shook his head with annoyance.

"I've been trying to convince Miss Schilders she should have a lawyer here before she answers any questions," he said. His English was almost as good as Jet's, with only the slightest trace of an accent. "But she tells me she doesn't know any lawyers, and she doesn't want to have to face another stranger tonight. She says she wants *you* to look after her interests for her."

I swallowed. "Jet, I—jeez, I'm glad you trust me, but I—I think Lieutenant Smit's right. Hell, I don't know much about *American* law, let alone—"

She looked up at me stubbornly. "Please, Jack. Stay with me. I don't want to—"

"I'm not going to leave you alone, precious. I just think you ought to have someone here who knows which questions it's okay for you to answer and which ones—"

She showed me a smile and patted my hand. Amazing: *she* was comforting *me*. "I'll answer anything the lieutenant wants to ask me. I don't have anything to hide."

"Sure, I know that, but—"

I could see I wasn't getting anywhere, so I followed Smit's lead and quit arguing. I squeezed her shoulders and returned her smile and sighed. "Go ahead, Lieutenant."

He clicked his ballpoint pen a couple times, retracting the point and popping it out again. "The name on the door downstairs is Moen," he began. "The woman in the bed is Mevrouw Moen, then?"

"Yes, that's right. Ans Moen."

"And you are—?"

"Her nurse."

"I see. Do you live here in the house, Miss Schilders?"

Jet nodded, but the lieutenant was writing in his notebook and missed it. There was a brief silence, and then he looked up and said, "Miss Schilders?"

"Yes?"

"Do you live here in the—"

"I'm sorry. Yes, I do. That is, I *have* been. I—I don't know what will happen now."

I moved my hands a little, just to let her know I was there with her.

"When did you move in here?"

"Four months ago. A little more than that, really. I started working on the tenth of February."

"And how did the two of you get along?"

Jet glanced up at me for a moment. "She was a difficult woman," she admitted. "Very picky, not easy to please."

"So you had problems with her?"

"Not problems, no. But—well, when I first came here, I hoped that she and I would be able to be friends. That's not the way it worked out, though. She was my patient, my employer, but not my friend."

"Did you hate her, *zuster*?"

I started to protest, but Jet shushed me. "No, Lieutenant, I did not hate her. I—"

"Did you *like* her, then?"

Jet frowned, and, as she considered the question, I heard the two patrolmen in whispered consultation with the police photographer. One of the cops said something in Dutch to Lieutenant Smit, and, at his reply, the three of them gathered their equipment and left the room.

"*Ben jij ook al klaar*, Kees?"

The assistant medical examiner sucked a tooth. "*Ikke wel*," he said. "*Mag ik 'r wegslepen, of heb je haar nog steeds nodig?*"

"*Neem maar weg*," said Smit, and the doctor closed his bag and went away.

"Where will you take her?" Jet said softly.

"The City Morgue. There'll have to be an autopsy, they'll do that in the morning. You were about to tell me if you liked Mevrouw Moen, *zuster*."

"Yes, of course. I—no, Lieutenant, I can't say I liked her."

"But you had no reason to kill her?"

This time I *did* protest. "Come on, Lieutenant," I growled, "that's ridiculous! Granted, the old lady was a crab—I only spent fifteen minutes with her, but that was plenty long enough to see she wasn't exactly Miss Conviviality. That's no reason to stick a knife in her, though! And you can't tell me this poor girl looks like a murderer. I mean—"

"Can *you* tell *me* what a murderer looks like, Mr. Farmer? Three weeks ago, we pulled the body of a seven-year-old boy out of a canal, not too far from here. He'd been stabbed seventeen times in the chest and stomach, but that wasn't what killed him. He was still alive when he was thrown into the water, but he couldn't swim, so he drowned."

Jet moaned, and buried her face in her hands.

"I'm sorry, *zuster*. It turned out his sister was the one who did it. The family was Turkish—there were eight of them living in a three-room apartment in the Jordaan. Mama and Papa said it was the little boy's turn to have the bed for a month, and the sister didn't want to have to go back to sleeping on the couch."

"So she—she *killed* him?"

"Stabbed him seventeen times and tossed him in the canal. His big sister. She was fourteen, and the sweetest child you'd ever hope to see. So you tell me what a murderer looks like, Mr. Farmer, I'd be grateful for a reliable description."

Jet wiped her eyes. "I didn't have any reason to hurt her, Lieutenant. I didn't like her very much, but I didn't have any reason to kill her, and I *didn't* kill her."

He turned a page of his notebook. "What *did* happen, then?"

"I always look in on her before I go to bed, to make sure everything is all right. Tonight, when I opened the door, I—she doesn't really snore, Lieutenant, but she breathes quite loudly when she's asleep. Tonight, I didn't hear her breathing, and that frightened me. I came into the room and went to her bedside. And she—she was—"

I knelt beside her and put my arms around her, pressed her cheek to my chest and stroked her long blond hair. She was sobbing again, and the strangled sounds which escaped her were the cries of a wounded animal in pain.

The medical examiner came back into the room, followed by two ambulance attendants carrying a stretcher and a folded white hospital sheet. I held Jet close, so she wouldn't have to see them pull back the old woman's blanket and transfer her lifeless body to the stretcher. They draped the sheet over her and took her away, and all the while Jet shivered helplessly against me and I smelled the apple freshness of her hair as her tears soaked into my shirt.

"Mr. Farmer," Smit said, and I opened my eyes to find the three of us alone in the room. "I'm sorry, but I do have some more questions. I'd like to hear *your* story, too, if you don't mind."

"I don't mind, but it's not much of a story." I kept my arms wrapped tightly around Jet as I told him. "I'm staying in the Begijnhof this week, doing some research for one of my college professors in America. I only got here today, and Jet was one of the—Miss Schilders was one of the first people I met. We went out to dinner together, then came back here. We said goodnight at the front door, downstairs. She let herself in, and a couple minutes later I heard her scream. I broke open the door and ran upstairs and found her in here."

He scribbled rapidly in his notebook. "What time did you return to the Begijnhof from your meal?"

"I'm not sure, exactly. Around eleven thirty, I think, maybe a little later than that."

"And you said goodbye to Miss Schilders at the front door?"

"Right. We talked for a minute or two, and then she went in."

"At approximately eleven thirty."

"Yes."

"I see. And how much time would you say elapsed between Miss Schilders entering the house and her scream?"

I could see the importance of the question, and I thought about it carefully, but it was no use. I'd been so blown away by Jet's kiss that I hadn't paid any attention to such trivial matters as time. "I'm not sure," I said grudgingly. "It might have been a minute, it might have been five."

"It might, in fact, have been long enough for Miss Schilders to have gone to the kitchen for a bread knife and climbed the stairs to this—"

Jet stiffened in my arms.

"That's out of line, Lieutenant," I said. "She's already told you she didn't kill her."

"I know what she told me, Mr. Farmer. My job is to get at the truth, and not everyone *tells* the truth in a murder investigation. Would you prefer to call in a lawyer before we go any further?"

"Jet? I really think it'd be better if we did."

"No," she said, her voice muffled against my chest. "I want to get this over with. Just answer him, Jack."

The lieutenant repeated his question: "Would the *zuster* have had enough time to fetch a knife and come upstairs and stab Mevrouw Moen before she screamed?"

"I don't know," I had to admit. "It's possible, I guess—as far as the time element goes, anyway—but it's the stupidest thing I ever heard in my life."

"When you heard the scream," Smit went on, ignoring my editorial comment, "you broke open the door and ran upstairs to this room?"

"Yeah, that's right."

"And where was Miss Schilders when you got here?"

I hesitated. "She was standing by the side of the bed."

"Bent over Mevrouw Moen's body?"

"She wasn't actually 'bent over' the body, no."

"But she was standing by her side?"

"Well, yes."

"Did she have anything in her hands?"

I licked my lips.

"Did she have anything in her hands, Mr. Farmer?"

I was trying to figure out how to avoid answering him, but Jet twisted away from me and cried, "Tell him, Jack! If you won't tell him, I will! I won't let you lie to him!"

She was breathing heavily. Her hair was wild, her lovely face was red and streaked with tears.

"Oh, shit, Jet," I sighed.

I reached out for her, but she pulled away from me and shouted, "*Tell* him!"

So what could I do?

I told him.

CHAPTER 8

Jet licked my cheek with her cold sandpaper tongue and purred contentedly. Nobody'd ever licked me like that before, and, *damn*, it made me tingle. I wrapped my arms around her and stroked her soft blond fur. She was—

Uh, wait a second. Her cold sandpaper tongue? Her soft blond fur?

I opened my eyes and found myself hugging poor Dropje, who was squinting down at me with a look of exasperation on her face, like a cat with other things on her mind than interspecies sex.

"Oops," I oopsed, and I gave her wet little schnoz a platonic smooch and lowered her to the floor and got out of bed. It was a little after eight, and I was groggy as hell. I hadn't hit the hay until almost three, and my brain had a neon sign on it flashing, "Serious Jetlag. Closed Until Further Notice."

What I needed was about another day and a half of rack time. What I *did* was shatter the Olympic record for showering and shaving, fling on some clothing and stumble down and out. Dropje bitched at me as I was leaving, but I told her I had to check on Jet and promised to come back and feed her as soon as I could.

It was a dismal morning, the sky blanketed with dense gray clouds and the air sharpened to a chill that made me uncomfortable in my short-sleeved OP shirt. The Begijnhof was deserted, white curtains pulled closed at every window.

Number 33 looked quiet, and it wasn't until I was about to start pounding on the door that I remembered Jet hadn't gotten to sleep until early this morning, either. Boy, I really *was* logy. She hadn't wanted to stay on in Mrs. Moen's house at all, after what had happened, but Lieutenant Smit had ordered her to stay close to the scene of the investigation. For a while there, I was afraid he was going to arrest her, after I told him about finding her with the knife in her hand, but Jet insisted she'd discovered the old woman with the blade sticking in her chest and had pulled it out automatically, too stunned by the terrible sight to realize that she might be covering over the murderer's fingerprints.

Smit tried hard to break her down, but she stuck to her story, bless her, and he finally compromised and said he wouldn't run her in if she'd agree to stick around, with a police matron on hand to keep an eye on her. There was a guest bedroom right next to Jet's, and she wanted me to use it, but the lieutenant vetoed that idea. He called in a doctor to give her something to help her sleep, and, once she'd dozed off, he sent me home. He was still there when I left, waiting for the matron to show.

So here it was, a quarter to eight, and I tapped lightly and waited, and a minute later I heard soft footsteps approaching from within. The door was opened by a woman in her forties, a kindly soul in conservative street clothes and a frizzy auburn perm. Smit had obviously briefed her about me, because she put a finger to her lips and shushed me and whispered "She's sleeping" in respectable English before I had a chance to get a word out.

"Are you the matron?" I whispered back.

She nodded, came out to join me on the top step and eased the door almost shut behind her. "Ineke Koot," she introduced herself, speaking now at normal volume. "And you are Mr. Farmer?"

"Jack," I said. "You can skip the 'mister.' Every time I hear somebody say 'Mr. Farmer,' I turn around and look for my father. How is she?"

"She's sleeping peacefully. I don't think it's a very good idea to wake her."

"No, no, she needs the rest. I'll come back later. How long will you be here?"

"Until eleven. Lieutenant Smit should be back by then. Otherwise, he'll send someone to replace me."

"Any idea how long she'll sleep?"

She pursed her lips. "At least a few more hours. The lieutenant said she was given a fairly strong sedative."

"All right, then. I'll check back around ten or so."

I returned to the Wooden House and whipped up some grub for Dropje. I was feeling a tad peckish myself, but the kitchen cupboards were bare. Then I remembered the free breakfast I had coming to me at the Nova, and, since Jet was snoozing anyway, decided I might as well take advantage of it.

On my way out the door, though, I spotted the slip of paper on which I'd written the number of Gerrit Rombach's hotel up north and figured I'd better let him know what had happened.

A switchboard girl rang me through to his room. He was already up, going over his notes for the speech he was due to give at ten. Needless to say, the news about Mrs. Moen practically knocked his block off.

"*Lieve hemel,* she is *dead*? I—"

"I know how you feel, sir. It's horrible. I can still hardly believe it."

"When did it happen? Was it—?"

"Last night some time. They're not sure exactly when, yet, but it—"

"Last night? Why didn't you telephone me right away, Mr. Farmer? I could have—"

"I'm sorry, sir. Maybe I should have, but it was like after two o'clock this morning before the police got through questioning me, and I—"

"The *police*? Questioning *you*? What in heaven's name has been going *on* down there?"

So I told him the whole story, Jet and the knife and the lieutenant and all, and when I finished there was a long silence at the other end of the line. Finally, he sighed, and when he spoke again his voice was dull and very tired. "I will leave here immediately," he said. "If there isn't very much traffic, I can be back in Amsterdam by—"

"No, really, Mr. Rombach, that's not necessary. There's nothing you can do here, the police are handling it. You just stay up there and give your speech. I'll call you again if we need you."

He didn't much like the idea, but I talked him into it. My motives, I must admit, were selfish: once he was back on the scene, he wouldn't need me to feed his cat anymore, and I wanted to stay as close as possible to Jet for the next couple days.

"What about the *zuster*?" he asked, as if he'd been reading my mind.

"She's pretty badly shaken, sir. This is going to take a lot of getting used to, but I think she'll be all right."

"Where is she? They haven't—they haven't taken her away, have they?"

"No, sir, she's still next door. They didn't have enough evidence to arrest her, but—well, it's crazy, but the cop in charge seems to think she might have done it, and he wants her close at hand during the investigation. She's sleeping now, and there's a police matron staying there with her. Don't worry, I'm taking care of her and Dropje both."

Another silence. Then, slowly: "Mr. Farmer, under the circumstances I hesitate to ask, but—"

"She's fine, sir. I just fed her. She'd be happier if you were here."

And so would I, I thought, but I kept that to myself and again reassured him that he might as well stay up north for his conference and rang off. He was devastated about the murder, and I probably ought to have stayed on the line with him for a while longer, but I figured the best thing I could do was give him time to get his head together before his speech.

The Begijnhof was still quiet when I left the Wooden House, and I wondered if Ineke and Jet and I were the only people there who knew about the murder as yet. Jet's scream had seemed pretty darn loud to me, and I'd've expected *somebody* else must have heard it, but apparently no one had. Sound sleepers, the Dutch.

Word would spread quickly enough, though, if it hadn't already, and the old ladies would absolutely spaz out. Ellen Antonie would be horrified and deeply saddened, Mrs. Boonstra would be flustered and frightened, and the de Klerk woman would be mad as a hornet that someone had dared to invade the serene security of her neighborhood.

And the rest of them, the couple dozen other old spinsters who called the Begijnhof home? They'd be horrified and saddened and flustered and frightened and pissed—and was it possible that some of them might be *glad*? Now that she was dead, I was already beginning to forget what a crabby old busybody Mrs. Moen had been. But many of these women had lived there with her for years and years. Some of them—hell, maybe *lots* of them—must have disliked her nasty nosiness pretty intensely. Was it possible that one of them might have *hated* her, hated her enough to kill her? That was a thought worth passing on to Lieutenant Smit.

I met Henk Kleijwegt in the time tunnel, coming in as I was leaving, wearing the same work clothes he'd had on yesterday, chewing sourly on the same beat-up old pipe, carrying a plastic shopping bag labeled HEMA that bulged with God knows what. He had a little English, I remembered, so I stopped and told him about the murder.

"Ans Moen?" He didn't seem especially surprised to learn that she was dead. He didn't seem especially disturbed about it, either.

"Can you think of anyone who might have had a reason to kill her, Mr. Kleijwegt? It's stupid, but the police think the *zuster* might have done it, and I'd—"

"The *zuster*? *Belachelijk*! I could tell them some things about Ans Moen, if I wanted to. The *zuster*. Hah!"

"What kind of things?" I asked, but the caretaker shook his head angrily and spat out a mouthful of blue smoke and disappeared into the courtyard. I considered going after him, but the inner man was clamoring for attention, and I decided Kleijwegt could wait.

When I came out at the far end of the time tunnel, the bustle and noise of the city startled me. I'd spent less than twenty-four hours in the Begijnhof, but already I'd come to think of *it* as the real Amsterdam, and this confused tangle of crowded streets and dirty canals and blaring horns and rattling streetcars as an unappetizingly modernized imitation.

It wasn't all disappointing, though. The clouds were beginning to burn off, and the air was slowly warming, and breakfast at the Nova was a treat. Fresh-squeezed orange juice, beautiful whole-wheat bread, the best Gouda cheese I ever ate, and a gallon of superb coffee to wash it all down with. (Excuse me, make that four *liters* of coffee.) I'd been hoping for some bacon and eggs, actually, but the bread and cheese was ten times tastier. They had it set up as a giant buffet, sort of a rise-and-shine *rijsttafel,* and there were about eighty other items I passed on only for want of sufficient gastrointestinal capacity. The weirdest offering on display was this big bowl of brown stuff which turned out on closer inspection to be chocolate sprinkles. I took a rain check, naturally, but a kid at the table next to mine heaped about four spoonfuls onto a slice of buttered bread and gobbled it down with what appeared to be genuine enjoyment. A chocolate-sprinkle sandwich—for *breakfast,* no less! No wonder Holland's no longer a major world power.

By the time I got back, it was almost ten, and I crossed my fingers to wish Gerrit Rombach luck with his speech and headed straight for #33. Ineke Koot told me she thought Jet was still sleeping, and I latched onto that "thought" and asked her to please go up and check. She did, and Jet *was* still sleeping, so I said I'd try again in an hour and went next door. Dropje seemed glad to see me, and I gave her some of the attention I'd've much rather lavished on Jet.

With nothing else to keep me occupied, I figured I might as well start digging some of the information Dexter Harriman had sent me for out of the Wooden House's archives. About five minutes into the files, though, a groggy little voice in the back of my head began suggesting that enough was enough, already.

"A nap," I said aloud, and Dropje padded over to rub against my leg at the sound. "Now *there's* an intriguing idea."

Half an hour, I promised myself, and dragged my tired bones upstairs and stacked them carefully on the narrow cot.

About two minutes later, the doorbell rang.

"Half a lousy hour," I grumbled. "Is that too much to ask?"

I opened my eyes and looked at my watch, and it was a little after noon. I'd been asleep for close to two hours.

The doorbell rang again.

"All right, all right," I yelled. I jumped out of bed and pounded down the wooden steps to the office and threw open the door.

And there was Jet, looking sad but ravishing in a knee-length denim skirt and a short-sleeved plaid blouse, her hair drawn back in a ponytail like she'd been wearing the first time I saw her. God, was that *yesterday*? Hard to believe. I felt like I'd known her for months.

"Hi," she said, and the sadness was in her voice, too. "We were going to take a walk, remember?"

"Yeah, sure, of course I remember. I—"

"I didn't have to get Mevrouw Moen her lunch, you see, because—"

And then those beautiful sapphire eyes filled with tears, and I put my arms around her and held her and the crying was bad for a while. I rubbed her shoulder blades and the back of her neck as gently as I could, and whispered the sort of stuff you whisper when you don't know what to say.

"I went over to see how you were," I told her, when she'd quieted a little.

"Twice. I know. Ineke told me."

"She seems pretty nice."

"Yes, she is."

"I'm sort of surprised she let you come over. I thought she was supposed to be keeping pretty close tabs on you."

And Jet looked up at me and smiled mischievously and dropped her bombshell. "She's in the kitchen with Lieutenant Smit," she said. "They don't even know I'm gone."

CHAPTER 9

"They excuse me?"

Jet winked at me slyly. "They don't know I'm gone. I sneaked away."

"You *snuck* away," I said. I couldn't help myself—it's the grad student in me.

"Yes, sorry, *snuck* away."

"Jesus," I exploded, letting go of her and backing off a step, "I don't care if you *snook* away! Mrs. Moen is *dead*, Jet, she's been *murdered*, and, whether you like it or not, Smit's got you involved in the investigation. You can't just run away from it. He'll think you're admitting you killed her."

Bull's eye. She sobered up like a shot, covered her mouth with both hands and stared at me, riveted by the thought. "You're right," she said. "I wasn't thinking. I can better go back."

I pulled her hands from her mouth and cupped my own big mitts around them and corrected her grammar once again, this time focusing on pronoun usage. "*We* can better go back," I said.

❧

Lieutenant Smit and Ineke Koot were still in #33's narrow kitchen, seated at a small wooden breakfast table with coffee at their elbows and Smit's notebook open between them.

"Djack," the matron greeted me, having a little trouble with the J. "I didn't hear you ring."

"He didn't ring," said Jet. "I let him in."

Ineke's brow furrowed. "But how did you know he—?"

"From the outside. I—"

"We had a date to go walking," I explained. "We made it before—last night. Jet thought you might not approve, so she—"

"I snuck away," she said contritely.

Smit raised his cup and sipped coffee, then set it down again with a sigh. "Thank you for bringing her back, Mr. Farmer. You did the right thing. *En jij, zuster, je moet je schamen. Da's geen manier van doen onder zulke omstandigheden.*"

Jet hung her head. "I know. I'm sorry. I won't do it again. It's just that I—"

"You wanted to get away for a while," Ineke nodded. "That's understandable. It's not wrong to feel that way, *zuster*—it's only wrong to *act* on the feeling. You don't have to be afraid of us. We're only here to find out what happened."

"Best thing *we* can do," I put my two cents in, "is cooperate. The sooner they figure out who killed Mrs. Moen, the sooner things around here'll get back to normal."

Jet tried to smile. "Things around here will never get back to normal," she said.

There was no answer to that, and the silence which flooded over us threatened to wash us all out to sea.

"Coffee?" Ineke suggested at last.

"Coffee, yeah, please." I steered Jet to an empty wooden chair, mouthing a "thank you" at the matron over her shoulder.

"Some questions," said Lieutenant Smit, sliding his notebook towards him. "Actually, Mr. Farmer, I'm glad you're here. Last night, you told me that you and Miss Schilders returned to the Begijnhof"—he flipped back a couple pages—"*ja, hier is 't,* 'around eleven thirty, I think, maybe a few minutes later than that.' Those were your words?"

"Near enough. What's this—?"

"Could it have been as late as eleven forty-five, do you think?"

I traded uncertain looks with Jet. "Maybe, but I—"

"Could it have been as early as eleven fifteen?"

"Now that's a different story. I'm pretty sure it was later than—"

"But is it *possible* you were here at eleven fifteen?"

"Well, yeah, I guess it's—"

"And is it possible that it was only eleven o'clock?"

This time it was Jet who answered. "No," she said, and her voice left no room for argument.

"No? And what do *you* say, Mr. Farmer?"

"I—"

"The bells," said Jet.

I snapped my fingers. "Yeah, right! At eleven o'clock, we were walking past some big old church—"

"*De Nieuwe Kerk.*"

"The New Church, right—although it didn't look much newer than the Old Church over in the red-light district, to me—anyway, we'd just come across Dam Square and we were walking past the church when we heard the bells strike eleven."

I answered Smit's question before he had a chance to ask it: "We counted them, Lieutenant. We stopped walking and counted them. It was eleven o'clock, not ten, not twelve—eleven. And then we must have walked for at least another twenty minutes after that before we wound up back here."

"*Melk en zuiker?*" Ineke Koot asked from the stove, and reached for the milk and sugar when Jet said "*Graag,*" which even from Jet has got to be the single ugliest syllable I have ever heard in my life. It sounded like she was hawking up a gob of phlegm and getting ready to spit.

"No *graag* for me," I gagged. "I'll take mine black and beautiful. Listen, Lieutenant, why is the exact time we got here so important, all of a sudden?"

"*Voor mij ook zwart.* It's important, Mr. Farmer, because I got the preliminary results of the—how do you call it?—the *lijkschouwing* about a quarter of an hour ago."

"The post-mortem," Ineke supplied, setting a china cup before me.

"*Ja, bedankt,* the post-mortem. In a detective, you know, the doctor takes one look at a body and tells you how long it's been dead to the nearest minute."

"A detective?"

"A detective story," Jet translated.

"But that's not the way it really works. There are too many variables involved. Our medical examiner thinks Mevrouw Moen was probably stabbed some time between half-ten and—no, sorry, between nine thirty and ten thirty last night, with a margin of error of perhaps half an hour in either direction."

It took me a second to do the math. "Well, hey, then that lets Jet out of the picture!"

"It's not quite that simple," Smit frowned. "I already said it, establishing a time of death isn't an exact science. The doctor says she *probably* died before ten thirty, but it might well have been as much as half an hour later, and it *could* have been even later than that. Unless the two of you are lying about the time you returned to the Begijnhof, though, it—"

"Lying!" I sputtered. "Come on, Lieutenant, that's—"

"Unless you are lying," he repeated, "then you're right, the *zuster* may well be in the clear. I have to consider the possibility that you might *be* lying, though, Mr. Farmer. You're obviously, ah, fond of each other, and—"

"We haven't even known each other for twenty-four hours, and you think we cooked up some conspiracy to commit a murder?"

"I don't know what to think. All I know on this moment is that an elderly woman has been stabbed to death, that Miss Schilders was her nurse, and that the two of them were not on the closest of terms. The two of *you*, however—well, I'm not blind, Mr. Farmer."

Jet's hands were folded in front of her, motionless on the tabletop. I scooted my chair a couple inches closer to hers and touched her slender fingers protectively. She turned up her palms and squeezed my hand.

"So, what happens now?" I asked.

Smit sighed. "Given your statements and the medical examiner's estimate of the time of death, I'm going to release the matron to another assignment. But I'd like you to stay on here in the Begijnhof, *zuster*, until we've completed our investigation."

"You mean I—I'm still a suspect?"

Smit looked uncomfortable. "Yes," he acknowledged. "You were found beside the victim, with the murder weapon in your hand. The knife came from the kitchen of this house, where you have been living. The only fingerprints on the handle are yours. Until we can—"

"God, Lieutenant, don't you have gloves in Holland? Or maybe the killer wiped off the handle after stabbing her—I *know* you've got handkerchiefs, I've seen them. You can't—"

"Until we can show that someone else committed this crime," Smit said doggedly, "we're going to have to consider you still under suspicion, *zuster*. I'm sorry."

"The lieutenant will be working on the case," Ineke murmured. "He'll be looking for motives, looking for a witness who might have seen someone enter the house last night, while you and Djack were away."

"Somebody must have seen *something*," I agreed. "It shouldn't take all that long to find out who and what."

Jet toyed restlessly with her cup and turned to Smit. "Can we go now?"

"You haven't touched your coffee."

"I'm not—I don't really want it," Jet said. "I'd like to walk for a while, if it's all right."

"I have some more questions."

"They can wait," I said. "Can't they?"

Smit considered it. "*Goed*," he decided. "There are some things I need to do here in the house. I'd like you back in an hour."

"No problem," I promised, and got quickly to my feet.

"*Sterkte*," said Ineke Koot encouragingly.

Jet smiled wan thanks, and I got us out of there before the lieutenant had time to change his mind.

∾

Ellen Antonie and Mevrouw Boonstra were standing with their heads together on the brick path between Ellen's house and the bleaching green when we came out of #33. Jet grabbed my elbow and steered me in the opposite direction, towards the time tunnel.

"If they haven't heard about it yet, we'll have to tell them, and, if they have, they'll want to talk about it—and I can't right now, Jack. Not yet. I need some more time."

I put my arm around her. "You take all the time you need," I said.

We caught a tram and rode it for ten minutes down a busy shopping street and through a bustling square, the Leidseplein, which was crammed full of white tables with people drinking coffee and reading newspapers on one side of the tracks and a circle of spectators watching two jugglers toss Indian clubs back and forth on the other. I'd've liked to get off there and check out the scene for a while, but we stayed on the tram for another couple minutes, instead, past the American Hotel and across a wide canal.

When we finally disembarked, a short walk brought us to a lovely city park, the Vondelpark. I got the name from a sign at the entrance, not from Jet, who hadn't said a single word since we boarded the tram. I might have thought she was mad at me, except she seemed content to have my arm around her waist. She *did* need time, I figured, and, if there wasn't much else I could give her, at least I could give her that.

The park was as serene as the Begijnhof, and I could see why Jet had brought us there. The day was warming up—although the sun had yet to put in an appearance—and this was a perfect place to forget about the murder for a little while and just *be*. There were couples lying on the grass, there were Frisbees sailing through the air, there was a general sense of peace-on-Earth-good-will-toward-man.

Not far inside the gate, we came to a stream, and we followed it aimlessly for a while, until it widened out into a small lake. Jet plopped herself down by the water's edge and smoothed out her skirt. I sat beside her and watched her, waiting.

In the center of the lake, a fountain shot a plume of water high into the sky, where it turned into rain and fell back to ripple the surface. On the far side, a gold-and-white Sheltie frolicked in the descending mist.

"Jack," said Jet. It came out sort of strained, and she coughed and said it again.

"I'm here."

She turned away from me. "I didn't kill her."

"Oh, God, Jet, I know that." I got to my knees and pulled her back around to face me. "Look at me. No, come on now, *look* at me. That's it. Now read my lips. There is no hesitation in my mind, Jet. I know you didn't kill her."

"But—" Her lower lip was trembling, and tears welled up to blur the sapphires. "But the knife!"

I sighed. "All right, look. I don't need to hear this. I'd bet anything—I would bet money, I would bet my *life*—you had nothing to do with Mrs. Moen's death. And you already explained about the knife last night, and I didn't even need to hear it *then*. But if *you* need to tell me about it again, Jet, I will sit here and listen."

She swallowed heavily. "After we said goodnight, I went upstairs to check on her. I couldn't hear her breathing, so I went closer and—oh, Jack, she was lying there with it stuck into her! I thought—I don't know what I thought. I screamed. And then—"

"—and then you pulled out the knife. I knew that the second I saw you standing there. You couldn't just let her *lie* there like that, could you?"

"You knew?"

"Of course I knew. What do you—?" I stopped for a moment. "Jet, you didn't think I thought—? You didn't think I thought you *did* it, did you?"

She stroked my cheek with the backs of her fingers. "I don't know. I was afraid maybe you weren't sure."

I stroked *her* cheek with the backs of *my* fingers. "Don't be afraid," I said. "I'm sure."

CHAPTER 10

The sky was clear and the sun was warm, so we decided to walk back to the Begijnhof, retracing our route alongside the tram tracks. The jugglers we'd seen in the Leidseplein were gone, and a Jamaican steel band had taken their place. Again I was eager to pause for a coffee and a listen, but Jet reminded me that the lieutenant wanted us back in an hour and our time was almost up, so I agreed to take a raincheck. I did a lot of window-shopping in the Leidsestraat, though, and she had to keep tugging on my arm to stop me from drifting into every other *winkel* we passed. They've got some ritzy emporia along that stretch of real estate; in the Dutch-language edition of Monopoly, Jet told me, the Leidsestraat is the equivalent of Park Place. (And you collect two thousand Euros when you pass "Go," not a measly two hundred bucks!)

We swung left at Konigsplein, dodged students entering and leaving the University of Amsterdam's library with its distinctive bright-red shutters, hung a right into the Spui. I waited for a break in the traffic and bolted—and, halfway across, I realized I was alone. I spun around and looked back: Jet was standing frozen on the curb, staring past me at the entrance to the Begijnhof.

A Citroën 2CV with an enormous sticker of a duck in a cowboy hat plastered across its hood just managed to avoid running me down. The driver leaned out his ridiculous folding window and swore at me, but I was so preoccupied with Jet that I forgot to give him the finger.

I darted back across the street. "What is it?"

She put a fist to her mouth. "Oh, Jack," she said softly. "If only I hadn't left her alone, last night. She—maybe she'd still be alive."

"Right, sure. Or maybe the *both* of you would be dead. Jet, listen, you can't think like that. God knows why somebody wanted to get rid of her, but somebody did, and you can't blame yourself for what happened. Whoever it was, if they hadn't of gotten to her last night, they'd've waited for another opportunity and done it then. You couldn't have protected her. You were her nurse, not her bodyguard."

She tore her attention from the doorway. "I know," she said. "I know. But I can't help thinking there must have been *something* I could have done to have saved her." She squeezed my arm. "I want them to find out who killed her, Jack. I want him caught and punished."

"They'll catch him," I promised—and at that moment I remembered a couple things I'd been told over the last twenty-four hours. I remembered Jet saying the door across the street from us was locked up every night at nine. I remembered Smit saying Mrs. Moen had died sometime between roughly nine thirty and ten thirty. And I remembered both Gerrit Rombach and Ellen Antonie mentioning that all of the Begijnhof's residents were women.

"*Him,*" I hummed. "Hmm…."

✧

Jet veered left toward the picket fence that protected #33's pocket-sized front garden from the tourist trade, but I grabbed her hand and pulled her in the opposite direction. "Let's cut over here a second, first. There's something I want to check out."

"Jack, the lieutenant said to be back in an hour. We're already—"

"I know, we're already ten minutes late. So another three minutes won't make that much difference, will it? What's he going to do, put out an APB on us?"

"A what?"

"An all-points—oh, never mind the English lesson. Come on!"

We found the Reverend William Llewellyn Jones hunched over a black-bound ledger in a small office off the English Reformed Church's paneled vestibule.

I cleared my throat in the doorway, and he looked up absently. Then he pulled off his hornrimmed reading glasses and saw who we were, and a smile of welcome lit up his thin, pale face.

"Miss Schilders," he beamed. "And Mr. Farmer! What a pleasure!" He laid the glasses carefully on his desk, shut the ledger and put it away in a drawer, and only then got to his feet and came towards us. "I didn't hear you come in. Well, I see it didn't take you two young people long to find each other in this community for the elderly. Do sit down. May I offer you a cup of tea?"

"We can't stay," I said, settling into the shaky folding metal chair he'd indicated. "You haven't heard the news, yet, have you?"

"The news?" He peered from me to Jet and back again. "I listened to the BBC World Service earlier this morning, but—"

"The local news," I said. "The here-in-the-Begijnhof news. About Mrs. Moen."

"Mrs. Moen?" He blinked rapidly. "No, I'm afraid I—I don't understand."

"She's dead," said Jet, in a very small voice. "She was murdered."

"Dear Lord," he whispered. "Murdered? That's—" He bowed his head and clasped his hands and closed his eyes, and his lips moved in silent prayer. When he looked up again, the energy had drained out of him, and he seemed a shade whiter than usual.

"What can I do to help?" he asked.

So I told him about my brief encounter with Henk Kleijwegt earlier in the day, and about the gruff old caretaker's broad hinting that there were secrets he could reveal about Mrs. Moen if he was in the mood. "I asked him what he was talking about, but he just shrugged his shoulders. He wouldn't say another word."

Reverend Bill unfolded his glasses and sucked thoughtfully on one earpiece. "Secrets," he repeated, apparently mystified. "No, I'm afraid I haven't a clue what he meant."

"But what about Kleijwegt himself? Do you think there's any chance he really *does* know something important?"

"Well, it's difficult to say, really. He's been here forever, of course, at least twenty years, and I've spoken with him often. I—"

"Is he a religious man?" asked Jet, surprised at the concept.

"No, no, quite the contrary. But the church is always in need of minor repairs, and he's in and out of here, oh, two or three times a week, I'd say. He acts as if the Begijnhof is his own private estate, and I think he'd quite prefer it if there weren't all these nasty *people* about, making such a mess of things. I found his—superior attitude rather annoying at first, but I've grown used to him by now. I wouldn't be a bit surprised if he *does* know things no one else is aware of—but, on the other hand, he does always seem to be dropping mysterious hints about one thing or another, and nothing ever seems to come of any of it. I expect it's just his way of making himself appear more significant than he actually is."

In other words, maybe Henk Kleijwegt was a lead worth pursuing, and maybe he wasn't.

Wonderful.

At least we were getting somewhere.

Not.

"Interesting," said Roelof Smit. "And what is *your* impression of him, *zuster?*"

Jet thought it over before replying. "I'm not sure," she said at last. "I've only talked with him a few times. He always seems to be angry about something. I think he's very impatient with the bureaucracy he has to go through whenever he wants to do anything that's going to cost any money. I can't say I ever thought he was trying to make himself seem important."

"And did he lock up at nine o'clock last night, as usual?"

The abrupt change of subject threw her for a moment. "I don't know. We were still at the restaurant at nine."

"Mr. Farmer?"

"*I* don't know. I didn't even know the door was ever supposed to be locked at *all* until we got back from dinner and I tried to be chivalrous."

"But Kleijwegt didn't say anything to you this morning about locking up last night?"

"No, not a word. We only talked for two minutes. He dropped his little hint about Mrs. Moen, and that was it."

"I'll have to question him myself, of course. About locking up last night, and about whatever he thinks he knows about Mevrouw Moen. Do you know where I can find him now?"

Jet shook her head. "He's usually putting around—*nee, wacht even*—puttering around here somewhere."

"I'll find him. And I appreciate your passing on this information. From now on, though, I'd be grateful if you would leave the detective work to the police. And, *over detectivewerk gesproken*, I have some more questions for the two of *you* before I go on to anything else."

The matron was gone, and the lieutenant was holding the fort on his own. Ineke'd left him a pot of coffee, but it was empty by now, and when Jet offered to brew some more he gargled out a *graag*. She got busy at the stove, and Smit addressed himself to her ponytail.

"The motive," he said. "Someone killed her, so someone must have wanted her dead. If it wasn't you, *zuster*, it must have been someone else. Who?"

Jet measured coffee grounds into a filter, then leaned forward and planted her fists on the countertop. "I don't know," she said tightly, her back to us. "I told you before, she wasn't an easy woman to get along with, but I can't imagine anyone hating her enough to want to kill her."

"Mr. Farmer?"

"Don't ask me. I only met her yesterday. She was pretty offensive—I don't have any trouble imagining someone hating her. But I wouldn't know who. If Jet says there wasn't anyone, that's good enough for me."

"What about money? Did she have any? Did she have a—*hoe zeg je 't?*—a testament?"

"A will," Jet said. "I don't know. She wasn't poor, but I don't think she can have had very much money."

"Testament's acceptable," I put in, "but it's kind of old-fashioned. Will's more commonly used. It must be possible to find out if she had one."

"What about bank accounts?" the lieutenant tried.

The water boiled, and Jet took the kettle off the burner and poured. "She sent me to the *giro* a few times. Always withdrawals, never a deposit. There wasn't much in the account."

"But she might have had other accounts?"

"It's possible. I don't know."

"We'll check it," said Smit, scribbling. He turned a page as Jet brought over the coffee pot and three fresh cups. "*Iets anders.* The front door is the only entrance to this house. You were able to lock it when you got in last night, *zuster*, so it seems unlikely the killer had forced it open. Impossible to tell for certain now, since Mr. Farmer *did* force it when he heard your scream. I'm having someone come by this afternoon to repair the lock, by the way. *In ieder geval*, if the killer *didn't* force his way in, that means either someone let him in from the—"

"Him or her," I said.

Smit nodded impatiently. "Yes, of course. Him or her. Either someone admitted the killer from the inside, or else someone outside let himself in with a key. Or herself. How many keys for that door are there?"

Jet set the pot on a candle-powered warmer and sat beside me. "Only two that I know of. I have one, and Herr Rombach has the other."

"Which means *I* have the other one, now," I said. "At least I guess I do. Mr. Rombach left his keys with me. Is it one of these?"

"*Wacht effe.*" Smit took the ring and went to the front of the house. He was back in a minute, working loose one of the keys. "Yes, it's this one. I'll keep it with me, if you don't mind. You were carrying these last night?"

"Fine with me, as long as you get it back to Mr. Rombach when you're finished with it. Yeah, we both had our keys on us. I used mine to let us into the Begijnhof, and Jet used hers to get into the house."

Smit blew steam from his cup and took a sip. "Mmm, *heerlijk is dat*. So, unless there are other keys you don't know about, Mevrouw Moen must have admitted her killer herself."

"Is that possible?" I wondered, doubting that it was. "I mean, she was an invalid. She could manage the three steps from her bed to the window seat, apparently, but was she capable of getting herself all the way down those stairs to the door?"

The lieutenant's brow crinkled. "She didn't have to go downstairs. She only had to pull on the—*ja, nou, wa's 'trekker' in 't Engels?*"

Jet pursed her lips. "I don't know. I don't think there's a word for it. Maybe they don't have them in America. It's a rope, Jack, or sometimes a wire; you pull on it from upstairs, and downstairs the front door opens. Probably every house in Holland has one. Usually it's in the upstairs hallway, but, because of Mevrouw Moen's condition, she had one built in right next to her bed. All she had to do to let someone in was reach out her hand and tug on the rope."

Smit tossed down the rest of his coffee and flipped his notebook shut. "Lots of work to do, then: testament, bank accounts, Henk Kleijwegt, see if any of the neighbors noticed someone entering this house last night. I've got some other things that will keep me busy for three or four hours, but I'll be back here later on this afternoon and see what I can see."

"This afternoon?" I figured I must have heard him wrong. "Lieutenant, there's been a *murder* here. What the hell 'other things' do you have to do that are more important than that?"

"Mr. Farmer," Smith sighed, "if this was one of van de Wetering's pretty little detectives—excuse me, detective stories—my kindly old commissaris would have me working on it full-time, with a handsome sergeant to do all the dirty legwork for me." He smoothed down the ends of his bushy mustache. "But it doesn't go that way in real life. Amsterdam used to be a nice, peaceful city, but over the last decade the crime rate's grown ten times faster than the police force. I don't have anything to do that's more important than this case, but I do have other cases that are *as* important, and I've got to give them some attention today, too. I'll be back as quickly as I can, but it will take me a few hours. *Bedankt voor de koffie, zuster. Erg lekker, was 't. Tot vanmiddag dan maar weer.*"

And he scooped up his notebook and was gone.

જ

I fussed and fumed for a while, then finally chilled out enough to notice that Jet was waiting to tell me something. I sat myself back in my chair. "Sorry," I said. "It just seems so stupid that they haven't got enough cops to—ah, skip it. So, what's on *your* mind, my pretty?"

She seemed to come to a decision. "Jack, Mevrouw Moen may not be *his* only case, but—well, she was *my* only case. My first and only. And I don't think my responsibility's over, just because— just because of what happened. Lieutenant Smit wants me to stay on until the investigation is over, and I guess I don't have much choice about that, but I have to *do* something while I'm here. I can't just sit around and wait."

"Oh, no," I said. "No, Jet, you heard the man: thanks very much for the information, but from now on leave the driving to us. You can't—"

"I know the people here, Jack! I knew Mevrouw Moen. If I ask enough questions—if I ask the *right* questions—I'll bet I could figure it out. I'm *sure* I could do it! And I'd be even more sure if you'd help me. If we looked into it together, Jack, don't you think we could find the answers?"

I thought the poor kid was nutso, that's what I thought. I thought she'd been watching too much television. I thought of us buzzing around reenacting old episodes of *Moonlighting* with a killer on the loose. I thought about the gasket D.S. Harriman would blow if he found out I was gallivanting around with Jet instead of devoting myself to the research he was paying me to undertake.

I thought Jet Schilders was the most wonderful woman I'd ever met. And, also, right now, the most forlorn.

"Please, Jack, I have to do this. I *have* to! Will you help me?"

So what would *you* have done, big shot, turned her down?

"Quick, Watson," I said, forcing a grin I didn't really feel, "the game's a third of a meter!"

CHAPTER 11

Fifteen minutes later, I was feeling even *less* gung ho about it. It's one thing to humor a sad-faced beauty by telling her you're going to help her solve a murder, but getting out there and actually *doing* it is something else entirely.

It was a quarter after two when the lieutenant left us, and the first item on my personal agenda was lunch. Jet wasn't hungry, but when I suggested I'd make a much better crimebuster if I wasn't faint with starvation, she bustled around the kitchen and came up with a couple thick ham sandwiches and two bottles of Grolsch. Terrific bottles, with ceramic caps and rubber stoppers attached to their necks by a cunning arrangement of wires. Terrific beer, too, cold and strong yet very smooth.

Jet picked at her *broodje* and drank about a third of her beer, while I polished off my own share eagerly. I wound up too full to eat the rest of her sandwich for her, but I was tempted to finish her Grolsch. She recapped it and stuck it back in the refrigerator before I could claim it, though, and all things considered, that was probably for the best. I mean, maybe his frequent consultations with the office bottle made Sam Spade a better detective, but I'm afraid another beer would have made Jack a dull boy.

While we ate, we planned strategy. Since Lieutenant Smit was going to be interviewing Henk the caretaker before the afternoon was out, we figured there wasn't much sense in *our* bothering him, especially since he hadn't been especially communicative on either of the two occasions I'd previously seen him. Instead, we decided our best bet would be to tackle the Mevrouws Antonie, Boonstra and de Klerk, the three women who, as far as we knew, were the last people to have seen Mrs. Moen alive—except for Jet when she brought up the old lady's supper and, of course, the murderer.

Jet washed and I dried, and then I shrugged into my Inverness cape and adjusted my deerstalker at a rakish angle and shot up a seven-percent solution of cocaine, and we set off to catch a killer, humming that little thing of Chopin's that goes tra-la-la-lira-lira-lay and praying for surf.

❧

Ellen Antonie was wrestling her white bicycle down the three stone steps from her front door to ground level under a sky that was threatening to fill with clouds again when we turned in at her gate, and, from the way her youthful face shone when she saw us, it seemed clear that *she* hadn't heard the news yet, either.

Here it was three o'clock and we were sitting on a murder, and no one seemed to *know* about it! No one had heard Jet's scream but me, and no one had noticed the cops swarming in or the body going out on a stretcher late last night, and now it was fifteen hours later and it didn't seem like anyone had even been questioned. What the hell had Smit and his so-called Murder Brigade been *doing* all day?

Since I first saw the place yesterday morning, I'd been thinking of the Begijnhof as a peaceful island set down in the raging ocean of downtown Amsterdam—but it was beginning to look to me like fifty separate islands, not one, with each of them entire of itself and apart from the main.

"Mr. Farmer," Ellen Antonie beamed, "*en de zuster ook nog. Wat enig dat jullie gekomen zijn! Ach*—sorry, I mean, how wonderful! I was just going away to do some shoppings"—she waved an explanatory hand at the battered leather saddlebags hanging limply on either side of the rear wheel—"but I can just as good do that later. Come inside!"

I carried her bike back into the hallway for her, and leaned it carefully against the flowered wallpaper. She ushered us into a comfortable living room bright with cut flowers and green plants, and sat us side by side on an overstuffed Hepplewhite sofa that might well have been a hand-me-down from her parents' parents' parents.

"*Ik ga even 'n lekker kopje thee zetten,*" she announced, and headed for the kitchen, but Jet called her back with a somber sentence I didn't quite catch. Something about *naar nieuws*, which I took to mean bad news.

Mrs. Antonie lowered herself into a velvet armchair with a lacy antimacassar draped over its back and clasped her hands nervously. "*Is er iets met Ans?*"

Jet nodded. "*Ze is dood,*" she said. "*Gisteravond al.*"

The bicycle lady's jaw sagged, and all of a sudden she seemed thirty years older. "*Nee,*" she said. "*Oh, jeetje, dat kan niet!*"

"She was murdered," I added gently, as gently as it's possible to add something that horrible. "I'm sorry, Ellen."

"Murdered?" She echoed the word as if she didn't know what it meant, but I was certain she did. *"Hij bedoelt toch niet dat ze vermoordt is, zuster?"*

Jet moistened her lips with the tip of her tongue. "It's true," she said, in English now. "Someone—she was stabbed to death, sometime last night."

The old woman lifted her fingertips to her mouth in slow motion and spoke through them. "Stabbed," she whispered. *"Wat is dat voor een woord*, stabbed?"

I thrust a fist forward, thumb extended. "Stabbed," I said. "With a knife. The police seem to think Jet might have done it, Ellen, even though she was having dinner with me when it happened. There's an officer assigned to the case, but he's got other things to work on, too, and we're afraid it could take forever before he gets anywhere. So we thought we'd ask some questions ourselves, to try and—"

"Ze denken dat U het gedaan heeft, zuster? Heb ik dat goed begrepen?"

"Nou, niet helemaal. Hoewel ze het graag zouden willen denken, geloof ik."

"Maar dat is toch—het Engelse woord ken ik niet—dat is toch belachelijk?"

"Ridiculous," Jet supplied.

"You bet it's ridiculous," I said.

"Ik kan het haast niet—nee, wacht even—I can—it is—"

She couldn't find the words she wanted, in English *or* in Dutch, and she broke off in the middle of whatever it was she was groping for, quivering with frustration. A tear spilled from one gray eye, and she wiped it away and licked it absently from her finger. "Ans," she sighed, more to herself than to either of us. *"Oh, wat verschrikkelijk is dit allemaal."*

Then she remembered we were there and what we'd come for, and she leaned towards me and said, "What questions, Mr. Farmer? What you have to ask, I will answer."

❧

Ellen Antonie was perfectly cooperative, but she didn't have much to tell us. She'd been sound asleep by ten o'clock last night, she had not heard the scream, she hadn't spotted anyone suspicious lurking in the shrubbery before she went to bed.

What we were mainly interested in, of course, was who might have had a reason for offing Mrs. Moen, but the bicycle lady couldn't come up with a decent suspect. Yes, she realized Ans had been a difficult woman, but, no, she had no idea who might have hated her enough to kill her.

What about someone from her past, Jet suggested, someone who'd held a grudge against her for many years, and had only now chosen to do something about it? Ellen reached back through her memory and told us the very little she knew about Moen's life: childhood on a farm in Brabant, a twenty-five-year career as an administrator for the power and light company in Amsterdam, retirement and the move to the Begijnhof. It was all innocuous stuff, and none of it seemed to get us any forrader.

To get a better sense of the cast of characters, I asked her for thumbnail sketches of the Begijnhof's other residents, and she worked her way quickly around the courtyard, filling us in on the names and histories. The names were all different, but the histories were pretty much the same: ordinary childhoods, ordinary adulthoods, eventually the move to the Begijnhof and then ordinary golden years. The one exception to the pattern was Rietje de Klerk, who'd been as ordinary and likeable and sociable as anyone until seven or eight years ago, when she'd suffered some personal tragedy and closed herself off from the rest of them.

None of it seemed to get us any forrader, and, after a while, we thanked Ellen for her time and I carried her bike back outside for her and we parted; she set off for the time tunnel and the outside world to do her shoppings, and we headed up to #19 at the far end of the bleaching green to try our luck with Mrs. Boonstra.

She received us in a parlor the same size and shape as Ellen Antonie's living room, but the lady herself was such a diminutive creature that the room seemed enormous by comparison. She sat in an overstuffed Victorian chair that dwarfed her, wearing a pale-blue blouse and a skirt the exact shade of the veins traced on her papery skin like a carefully-drawn pattern on fine bone china.

Except for Mrs. Boonstra, everyone I'd met so far in Holland spoke at least a *little* English. She was the exception to the rule, though, so Jet did all the talking for both of us. And, no, this one hadn't heard that Mrs. Moen was dead, yet, either. She took the news better than Reverend Bill or Ellen Antonie, but blanched at the mention of the word murder and excused herself for what turned out to be almost five minutes. When she came back, she acted as if nothing out of the ordinary had happened, but her eyes were red and I was pretty sure she'd been crying.

She hadn't particularly liked Ans Moen, she acknowledged, but she certainly hadn't wished her any harm. And, no, she hadn't a clue as to who might have killed her, or wanted to. Within a quarter of an hour of our arrival, we were back outside.

The gathering clouds had thinned out again, and it looked like there was a chance the sun might favor us with another command performance.

"What do you say we take a break and sit for a bit?" I suggested, waving a hand at the kite-shaped lawn.

"Jack, no!" Jet cried, as I was about to step up onto the low brick wall that surrounded the grass. "It's forbidden to walk there. Didn't you see the sign?"

"Oh, yeah, right. Henk Kleijwegt was all steamed up because some tourists had a picnic out there yesterday. I forgot. What's the big deal, though? I mean, it's not going to hurt anything if we sit down for like five minutes."

"The big deal is this is a cemetery, *oen*, not a public park."

I backed off. "A cemetery? You're kidding."

"For the nuns, hundreds of years ago."

"Wait a second, don't tell me." I thought back to the pamphlet I'd leafed through yesterday morning in *het houten huys*. "The Sisters of St. Begga, right? The Beguines, as in Begijnhof?"

"Very good." She patted my cheek like a kindergarten teacher praising a five-year-old for coloring inside the lines. "Actually, there's an interesting story about the bleaching green. Would you like to hear a story?"

"A bedtime story?" I Grouchoed, waggling my eyebrows and tapping ash from the end of an invisible cigar.

"*Doe niet zo melig*," Jet scowled, hands on her hips. "And, no, it's not a bedtime story. It's a ghost story."

"Oooh, yeah, let's hear it." I took a seat on the wall and patted the bricks beside me, and Jet folded herself into the lotus position, facing me, with her knees touching my thigh and her hands in her lap.

"Once upon a time," she began, "there was a—"

"No good," I said.

She squinted at me. "What do you mean, no good? I haven't started yet!"

"You said 'once upon a time.' That's for fairy tales, not ghost stories."

"Well, how do you start a ghost story in English?"

I thought it over. "It was a dark and stormy night," I decided.

Jet grabbed my leg and shook it. "But it *wasn't* a dark and stormy night. It was once upon a time."

"All right, all right." I turned toward her and covered her hands with mine. This was the first time I'd seen her smile since yesterday, and I wanted it to last as long as possible. "Tell it your way. It's not gonna scare me, though. Once-upon-a-time stories are automatically never scary."

"This one is." She waited while a German couple with a baby in a stroller passed by, *ach-du-lieber*ing about the beautiful flowers, then leaned closer and started in again. "Once upon a time, long ago in the seventeenth century, the Begijnhof was the home of the Sisters of the Blessed Sacrament."

"The Sisters of St. Begga," I corrected her.

"It's the same thing. Now don't interrupt."

"Sorry."

"The Beguines were freer here than they would have been in a cloister: they didn't take vows, and they could own their own possessions. But their order was strict in other ways. They dressed very simply, and any type of showing off was forbidden. They weren't allowed to keep dogs or chickens, because those kinds of animals would disturb the quiet of the Begjinhof."

"They were, of course, permitted to possess one boyfriend apiece," I put in, "as long as they kept him from making any excessive noise."

"You interrupt me one more time," scolded Jet, "and you're going to get a spanking!"

"You promise?"

"*Hou nou op!*" She slapped my hand, then brought it to her lips and lightly kissed away the slap. "Do you want to hear this story or don't you?"

"Yes, ma'am," I said, and she jumped up and pulled me to my feet. The sun was out at last, but the chestnuts stippled the path with shade and narcissus perfumed the air. We rounded the top corner of the kite and walked slowly southward, toward the church. A whitehaired granny was pulling weeds at #10, her older sister sat in a bright-yellow lawn chair in the garden at #8, reading an oversized paperback with a photograph of a beautiful porcelain doll on the cover.

"If a nun broke the rules," my own beautiful doll went on, "she was expelled from the community. Otherwise, she lived until she died, and, *when* she died, she was buried here beneath the grass."

I raised my hand and waited to be called on.

"Mr. Farmer?"

"Why aren't there any gravestones?"

"Ah, because, you see, according to the Beguines' way of thinking, that would be—*verdikkeme*, what's the word I want?"

"Ostentatious?"

"*Precies*. Ostentatious. Well, there came a time when one of the sisters, Cornelia Arents, was suspected of doing something wrong. The legend doesn't say exactly what."

"It was that boyfriend of hers, I'm—"

"Jack!"

I zipped my lip.

"There wasn't any proof against her, so they couldn't throw her out of her house. But everyone was certain she was guilty, and, for the rest of her life, none of the Beguines ever spoke to her again." Jet came to a stop by the windowless concrete north wall of the church and looked out across the central green. "And when she died, they refused to bury her in holy ground. Can you guess where they *did* bury her?"

I didn't have the slightest idea, and admitted as much.

"You're standing on her," Jet smiled—and, sure enough, there was a long, flat tombstone set into the path beneath my feet!

CHAPTER 12

I must have jumped a half a mile. Or, excuse me, make that eight-tenths of a kilometer.

When I landed, Jet was doubled up laughing. "I thought you weren't going to be scared," she gasped.

"I wasn't scared. I'm just not exactly used to walking on some poor dead nun's grave, that's all."

The sapphires glistened. "Of course you weren't scared. You were only practicing your pole-vaulting for the summer Olympics, that's all."

"I wasn't scared," I insisted. "And, besides, you cheated. You said it was going to be a ghost story, but there wasn't any ghost in it."

Jet looped her arm through mine and led me to a wooden bench set against the blank wall of the church. "What I told you is the legend," she explained. "In the official version of the story,

Cornelia Arents *asked* to be buried in the gutter, as a way of doing penance for her sins. They ignored her wishes, though, and put her coffin on display in the church. The next morning, it was found out here on the path, and no one could say who had moved it. They brought it back inside the church, but, the next morning—"

"—it turned up out here on the path again," I guessed.

"Yes. That happened three days in a row, and finally they gave up and buried her in the gutter, after all."

"And at last her spirit was at rest. I think I like the legend better, even without a ghost."

"Me, too. I've told it before, but nobody ever jumped as high as you did."

"Is she really supposed to be under that stone?"

"They say so. And every year, on the anniversary of her death, the parish decorates her grave with flowers. If you come back some time on the second of May, you can see for yourself."

Which was the first time either of us had brought up the fact that I was going to be leaving Amsterdam, sooner or later. Sooner, if you want to be technical about it. In less than two weeks.

It was a troublesome thought, and a long silence fell between us.

"I'd like that," I said at last. "I'd like to come back and see the flowers."

જી

Mrs. de Klerk was not pleased to find us at her door, and she became downright *dis*pleased when we told her we wanted to come in and ask her some questions. When I sprang the news of the murder on her, though, she grudgingly stood back and let us pass. Mrs. Moen's death didn't seem to disturb her—it was, in fact, the first thing I'd said to her in our long and eventful relationship which *didn't* seem to tick her off. Jet and me invading the privacy of her home, however, was clearly an irritation, and the whole time we were there she looked like she was forcing herself not to go running for the bug spray.

The living room in which she seated us took me by surprise. Floral wallpaper, plush furniture upholstered in soft colors, a rosewood breakfront displaying china and assorted knickknacks, nineteenth-century landscapes and still lives that looked like originals, not prints, arranged tastefully on the walls. It was a sweetly feminine room, not at all what I'd've expected from the gangly woman in the slacks and mannish shirt who sat ramrod straight in the least comfortable chair available and waited impatiently for us to ask our questions and get out of her sight.

She didn't offer us tea. She didn't ask if the identity of the murderer was known. She just fussed a little with her snowy coiffure, which was precisely arranged and not at all in need of fussing, nudged her spectacles a centimeter higher on the bridge of her long, straight nose, then folded her bony hands in her lap and waited.

I cleared my throat. "We're trying to find out who had a reason for wanting Mrs. Moen dead," I began, "and we were wondering if you might have—"

"If *I* might have had such a reason?" she snapped.

"Well, actually, no, ma'am. I mean, if you *did* have a reason, sure, we'd like to know about it. But that's not what I was asking. We were wondering if you might have any *ideas*, if you might be able to suggest something. See, at this point we just don't really know where we ought to be looking."

"What I cannot understand," she said coldly, "is why you and Juffrouw Schilders are looking at all. If Ans Moen has been murdered, as you say, then the *police* should be doing the looking, not you."

Cha-ching!

Jet laid a couple paragraphs of Dutch on her, and de Klerk spat back a reply. I didn't understand a syllable of what they were saying, but the general tone of the conversation reminded me of that scene in *Citizen Kane* when Agnes Moorhead sells her son to Walter Parks Thatcher the banker for thirty pieces of silver, and little Charlie's father tries to reason her out of it. Tries in vain, I might add, and Jet's reasonableness now had about the same lack of effect on Rietje de Klerk.

Who stood up and rested a wrinkled hand on the back of her chair, her thin lips drawn even thinner in an angry frown.

"I'm sorry, Jack," said Jet. "She won't talk to us. She says if there's anything the lieutenant needs to ask her, he should ask her himself instead of sending us."

"He didn't send us," I griped. "And if she didn't want to talk to us, what did she let us in here for?" Then I realized I was griping at the wrong person, and aimed a salvo at the Bride of Frankenstein. "He *didn't* send us," I growled. "And if you didn't want to talk to us, then why the hell did you let us in?"

"You are right," she said tightly, "I should not have allowed you in my house. I apologize for my mistake, and I would like now to correct it. Please leave."

"Please leave," I mimicked her, pitching my voice an octave lower to get it right. "Sure, fine, we're on our way. But let me tell you something first, lady. There's been a murder here in Mr. Rogers' neighborhood, and your city cops are about half convinced Jet had something to do with it, in spite of the medical evidence. And I'm going to get to the bottom of it, whether you like it or—"

"Jack." Jet squeezed my arm, and I noticed that, somewhere along the line, we'd both gotten to our feet. "Let's just go. Yelling at her won't help."

I was hopping mad, and an hour of flat-out yelling probably *would* have helped. It would have helped me vent the anger I was feeling, for one thing. One look at the concern on Jet's face had much the same effect, though, and I took a deep breath and let it out, smiled a smile and touched her cheek.

"You got it," I said. "We're outa here. Don't think it hasn't been a pleasure seeing you again, Mrs. de Klerk, because it hasn't. No need to show us to the door. It probably hasn't gone anywhere since we came in."

"Mr. Rogers?" the old bag said as we breezed by her. "*Wie is in hemels naam* Mr. Rogers?"

❧

"Who *is* Mr. Rogers?" Jet wanted to know.

I made a noise which, in all honesty, could only have been called a snort. "Old American television," I said. "Don't worry about it, I was just blowing off some steam."

"I haven't seen that one. Is it anything like *CSI?*"

"Uh, no, not exactly. Mr. Rogers is a lot more, ah, grown-up than *CSI*. Do you get that here?"

"It's very popular. All the American shows are popular—except for the news and *Koot en Bie*, Dutch television is pretty terrible."

"*Koot en Bie?*"

"Old Dutch comedians. They used to be *very* funny, but they're not on anymore. Now it's just a lot of stupid variety shows and quizzes. Your programs are the best things we have."

"Funny. Most of the people I know back home think of American TV as a vast wasteland."

"Well, it's a wasteland here, too, only not very vast. We only have television a few hours a night, and there's only three nets to choose from."

"Nets?"

"Isn't that the word? Three—*weet ik veel*—three choices, three sets of programs. Nederland One, Nederland Two, and Nederland Three."

"Three *networks*. And how many local stations?"

"How many what?"

"Local stations. You know, like a station in Amsterdam with a transmitter that's only strong enough to reach a local audience, and then another one in Rotterdam and another one in The Hague and—"

"No, no, we don't have that. The country's too small. There's just the three nets, that's all."

"No kidding? You've got three channels, period? God, no wonder you people all learn eleven languages. What else is there to *do* around here?"

She sobered up at that. "There's *work* to do, Mr. Farmer. Now do you want to keep helping me do it, or would you rather go look at television?"

I checked my watch. "Ten after four," I frowned. "Won't be anything good on until later, so I guess I may as well stick with you. Lead on, MacWatson!"

✌

It took us the better part of an hour to question the ladies whose residences offered a view of Mrs. Moen's front door. Those of them who were in, that is, which turned out to be most of them. When you're living alone in the Golden Palace, I guess there's not too many other places worth going on a Monday afternoon in Amsterdam.

Anyway, what we were looking for was someone who'd spotted somebody entering Moen's house the night before—and, hopefully, for a useful description of the caller.

What we came up with was nothing.

Including Rietje de Klerk's #40, we counted nine houses from which #33 could be seen—plus the English Reformed Church and *het houten huys*, of course, but both of those had been empty during the relevant time period. Two of the nine occupants we were interested in were out when we rang, so we didn't get to talk with them, and de Klerk hadn't told us a thing worth hearing, leaving an even half-dozen—or, if you want to be all metric about it, six.

Of those six, two had been watching *Idols* on Nederland One while Mrs. Moen was getting herself killed, two had been watching a subtitled rerun of *The Commish* on Nederland Two, one had been knitting a sweater for her sister's granddaughter, and one had gone to bed with a headache at seven thirty. They'd all been sound asleep by the time Jet and I returned to the Begijnhof, and none of them had heard Jet's scream or the comings and goings of Lieutenant Smit and his entourage.

The old-biddy grapevine had kicked in at last, though, and most of the ladies we questioned had heard about the murder by the time we got to them. Everyone was horrified by it, but no one could suggest a motive—and, although two of them recalled glancing out their windows at least once during the course of the evening, neither could remember seeing anyone approaching or entering or even passing #33.

In other words, we came up with zip.

No witnesses, no clues, no suspects, no leads.

As Nick and Nora van de Charles, we weren't exactly making what I would call remarkable progress.

CHAPTER 13

We went back to the red-light district for dinner, quesadillas and a pitcher of icy margaritas at a crowded Mexican restaurant in the Warmoesstraat. The food and drink were fine and dandy, and there was even a floor show, which took the stage shortly after we were seated: a kilo and a half's worth of dachshund attacked this enormous German shepherd and sank its teeth into the poor brute's neck, and the chef had to come out and pry the little bastard's jaws apart with a long wooden spoon from the kitchen to get him loose. The dogs' owners, at opposite ends of the dimly lit dining room, went on eating as if this sort of thing was a regular Café Pacifico attraction, but Jet and I were scared to death Rover and Fido would tip over our table and waste a liter of perfectly palatable tequila.

Our conversation was subdued. We were both depressed about our failure to get anywhere on the killing, and, every time one of us suggested an item for tomorrow's agenda, the other one glumly shot it down.

"Maybe we should just forget it," said Jet at last. "Maybe we should listen to Lieutenant Smit and mind our own business and let him do the detective work."

I guacamoled a nacho in silence.

"Do you think we're making a mistake, Jack? Do you think it's wrong for us to—how do you say it?—to stick in our noses?"

"To stick our noses in," I amended. "Hell, no, I don't think it's wrong. Listen, you feel some guilt about leaving her alone last night, you feel like you're responsible to some extent for what happened. And, not only that, you've got this dimwit Smit who's half-convinced you *dun* it. It's not wrong for you to want the thing cleared up and out of the way as soon as possible, so you can get on with the rest of your life."

"But what about you? It's your first time in Europe, and you've got all that work you're supposed to be doing in the Wooden House, but, instead of seeing the sights or getting your job done, you wasted your whole day helping me. Isn't *that* wrong?"

I thought it over. "I don't know, Jet. Wrong's a pretty heavy word. I could care less about the sightseeing, really, but I probably *should* be getting Prof Harriman's research done for him. This is about eighty thousand times more important, though. There's been a *murder*, for God's sake, and you're a *suspect*. What am I supposed to do, sit around and make notes about some shit that happened three hundred years ago, while Amsterdam's finest puts in overtime trying to send you to prison?"

She leaned forward and planted her elbows on the table, her chin on the backs of her hands. "You know," she said, "you come across as very—is 'flip' a word?—very flip a lot of the time, but underneath all that you're a warm, understanding man. Are you scared to let people see that side of you?"

A hit, a palpable hit. There was still some salt on the rim of my glass, and I lined it up with my mouth and drank. "You've known me for an entire day and a half," I said, "and you just summed me up better than friends I've been close to all my life. How do you do that?"

She smiled. "I don't know. I just look at you, and I see a good person who's afraid he has something to hide."

"Uh-huh. Yes, well, um—oh, Christ, here I go again. I've got this little voice in the back of my head yelling, 'Don't take it seriously! Turn it into a joke!'"

"And?"

I paused. Then: "And I'd really rather not. I like to kid around, Jet, I enjoy it. But I like to be serious, too, sometimes—and, back home, it seems like that doesn't work out real well for me. It's kind of like I've been typecast as Jolly Jack the Joker, and that's the only part I'm allowed to play."

She was quiet for so long I began to think she'd drifted into a daydream. Then she smiled again and said, "Who did the casting, Jack?"

I opened my mouth to blame my parents, my friends, the rest of the world—and suddenly I got it.

"Me?" The possibility amazed me. "You mean I did it to *myself*? That's—I want to say that's ridiculous, except, when I think about it, it's got this weird ring of truth to it."

"Maybe it's true, then," said Jet.

"Maybe it is," I mused. "Jesus, maybe it is."

❦

"Hey," I asked her, later on, after we'd gorged ourselves on sopapillas rich with chocolate and honey, "you're not—well, sort of *going* with anybody, are you?"

"You mean do I have a friend?"

"A boyfriend, yeah."

"Boyfriend, yes, I forgot. In Dutch we just say *vriend*, the same for a regular friend as for a boyfriend."

"You haven't answered my question."

"I know." She raised her cup to her lips, though I'd seen her finish off her coffee five minutes earlier and decline a refill. "No," she said, "I don't have a boyfriend. Boys don't seem to be very interested in me."

"Not—" I shook my head. "Listen, about an hour ago you dug up one of my best-kept secrets and made me look at it. Now let me tell you something about *you*. Boys are definitely interested in you, *zuster*. I guaran-damn-tee it."

"You can guarantee it all you want, but that doesn't make it true."

"It *is* true. Boys are nuts about you, I promise."

"Then why don't they ask me to the film, to a party? Why don't they ask me anywhere?"

I sniffed out a chuckle. "They're afraid of you, Jet."

"*They're* afraid? Of *me*?" She seemed truly baffled. "But why?"

"Because you're so damn *beautiful*, that's why. Every guy who sees you wants to ask you out, trust me, but he knows for a fact you've got eight thousand other guys after you, and all of them are bigger and stronger and smarter and handsomer than he is, so he hasn't got a chance. He's afraid you'll turn him down cold, so, to avoid the rejection, he doesn't even ask."

She mulled that over as if she'd never before considered it. Probably she hadn't. It's bizarre, but the lovelies never do. All they see is the rest of the world avoiding them, and they wind up convinced there must be something terribly wrong with them.

"What's the answer, then?" she demanded. "If I like a boy, how do I get past his fear?"

"You don't wait for him to come to you," I said, uncomfortable about playing Ann Landers under these particular circumstances. "You have to go to *him*, let him know you like him. Why, is there—have you got somebody special in mind?"

She messed around again with her empty cup. "Yes," she said. "Actually, yes, I do."

I drew a breath and sighed it out.

"Oh," I said. "That's—I mean—"

"*You*, you silly American. I like *you*."

Something flip tried real hard to come out of my mouth, but I managed to bite it back. Wasn't easy, but I did it.

"Thank you," I said. "I like you, too."

ↃↃ

The time-tunnel door was locked when we got back to the Begijnhof at eleven. Jet handed me her key, and I opened the door and escorted Jet to #33. Then I folded my arms around her and kissed her. The sky above was a blanket of gray velvet, the moon hidden away behind steely clouds, but twin stars twinkled in the depths of her sapphire eyes.

"Let's get an early start tomorrow," I said. "How's breakfast at eight sound?"

"We haven't even decided what we ought to be doing next," she pointed out.

"Let's just sleep on it," I suggested, "and maybe we'll come up with an idea by morning."

"I don't know if I'll be *able* to sleep," she said, "alone in this house."

And my mind went ballistic.

Back before Pat and I tried living together, I'd spent a lot of time behaving like yer basic Wolfman Jack. I mean, if you had the curves, baby, I had the angles. When I think about it now, it seems pretty awful, but the truth is I went through a long period when I was more interested in quantity than anything else. I'd done a lot of playing around, but never with a woman as utterly desirable as this one. She was the sexiest human being I'd ever seen without a staple in her belly button, and she was warm and cuddly and smart and funny, and she seemed to like me as much as I liked her. And she was European, no less—and I'd heard all *about* European women, nudge nudge, wink wink, say no more.

And there she stood, telling me she didn't know how well she'd be able to sleep, all by her lonesome in Mrs. Moen's big old scary house. And—

And it was wrong. For the first time in my life, I found myself caring too much about a girl to try and maneuver myself between her and her Calvin Kleins at the first opportunity.

Not that I didn't want to. Godfrey Daniel, I most assuredly *wanted* to!

But not now. Not like this. Not yet.

"You slept okay last night," I said hoarsely.

"I was heavily sedated last night."

"Oh, yeah, right." I swallowed. "Well, listen, Jet, I'll be right next door if you need me. You've got the phone number, don't you?"

She smiled up at me. "Yes, *lieverd*. I have the phone number. *Welterusten*."

"*Welte* what?"

"*Welterusten*. It means have a good sleep."

"Ah. *Welterusten*, then. Sleep tight."

❧

Dropje was waiting up for me when I let myself into *het houten huys*, drumming her claws on the floor and looking impatiently at her watch.

"I'm sorry, I'm sorry," I said in a rush. "I had a flat tire. I ran out of gas. The bus was late. I couldn't get a cab. Can you possibly find it in your heart as big as all outdoors to forgive me?"

She threw me a haughty look and refused to talk to me, but, when I whipped up a bowl of cuisine and set it in front of her, she relented a little and mewed a thank-you before tucking in.

It'd been a hell of a day, and I probably ought to have been beat, but I didn't much feel like sleeping. I was tingling with the excitement of what was going on between me and Jet—and I imagine my circadian rhythms hadn't had a chance to catch up with local time yet, either.

Anyway, I was wide awake, so while Dropje chomped away at her *kattebrokjes*, I fetched a yellow legal pad from upstairs and settled down at Gerrit Rombach's cluttered desk to start earning my keep.

Prof Harriman was doing a book on the so-called "Miracle of Amsterdam," an episode which—strangely enough—had some features in common with the Cornelia Arents story Jet had laid out for me that afternoon.

It happened in 1345, a mere six and a half centuries ago. A man lay dying in a house in the Kalverstraat, not far from the Begijnhof. Last rites were administered and he was given Holy Communion, but, shortly after scarfing down the wine and water, he puked his guts out into a spittoon that had been left by his bedside. With the typical Dutch spirit of cleanliness-is-next-to-Godliness, the woman who was attending him dumped the yukky contents of the spittoon onto the fire.

Next morning, she discovered the consecrated Host floating above the flames, pure and untouched. Understandably, she freaked right out, grabbed the thing out of the fire and stashed it away on a clean white cloth in a wooden chest. Her husband ran off to find a priest, who carried the Host to the tabernacle of the parish church of St. Nicholas. But the next day, damned if the wafer hadn't disappeared from the church and reappeared back in the chest in the Kalverstraat!

So it was brought back to the church, and again it vanished, turning up once more in the wooden chest. This happened a couple more times, and eventually the Amsterdam clergy caught on that something unusual was cooking. The house in the Kalverstraat was turned into a chapel, special prayers were written, the Bishop of Utrecht put his two cents in, and blah blah blah.

What's all this got to do with the Begijnhof? Well, the chapel in the Kalverstraat was demolished in 1908, but the city still needed someplace to celebrate the Miracle of the Blessed Sacrament. The Begijnhof got the nod, and to this day it remains the official site of the holy miracle.

Fair enough, as far as it goes, except there are all kinds of gaps in the story, and that's why my portly professor had sent me to Holland. Who was the dying man, and what was he dying of? Who was the lady who found the Host in the fire, and who was the priest she delivered it to? I had a list of about twenty-five such riveting questions, and my job was to dig through the Begijnhof's records and ferret out as many of the answers as I could find.

I didn't get far, though, before my thoughts turned to a different set of problems. I ripped off the yellow sheet I'd been scribbling on and set it aside. I returned the files I'd selected to their assigned places in Rombach's archives. I went back to the kitchen and selected a beer from the crate beside the fridge and a glass from the cupboard.

Mrs. Moen, I printed at the top of a clean page. I poured some beer and drank it and thought. Then I started writing:

1. *She's dead and it wasn't suicide, so somebody must've killed her.*
2. *If somebody killed her, they must have had a motive.*
3. *If we could figure out* why, *maybe that would tell us who.*
4. *So, WHY?????*

So far, so good. Only that was as far as I seemed to be able to get. None of the people we'd spoken with that day had been able to suggest anything even remotely resembling a motive strong enough to justify stabbing the harmless old busybody to death, and no one had noticed a visitor entering the house last night. And, without a motive or a witness, there wasn't—

Wait a second. I refilled my glass and drank more beer and thought back to my one encounter with the dear departed. After a while, I set down the glass and picked up my pen:

5. *Maybe she* wasn't *so harmless, after all. She was a disagreeable old soul, sitting in that window for hours on end and minding the rest of the world's business for them.*
6. *Is it possible she might have seen something she wasn't supposed to see? Could* that *be the reason she was killed?*
7. *What did she see? Who* did *she see? When did she see it?*
8. *There are nine houses with a decent view of #33. Could* she *see into the same nine houses from her bedroom window? Check this out. And what about the church?*

I finished off my beer and got up to go for another one, and then I remembered a couple things Jet had mentioned in passing last night, just before we left the Chinees.

I sat back down again.

> 9. *What was Rietje de Klerk doing there yesterday afternoon? Jet doesn't think she'd ever been by before, so why the sudden social call?*
> 10. *And why were Antonie and Boonstra there on a Sunday, when they usually visited Moen during the week?*

These questions intrigued me, and I was ready to call Jet and risk waking her up to ask her about them when the telephone rang.

Communication, I thought, and scooped up the receiver with a grin. "Hiya! You having trouble sleeping after all?"

"Mr. Farmer? Is that you?"

Oops, I'd forgotten all about Gerrit Rombach!

"Yes, sir, it's me. How'd your talk go this morning?"

"My talk was fine, Mr. Farmer, but I haven't called you from the north of Holland at almost midnight to tell you about that." He sounded very annoyed, maybe an eight-point-five on a scale of ten. "What is happening there? Have the police made any—*vorderingen*, how do you say it?—progress, yes, any progress? I have been trying to reach you all day."

"Oh, gosh, I'm sorry about that, sir. Jet, uh, Miss Schilders asked me to help her nose around a little, and I spent pretty much all day with her. The police were supposed to have been here this afternoon, but we didn't run into them. I was just making some notes when you called, though, and I've got a couple of ideas I want to check on tomorrow."

"Tomorrow? But what about Dexter's work, Mr. Farmer? When does that get done?"

"I've already made a good start on it," I lied, "but it's not easy to concentrate on ancient history with this murder hanging over our heads."

"Yes, I understand. I sink, Mr. Farmer, that it is time for me to return to Amsterdam."

"Well, to be honest with you, sir, I don't really see what good that would do. The sister and I'll do some more digging in the morning, and Lieutenant Smit ought to be around. If you're not finished up there, I'd say you might as well stay on."

I could hear him debating with himself at the other end of the line. "*Dan maar goed,*" he said at last. "You have my number. You will telephone me if you need me?"

"Yes, sir. Absolutely."

"And tomorrow evening you will let me know if there is any news?"

"Sure, Mr. Rombach. I'd be glad to."

"Very well, then. Ah—Mr. Farmer?"

I grinned. "She's fine, sir. She's right here, looking up at the phone like she knows it's you. You want to say hello?"

"You won't sink it's very foolish of me?"

"No, no, not at all. Here, you go right ahead."

So I held the receiver next to Dropje's ear, and he murmured at her for a minute, and I'd swear she followed every word. She purred happily when he said goodbye, strolled over to her box and curled up like she hadn't a care in the world.

I said my own goodbyes and cradled the receiver. It was after twelve, and I decided my list of questions could wait until morning. If Jet was sleeping, it'd be a shame to wake her.

I sat there staring at my ten numbered points, and after a while I found that my attention was focused on the bottom third of the page, which was still blank. I grabbed my pen and divided the empty space in half with a vertical line. To the left of the line I scrawled a plus sign, to the right a minus.

Beneath the plus I wrote Jet's name, beneath the minus the words "twelve more days."

I yawned, and suddenly my eyelids felt heavy.

"Tomorrow is anothah day," I Scarlett O'Hara'd, and dragged my weary bones upstairs.

The narrow bed was very lonely.

CHAPTER 14

"Wat in hemelsnaam ben je nu aan 't doen?"

I smished the two slices of bread together and took a bite. "Huh?"

Jet was staring at me in horror. "What's that you're *eating*?"

"Peanut butter and jelly sandwich," I talked with my mouth full. "What's it look like?"

"You eat *pindakaas* and jam together? That's disgusting!"

I swallowed and licked my chops. "You think *that's* disgusting? Over at the hotel yesterday morning, I saw some kid eating bread and butter with chocolate sprinkles on it!"

"*Ja, lekker*," she nodded. "*'n Broodje hagelslag.*"

I knew the word *lekker*. I'd heard it at the Chinees, and again at Café Pacifico. It meant "delicious."

"A chocolate sandwich is *lekker*, but peanut butter and jelly's disgusting?" I shook my head. "Man, is everybody in Holland this weird about food, or is it just you?"

She shaved a last paper-thin curl from a thick wedge of Gouda cheese and arranged it neatly on her own slice of fresh brown bread, hoisted knife and fork and dug in.

It was around a quarter after eight. I'd dragged myself out of bed at seven thirty, grabbed a quick shower and a shave, slid a bowl of breakfast in front of Dropje and topped off her water dish, and at eight sharp I was ringing the doorbell at #33.

Jet was up and dressed, pretty as ever in a lightweight pink sweater over white slacks, but the paleness of her cheeks and a slight puffiness beneath her eyes told me she hadn't gotten much sleep after all.

She seemed cheerful enough as we ate our sandwiches and drank our coffee, though, and I figured I'd stall as long as I could before getting down to detective business.

As it happened, she was the one who brought it up. I was clearing the dishes from the kitchen table—hey, I'm no chauvinist!—and when I turned from the sink she was watching me, hands folded calmly before her.

"What is it?" I asked.

She moistened her lips with the tip of her tongue. "I spent most of the night thinking about Mevrouw Moen," she said, "but I still can't figure out why anyone would have wanted to kill her. It doesn't make *sense* to me, Jack."

So I opened my mouth to tell her my idea, and, at that moment, the doorbell rang.

Jet went to answer it, and came back to the kitchen with Reverend Bill.

"—pop by and see how you were doing," he was saying, rubbing absently at the mole on his chin with a long, thin forefinger. "Ah, Mr. Farmer, I see you've had the same thought."

I got up and shook his hand, while Jet fetched him some coffee and refilled our cups.

"Poor Mrs. Moen," he said, studiously measuring out three-quarters of a teaspoon of sugar. "What a dreadful tragedy."

"Yeah, the murder was pretty dreadful," I said, "but the tragedy is that the police have this idea that Jet might have had something to do with it."

He paused with his cup halfway to his lips. "But—but that's absurd!"

"Tell me about it. Try convincing the cops, though. They've already got their minds made up."

"It's not *that* bad," said Jet.

"It's bad enough."

The Rev frowned thoughtfully. "Well, is there anything at all I can do to help?"

"Yeah, sure: you can give us a positive identification of the person you saw coming into this house around nine thirty Sunday evening."

"The—the person I saw? But I—I wasn't even here at that hour. I left for home at, well, I suppose it must have been a little after seven."

"All right, so at least you could tell us who had a motive for butchering the old lady. That'd be a—"

I don't know which of them looked more stricken, Jet or Reverend Bill. "I'm sorry," I said. "I didn't mean to sound so cold-blooded. It's just, this thing's got me so uptight, I—"

"I only wish I *could* suggest a suspect," the reverend said wistfully, "but I'm afraid I didn't know her at all well. I've only had this congregation for just over a year, you see, and of course she's been an invalid for much longer than that. Even if she'd wanted to, she wasn't physically capable of attending our services. I called on her several times in the first weeks after my arrival, but she made it quite clear that she hadn't the slightest interest in the Church or in spiritual matters."

"And you've never heard anyone speak angrily about her?" asked Jet.

He sipped his coffee. "I know she was not a popular woman," he said slowly, "but, no, I can't think of anyone angry enough with her to have taken such a—to have done such an unspeakably evil thing as murder."

"Back up a second." Something he'd just said was confusing me. "I thought she'd only been confined to bed for the last four months, but—"

"Oh, no." Jet seemed surprised. "She's been ill for the last ten years. Didn't you—?"

"So she must have had other nurses before you then, right?"

"Yes, of course. I think the record holder made it through an entire seven months before Mevrouw Moen fired her."

"Fired her," I echoed. "That wouldn't have been the last girl who had the job before you took over, by any chance?"

"Ellie Hageman? No, she was one of the ones who quit. She only lasted five or six weeks. You know how difficult Mevrouw Moen was to—"

"I imagine she had a set of keys while she was working here, huh?"

"Keys? Why, yes, I suppose she must have." She got it, then, and drew in a sharp breath. "Jack, you don't suppose she—?"

"I don't know. But it's possible, isn't it?"

"What's possible?" Reverend Bill, who'd been shifting his attention back and forth between us like a spectator at a tennis match, had apparently lost sight of the ball. "What are you driving at, Mr. Farmer?"

It was Jet who replied. "Ellie Hageman obviously had problems with Mevrouw Moen. Otherwise, why did she leave so soon?"

"Ah, yes, quite. And perhaps those problems were serious enough, you're thinking, to have led her to the commission of murder?"

"Her or one of the ones who came before her," I said. "Every one of them must have had her own set of keys, and plenty of opportunity to get copies cut, so any time after they quit or were fired, they could have let themselves back into the Begijnhof and—"

"But why would they have waited until *now*, Mr. Farmer? Ellie Hageman left Mrs. Moen's employ back around February, if I remember correctly, and her predecessors have been gone for even longer than that."

"Maybe one of them's been, uh, sort of nursing a grudge ever since she left, so to speak," I began, but the explanation was as lame as the gag, so I let it drop. The rev had a point: hell may have no fury like a *zuster* scorned, but would a scorned *zuster* let four or more long months go by before she got around to doing something about it?

Possible, but not bloody likely.

The three of us were still trying to figure out a way around the snag when the doorbell rang again. Jet went off to answer it, and came back with a soggy Roelof Smit. His brown curls were damp, his mustache was waterlogged, there were chocolate sprinkles on the shoulders of his tan trenchcoat.

"You're wet, Lieutenant," I greeted him. "Is it raining?"

"Just a little." He shrugged out of the coat and draped it over the back of a wooden chair. "How do you say it in English— dribbling?"

"Drizzling. So what happened to summer?"

Jet set coffee in front of him, and he cupped his hands around it and hunched over it and sucked in some steam. His walrus mustache probably strained all the flavor out of it, but I imagine he was only after the warmth, anyway.

"This *is* summer," he said ruefully. "The only difference between Dutch summer and the rest of the year is that, in the summer, there aren't any R's in the names of the months."

"Lieutenant." Jet leaned toward him eagerly. "Have you found out anything?"

He blew on his coffee and drank some. "A few things, *ja*. I had a talk with Henk Kleijwegt, and you were right, Mr. Farmer, he's full of little hints and suggestions. It's hard to tell if there's anything really relevant underneath all the words, but I get the impression that he *is* holding something back. He wouldn't tell me what it was, though."

"Can't you sort of toss him in a dungeon somewhere and sweat it out of him?"

"Is that the way your American police would handle it?" Smit's condescending sneer would have withered a geranium, if there'd been a geranium on the premises, which there wasn't. "I will talk with him again, Mr. Farmer, but I can't force him to tell me anything he doesn't want to tell me. This is Amsterdam, not Chicago."

He pronounced the "Ch" incorrectly, like in "chicken," and I gave him a condescending sneer which would have withered a tulip, if there'd been a tulip on the premises, which there wasn't.

"He did confirm that the Spui door was locked at nine o'clock on Sunday, as usual," Smit went on, "and he took me around and showed me the other entrances."

"The other entrances? I thought the door off the Spui was the only way in."

"Oh, no," said Reverend Bill, clearly pleased to be able to make a contribution, "there's an iron gate at the back, between #12 and #14, that leads to the Historical Museum, and a heavy wooden door between #1 and the back of the church that opens into a narrow alley, the Begijnsteeg."

"We passed it yesterday, Jack, just a few meters from the place where Cornelia Arents is buried."

"So the fact that the Spui entrance was locked doesn't mean anything," I pounced. "The murderer could have come in through Cornelia's door or the gate!"

Smit shook his head. "Kleijwegt locked the gate at five, when the museum closed, and the door to the Begijnsteeg at seven. The gate, *trouwens*, is four meters high, with iron spikes at the top, so it would have been almost impossible to climb over without anyone noticing. Besides, the museum has alarms hooked up to both of its doors. To get into the Begijnhof through the gate, first the murderer would have had to break into the museum without setting off the alarms, then—"

"Not necessarily," I tried. "He could have hidden himself in the museum while it was still open, and then, after closing, all he'd have had to do was—"

"But the Spui door was open until nine," said Jet reasonably. "Why would anyone want to hide in the museum and then have to worry about climbing the gate, when he could walk right into the Begijnhof as much as several hours later and hide in here until he was ready?"

"Oh. Good point." I poured the lieutenant and the reverend each another half-cup of coffee, finishing the pot. "But, wait a second, where is there to hide in here? There aren't any nooks and crannies."

"*Precies*," Smit nodded. "And this is why I'm sure it was someone who lives in the Begijnhof who did the murder. Yes, maybe it's possible some outsider found a place to hide, after all, or hid in the museum and climbed over the gate, or broke in through the Begijnsteeg door or the Spui door without attracting any attention or leaving any traces, but it's much more likely that it was someone who was here on the scene anyway."

Jet and the reverend and I all eyeballed each other glumly. "He's probably right," I admitted. "Okay, Lieutenant, but listen, forget about all that for now. I had this idea last night, and I want to run it past you and see what you—"

I never got the chance.

"I didn't only come to tell you about Henk Kleijwegt," Smit cut me off. "I also have some information about Mevrouw Moen's finances, and about her testament. Her will, *bedoel ik*."

"How'd you dig that up so fast?"

"When I came back to the Begijnhof yesterday afternoon, I rang the bell here, but no one answered. So I let myself in with the key I got from you, Mr. Farmer, and searched the old woman's bedroom. In the night table beside her bed, buried beneath a pile of other papers, I found a bankbook on the Algemene Bank Nederland and a copy of her will."

"So she *did* have some money stashed away! How much? I bet it turns out she was stinking rich!"

"Stinking rich," he repeated. "That's interesting. We say it the same way in Dutch: *stinkend rijk*."

"Yeah, right, fascinating. Come on, Lieutenant, what was she worth? A million? A couple million?"

"*Ongeveer dertig duizend. Iets minder, eigenlijk.*"

I turned eagerly to Jet for a translation.

"About thirty thousand Euros," she said. "A little less, actually."

"Well, shit, that's no big deal. It's like, what, maybe forty thousand dollars?"

"It's a lot of money," Jet protested. "More than I can earn in a year. Where in the world did she get it?"

"When I'm lucky," said Smit, "I'll have an answer to that sometime today."

"But, meanwhile," Reverend Bill mused, "there's another rather important question, isn't there? *Cui bono?*"

"Ah, yes," I nodded sagely, "Sonny Bono's Dutch uncle Cui. I understand he's a—"

Jet slapped my arm to shut me up. "It's not Dutch, you *oen*, it's Latin. 'Who benefits?'"

"Who—? Oh, right, sure, the will. If the old lady had a will, that means she had beneficiaries. And if she had beneficiaries, that means there were people with a built-in motive for killing her. All right, Lieutenant, spill it: *cui bono?*"

I should have seen it coming. In retrospect, I can't believe I didn't. As it happened, though, it was like a smack upside the head with your well-known blunt instrument when Smit put a fist to his mouth and forced an unnecessary cough and pronounced Jet's name.

CHAPTER 15

The furniture was Paleozoic. Wardrobe, dresser, desk, chair, bed—all were bulky oaken pieces that had already been antiques in Cornelia Arents' time. The curtains were standard-issue white gauze, the floor was weathered wood, the comforter on the bed was proof positive that a ton of feathers weighs just as much as a ton of gold.

Only the personal touches scattered here and there distinguished the room from Mrs. Moen's boudoir down the hall. A studious gray teddy bear in bifocals and a plaid scarf sat beside a Snoopy in a red nightshirt atop the dresser, with an assortment of tubes and jars of girl stuff and a pale-blue alabaster bowl filled with earrings at their feet.

The desk was cluttered with papers and photographs and, behind them, a dozen paperbacks; the books were mostly Dutch, but there were well-worn English copies of Updike's *Rabbit, Run* and Nabokov's *Pale Fire* there, too.

Where the old lady's walls were bare, except for a single small oil painting of contented cows in a misty landscape, Jet had covered hers with a riot of posters: an abstract figure in shades of blue and purple advertising a Paul Klee exhibit in Florence, Mickey Mouse as the Sorcerer's Apprentice, Dragan Maksimovic crossing the bridge to knowledge in a scene from the film version of Gurdjieff's *Meetings With Remarkable Men*, fourteen happy toucans promoting Conservation International, others. My favorite was a stylized Oriental print of two craggy green peaks staunchly holding their heads above a boiling yellow sea. The caption, by an anonymous Japanese poet, read: "I am moving all day and not moving at all. I am like the moon underneath the waves that ever go rolling."

And that, of course, was Jet, and had been for the last two hours. She lay beneath the heavy white comforter, tossing restlessly from stomach to side to back to side to stomach, asleep but not at peace. I sat close enough to stroke her forehead when the dreams got bad, and when I did, she'd settle down again for a while, until the monsters returned.

She woke up around eleven, just as I finished counting the toucans for the umpteenth time, saw the ceiling above her and turned her head and saw me and blinked her eyes.

"What happened?" she said. Her voice sounded perfectly normal.

I skootched a little closer and touched her cheek. "How do you feel?"

She took inventory. "Fine, I think. A little tired. What *happened?*"

"Lieutenant Smit and the reverend were here. Do you remember?"

She blinked again, and I could see the memory come back. "Oh, Jack, yes. That poor old woman! She didn't have anyone else, so she put me in her will."

"You didn't know about it?"

"No, she never told me. A lawyer came to the house about a month ago, but she didn't tell me why, and of course I didn't ask. She never talked about personal things with me. I always thought she was so cold, but—I can't believe she put me in her will. What a sweet thing to do. I wish I'd known about that side of her before she—before she died."

She threw back the comforter and sat up, her legs draped over the edge of the bed. "Did I faint?"

"You sure did." I smiled. "That's the first time I've ever actually seen that happen. Here's me with my giant intellect, I go, 'Gee, Lieutenant, probably whoever she left her money to's the one who killed her,' and Smit licks his lips and twirls his mustache and goes, '*Nyah*-ah-ah!'"

I stopped smiling. "It just doesn't add up right, because of the medical evidence, but now that he figures you had a motive, I think he's really convinced you did it after all, Jet." I sighed. "The jerk."

I looked up and saw tears in her eyes.

"What am I going to do?" she whispered.

I took her hands. "Wrong pronoun," I said.

She didn't follow at first, but then she got it and wiped away the tears, and the sun peeked out a little from behind the clouds. "We," she said. "What are *we* going to do?"

❧

"… six, seven, eight," Jet counted. "Nine, if you include that little bit of #46 that sticks out from behind the corner of the church."

"Include it," I said. "There's enough of the window visible for Mrs. Moen to have spotted something going on behind it."

"What, though? What could she have seen that would make someone want to kill her?"

"No idea. But I was thinking, while you were asleep. You said it yourself. That thirty thousand Euros she had in the bank. Where did she *get* that money?"

"I don't know. I didn't even know she had it."

"Well, I'd sure like to find out. Wouldn't it be interesting if somebody's been sticking, say, a couple hundred Euros a month in that account for her?"

Jet frowned. "You mean—?"

"I mean blackmail. What if Mrs. Moen saw somebody up to something weird in one of those nine houses and started blackmailing her, and—"

"Jack, they're all little old ladies! What could they possibly have been doing that was so horrible?"

"You got me, honey. But then, what was Mrs. Moen doing that was so horrible it got her murdered? If she saw something she wasn't supposed to see and was bleeding one of her neighbors to keep quiet about it, maybe the victim got tired of paying her off or ran out of money or something, and decided to kill her and get it over with."

We were sitting on the window seat in Mrs. Moen's bedroom, me in the old crow's favorite vantage point and Jet beside me. After I'd finally explained my idea to her, we'd trooped down the hall to check out which of the Begijnhof's houses could be spied on from Moen's window. There weren't all that many of them that fit the bill, just numbers thirty-eight through forty-six, all of which fronted the south wall of the English Reformed Church and had the Spui at their backs—the same nine houses we'd previously figured had offered their residents the opportunity to see someone entering #33 on Sunday night. The stained-glass windows high in the south wall of the church were invisible from our position, and there weren't any windows in the western façade that faced us from across the path or the blank northern façade that would have looked out across the bleaching green if there'd been anything to look *through*, so the church was out. If Mrs. Moen had seen anything that could have led to blackmail, it had to have happened in one of those nine houses—which meant, luckily, that the field of possible suspects was narrow.

"I'm betting on Rietje de Klerk," I said. "That's how come she came over here Sunday afternoon, to try and talk your boss out of bleeding her. She didn't get anywhere, though, so she figured she'd have to kill her. It makes sense, don't you think?"

"You're telling me Mevrouw Moen was a blackmailer and Mevrouw de Klerk is a murderer, and you want to know if I think it makes *sense*? No, Jack, I don't think it makes sense. I don't think *any* of this makes sense."

"But Mrs. Moen is dead," I reminded her. "And there *is* that thirty thousand Euros to account for."

"Yes," she sighed, chewing prettily on her lower lip. "There is all that."

We were silent for a moment, and then Jet looked up and demanded, "Why didn't Lieutenant Smit arrest me when he found out about Mevrouw Moen's will?"

I chuckled. "You were unconscious, that's the main reason. But once I'd carried you upstairs and tucked you in, he told me the rest of it. He got the autopsy results before he came over here this morning, and the medical examiner still figures it's unlikely Mrs. Moen was stabbed any later than about eleven o'clock at the outside. So if you didn't get back from dinner until eleven twenty—which I will testify is what happened—that puts you in the clear."

"But no one saw us, Jack! *We* know we're telling the truth, but the lieutenant must realize we could be lying."

"He sure does. He's suspicious as hell. Unless he can break down your alibi, though—meaning me—he can't arrest you."

Jet jumped resolutely to her feet. "Let's go down and talk with him," she said. "Maybe we can—"

"He's not here. He's out sleuthing, trying to find somebody who'll say she saw us in the Begijnhof before eleven Sunday night."

She slumped back onto the window seat, deflated.

"Hey," I said. "Cheer up a little. *We* know you didn't kill her, and sooner or later either we'll find the real murderer or Smit will."

"Sooner or later," she echoed woodenly.

"Sure. And once that happens, it's all over."

"And Mevrouw Moen is dead."

"Honey," I said softly, "there's nothing we can do about that. You've got to look at the bright side."

"What bright side? I'm the number-one suspect in a murder, Jack!"

"We'll clear that up. I promise."

"I don't have a job anymore."

"You'll find another job, Jet. Trust me."

"Trust *you!*" she snapped, sitting there by the window with her fists clenched and her brilliant sapphire eyes ablaze. "*You* promise! In two weeks, you won't even *be* here anymore! What good will your promises do me then?"

There had to be an answer to that one—but for the life of me I couldn't think what it was.

CHAPTER 16

I aimed a finger at Rietje de Klerk's doorbell, but before I could press it Jet pulled my hand off-course and turned me around to face her.

"I'm sorry I yelled at you," she said. "It's just that—"

"Hey, I understand. Jeez, your boss got murdered and you found the body, and now the cops are annoyed they can't find a way to pin the killing on you. If you *didn't* freak out from time to time, I'd start to worry about you."

The look in her eyes told me that maybe I hadn't understood her, after all. "Oh," I said. "You mean us."

She tightened and released her grip on my hand in an almost painful massage. "Yes, us."

I took a deep breath. What *about* us? We'd only known each other for like forty-eight hours. It was crazy to think there could be anything *important* going on between us that fast. I mean, sure,

Jet and I had forged a bond that was destined to last throughout all eternity—and, in the immortal words of those great Twentieth Century philosophers Wayne and Garth, "monkeys might fly out of my butt."

And yet....

I cupped her face in my hands. "I don't know about us," I said. "I know how I feel when I'm with you, when I touch you like this. And I know how I feel when I think about going back to Michigan and not seeing you again. But there's a lot of questions hooked up to those feelings, Jet, a lot of really major questions, and I don't know how to answer them yet."

"You're not just—playing, though? This isn't just Jack the Joker?"

I pulled her close and rocked her gently from side to side. "I'm not playing, and this is Jack the Very Serious."

She buried her cheek against my windbreaker for a moment, and when she looked up again, the sadness had left her eyes. "You promise?"

"I promise."

"Okay, then. I trust you."

We stood there on the stoop before Rietje de Klerk's front door, wrapped in warmth beneath a slate-gray sky that had stopped dribbling, but that looked like it was making up its mind to dump some heavy-duty rain on our poor little heads.

"Ring the doorbell," Jet whispered. "We've still got a murder to solve, remember?"

I kissed her and let her go and rang the doorbell.

No one answered.

"She's out shopping," Jet frowned. "What do we do now?"

"Hmmm. Well, two choices: we start checking out the other eight women Mrs. Moen could have spied on from her window, just in case, or we hit the bank and try to pry loose some information about her account. You pick."

She mulled it over. "I pick the third choice," she said at last.

"Say what?"

She took me by the arm and led me down the steps. "Lunch," she said firmly. "I'm famished."

❧

Instead of going out through the time tunnel, Jet led me around the church and past Cornelia Arents' grave and the chestnuts and narcissus. At the far end of the bleaching green, between the houses numbered 12 and 14, there was a shallow open space where #13 should have been. There aren't hardly any buildings tall enough for architects to leave out the thirteenth floor in Holland, so I guess they've found other ways to be superstitious.

At the back of the open area was the tall iron gate Reverend Bill had mentioned, its bars close together and newly painted black. We stopped to examine it and agreed that the height of the bars and the wicked spears at their tops and the narrow openings between them and the forbidding lock made it highly unlikely anyone had gotten in this way on Sunday night.

The gate was latched open now, and we went through it to find ourselves facing a long expanse of rusty brick with—I swear I'm not making this up!—a sort of greenhouse affair projecting out a couple feet from the wall and filled with half a dozen suits of armor.

"What the heck is *that?*" I demanded.

Jet looked at me like I'd asked her how much is two plus two. "It's armor," she explained patiently. "They wore it in the Middle Ages to—"

"I know what it *is*, Jet. But what's it *doing* there?"

She giggled. "It's an exhibit, *lieverd.*"

"Oh, right, the history museum."

"*Precies.* It used to be a—*ja, nou, hoe zeg je 'weeshuis' in 't Engels?*—a house for children who didn't have any parents."

"An orphanage?"

"That's right, orphanage. The city bought it up in the early sixties and spent ten or twelve years turning it into the Amsterdams Historisch Museum."

"Yeah, Professor Harriman said I ought to check it out. It's supposed to be pretty interesting."

"It is. Come on, here's one of my two favorite parts."

An automatic glass door whooshed open, and we entered a long gallery that had once been an alleyway between two of the orphanage's dormitories. The brick paving beneath our feet had been restored to its original glory, but an arched glass canopy two stories above our heads and tall glass walls at either end had turned the outdoor passage into an airy display room for the fourteen enormous paintings that hung on what had once been the outside walls of the dorms.

The paintings were wild. Every last one of them showed a different assortment of grim characters in baggy pantaloons and knee stockings, with Van Dyke beards and ruffles around their necks and plumed hats and plush sashes across their chests. Some of them wore armor, some carried swords or guns or pikestaffs, all stared out from the canvas as if they were trying to decide whether it'd be better to string up the artist before or after cocktails.

Jet looped an arm through mine and planted us in front of the largest of the portraits. "They're called *schuttersstukken,*" she said. "Around the beginning of the sixteenth century, there were three civic-defense guilds that kept the peace in Amsterdam, the *schutters.* You're the historian, Meneer Farmer, you ought to know about that."

"Don't get fresh, there, cutie. It just so happens I *do* know about the *schutters'* guilds. There was St. George's crossbowmen, and St. Sebastian's archers, and"—I searched my memory—"and another one," I ended lamely.

"St. John's. And two from three's not bad for an American. Anyway, each guild held a banquet, one time in the year, and—"

"Two *out* of the three and *once* a year. But that wasn't bad for a—ouch, that hurts!"

"—and every year they brought in a painter to do a picture of the group. Have you ever heard of the *Nachtwacht?*"

"The I'm sorry?"

"*The Night Watch*, from Rembrandt. That's the most famous of the *schuttersstukken*, you can see it in the Rijksmuseum. But there are about fifty more of them left in Amsterdam, I think, and this is the biggest collection."

"Way cool," I said. "I like them. What's your other favorite part?"

"We're on our way."

She led me through the other automatic door, at the far end of the gallery. To our left was a gorgeous courtyard—very classical architecture, four brick walls capped with a steeply sloping gray roof lined with dormers—but we headed right, under a dark archway and into the museum's café.

The moment we came through the door, I could see why Jet liked it. The room was big and crowded with tables, the ceiling high and half-timbered. And it's a good thing the ceiling was high, because, otherwise, Goliath would have been pretty darn cramped.

Goliath was—well, hell, he was Goliath. A big old dude, maybe twenty feet tall, in a leather skirt and chest armor, left arm akimbo and a spear even bigger than *he* was in his right fist. David was there, too, about life-size, sneaking up behind the big guy to let him have it with his sling. Both figures were carved out of wood and realistically painted. If Goliath had raised his spear and shaken it at me, I don't think I'd've been a bit surprised.

"They're terrific," I said. "I love 'em!"

We wound our way to an empty table. "They're a hundred years younger than the *schuttersstukken*," said Jet. "There was an amusement park, *De Oude Doelhof*, just outside the city in the seventeenth century, and they had a lot of these figures on the grounds. David and Goliath are the only ones left."

"They're great, Jet." I reached across the table and took her hand. "*You're* great. I like your taste."

"I like your taste, too," she smiled.

I arched my eyebrows. "Ah, yes. Yes, indeed," I said, doing my internationally acclaimed impression of W.C. Fields, "you can taste me any time you like, m'dear."

She blushed, and hid her face behind a menu.

❧

"Delicious," I said, forking a last bite of *pannekoeken* through the teeth and over the gums. Sort of a cross between a pancake and a crepe; I had mine with cheese and mushrooms, Jet's was apple and raisin and dusted with powdered sugar.

We'd managed to keep the conversation away from Mrs. Moen while we ate, but with lunch behind us it was time to get back down to cases.

"Let's try Mrs. de Klerk again first," I suggested. "I still think she's the likeliest. Then, if we don't get anywhere with her, we'll hit the other ladies and the bank."

"We're right around the corner from the bank now, Jack. Maybe we should go there first."

And so to the bank. Out the main entrance of the museum into the Kalverstraat, the long pedestrian shopping street we'd walked on my first night in Amsterdam, back around through a narrow alley to the Nieuwezijds Voorburgwal, and there it was: the Algemene Bank Nederland. The branch manager, Tom Veldhuysen, was a mousy little gentleman with a receding hairline and a handshake that would have scored Wimp on a test-your-grip machine at *De Oude Doelhof*. He seemed out of place behind his glass-and-chrome desk, in an office lush with ferns and framed abstracts.

He'd already spent some time with Roelof Smit, and he was very hesitant about releasing any information on Mrs. Moen's account to us. We finally managed to worm one very interesting fact out of him, though: the account had been opened about seven years ago with a deposit of four hundred Euros, and ever since—on the third of every month, as regular as clockwork—another four-hundred-Euro deposit had been posted.

We tried to get him to tell us where the money'd been coming from all that time, but he pressed his thin lips together and refused to say anything else but "*Goede middag*," which Jet translated as "Good afternoon" but I took to mean, "Hit the road, Jack, and don'tcha come back no more, no more, no more, no more."

"Four hundred a month," I said, when we were out on the street again. "That's, uh, forty-eight hundred a year, times seven years is a little more than thirty thousand Euros. Yeah, it checks."

"And you really think it's blackmail money?"

"What else *could* it be? Seven years ago, she saw something she wasn't supposed to see, and she's been squirreling away four hundred Euros a month in hush money ever since. Only the person she'd been bleeding finally got sick of it and put a knife in her."

"What did she see, though? *Who* did she see? And how can we find out, after such a long time?"

"Hey, hey!" I grinned confidently. "I'm quite the historian, remember? Digging up the past is my specialty. Give me another day or two, and—"

I stopped walking.

"Jack?"

I folded my arms across my chest and sucked my upper lip.

"Jack, what is it?"

"When we were talking with Ellen Antonie yesterday," I said slowly, "she told us Rietje de Klerk used to be as sociable as anyone else in the Begjinhof, until some kind of tragedy happened and she closed herself off from the rest of them."

Jet's perfect jaw dropped. "Seven or eight years ago," she said. "*Gossie.*"

"I'll drink to that," said I.

CHAPTER 17

"She had a brother," Ellen Antonie sighed, reaching back for a set of memories she hadn't used in years. "Ab, he was called. Ab de Klerk. He had a—a little *woning* in Amsterdam-Nord and—"

"An apartment," I said, remembering Gerrit Rombach's use of the term at our first meeting. Jet pursed her lips in grudging approval.

"He was coming all the time to visit her," the bicycle lady went on. "Sometimes two days in the week, sometimes three." She leaned back in her chair and gazed up into the past. "In those times, she wasn't how she is now. She was very happy, very friendly. She was a good friend to me." A smile illuminated her youthful face, and she lapsed into reminiscent silence.

"*Wat is er dan veranderd?*" asked Jet softly.

The smile flickered and faded. "*Hij is dood gegaan,*" she said, then caught herself and added a translation for my benefit. "He died."

"The brother?"

"Ab, yes. He died, and on that moment everything changed. Rietje closed herself away, she wouldn't see anyone, she became"— she tilted her head, as if listening for the English, gave up after a moment and turned to Jet for help—"*wat is 'bijna 'n heremiet' in 't Engels, zuster?*"

"Almost a hermit," said Jet, and the old woman nodded like she'd known it all along.

"Almost 'n hermit. I went to her house, I was afraid she wasn't eating, I brought food for her, but she wouldn't even let me in. She told me through the door to go away. '*M'n broertje is dood,*' she said. '*Ik blijf liever alleen.*'"

"'My brother is dead,'" said Jet. "'I want to be alone.'"

Greta de Garbo, I thought—but for once in my life I was tactful enough to keep my big mouth shut.

I let a couple seconds go by, then took a shot in the dark. "Do you know how he died, Ellen?"

"How he died?" She touched her salt-and-pepper coiffure distractedly. "No. No, I—no. She never talked about it. She never talked about Ab anymore. She never talked about anything, except one second to say hello if I passed her on the path. He was the only family she had left, and when he died, she—changed. From the time he died until Sunday, I almost never saw her again, and the times I did see her she was so—so cold. All the light was gone away from her, and she was dark and—*hoe zeg je 'bitter' in 't Engels?*"

"*Gewoon* bitter," said Jet. "It's the same word."

Ellen's black eyebrows dipped in puzzlement. "The light," she said.

"The what?"

"The light." She nodded, sure of it now, whatever it was. "You asked me yesterday did I see something Sunday night, and I only now remembered. There was a light on, inside the church, Sunday and again last night."

I glanced at Jet, and saw her gripping her knees tightly. *"Hoe laat was 't? Kunt U dat nog herrineren?"*

I knew exactly what she was thinking, despite the Dutch. Just this morning, Reverend Bill had told us he'd left the church a little after seven on Sunday evening. So how late was it when Ellen had seen the light, so to speak?

"Ongeveer negen uur," she said. *"Allebei de nachten."*

"About nine o'clock, both nights," Jet translated tightly. "But maybe he just forgot to turn them off when he left, Jack."

"Both nights? Maybe. Has he ever done that before?"

She considered it. "Not that I've ever noticed. It's always dark by six or seven."

"Huh. Listen, Ellen, I—"

But the bicycle lady's attention had gone back to Rietje de Klerk. "We were friends for ten years," she said, washing her hands fitfully in her lap, "but, suddenly, when Ab died, that didn't mean nothing anymore."

Jet touched my arm. "We have to go," she said.

"Yeah, okay, in a couple minutes. I—"

"It's almost three, Jack. We're supposed to meet Lieutenant Smit, don't you remember?"

I narrowed my eyes. "What do you—?"

"Jack." There was an edge to her voice. "We shouldn't keep him waiting. Let's go, please."

Well, hey, I may be dumb, but I'm not *stupid*. I took the hint, and we got out of there.

❧

"What was *that* all about?" I demanded, as Ellen Antonie's gate swung shut behind us. "We're not supposed to meet Lieutenant Smit. Hell, he's the *last* person we want to see. And I had some more questions I wanted to ask her about brother Ab."

She raised her fine blond eyebrows and looked up at the leaden sky and shook her head. "She was in pain, Jack, couldn't you see that?"

"Of course I saw it," I growled, automatically defending myself, but then I woke up and saw what I was doing. "No, strike that," I said. "I saw it, but I didn't pay any attention to it. You were right to stop me. *Bedankt.*"

Thunder grumbled irritably in the distance, and Jet paused to button up her pale-yellow cardigan. "Where to now?" she said. "Reverend Bill?"

"Either him or Rietje. This thing about Bill is pretty provocative, but I still think she's our best bet. I mean, Ab de Klerk dies of unknown causes around seven years ago, and his grieving sister abandons all her friends and turns into a loner—which I guess would be understandable enough, all by itself—only right around the same time, four hundred Euros a month start showing up in your busybody boss's bank account. Okay, maybe there's no connection, but I'd sure like to have a long talk with Rietje de Klerk."

Fair enough, except there was still no one at home at #40, and today the English Reformed Church was locked up early for a change.

Where the hell was Rietje? Why had Reverend Bill lied about the time he went home on Sunday night, and where was he now? What, if anything, was Henk Kleijwegt holding back?

Nice questions, but neither Jet nor I had anything even remotely resembling answers—so we spent the next couple hours dodging hot, heavy raindrops and making a second go-around of the old ladies in the other houses within line of sight of Mrs. Moen's bedroom. We tried to keep an open mind about it and picture each of them as a woman with a secret, as a victim of blackmail, as a murderess, but it was no good. They were sweet little old ladies, one and all, and the only information they had to offer us was confirmation—several independent confirmations—that there'd been a light showing through the stained-glass windows of the south wall of the English Reformed Church as late as nine thirty on the night of the murder, and even a bit later last night.

We must have rung Rietje de Klerk's chimes a dozen times during the course of the afternoon and early evening, and at seven—with her still among the missing and the church still dark—we finally gave it up and broke for some R & R. Our first stop was *het houten huys*, where Jet took care of Dropje's inner cat while I called Gerrit Rombach at his hotel in the north of Holland to report on the day's events. Or, more accurately, the day's non-events. Same as yesterday, he offered to skip the rest of his conference and return to Amsterdam—and, same as yesterday, not wanting to have to give up being close to Jet, I managed to talk him out of it.

Dinner was a wooden platter piled high with charcoal-broiled lamb chops and I forget how many glasses of *heerlijk, helder* Heineken at the Café de Klos, a crowded but *gezellig* bar on a narrow side street just off the Leidsestraat.

Heerlijk, helder I can put into English for you: it means "delicious, clear" and, according to Jet, it's the "Coke is it!" of Dutch advertising. Don't ask me about *gezellig*, though. *I* asked, and all I got was some vague equivocation about cozy, or maybe comfortable, or maybe homey. However it translates, it refers to a place you feel good to be in, and, with fine food and beer in front of me and Jet beside me, the Café de Klos was as *gezellig* a spot as I've ever occupied.

We talked and talked, then talked some more. The usual stuff: our memories of the past, our feelings in the present, our dreams for the future. Jet told me about her mother and father, who had passed away within six months of each other when she was twelve. Lung cancer, both of them, in a country whose population boasts the world's highest per capita consumption of tobacco products. Up till then, Jet hadn't had much of an idea what she wanted to do with her life, but the kindness the hospital's nurses had shown her parents as they lay there dying had reached inside her and given her a direction she would travel faithfully from that moment on.

And, for the first time I could remember, I shared my feelings about *my* folks, who'd checked out in a freeway smashup while I was still in diapers, and realized in the telling that—just as the loss of her parents had driven Jet into nursing—it had perhaps been the never-having of mine which had been the guiding force that pushed me into history, the study of the otherwise inaccessible past.

An interesting thought to come up with, at the advanced age of twenty-four.

> Jack be nimble, Jack be quick,
> Even an old dog can learn a new trick.

We talked about the murder, too, of course, and our growing conviction that Rietje de Klerk must have had something to do with it.

And maybe we were just plain dumb, but neither one of us considered the possibility that the old lady had bolted until we got back to the Begijnhof a little after eleven and found the windows of #40 still as black as the starless sky above.

"Where could she *be*?" wondered Jet, as we stood there staring up at the blank façade. "She almost never leaves her house, but now all of a sudden she's been gone all day. Jack, you don't think she could have run away, do you?"

I ran that up the flagpole: blackmail, murder, flight. "Sure," I saluted. "Say she went over to your place on Sunday afternoon to try to talk your boss into letting bygones be bygones, but Ellen Antonie and Mrs. Boonstra showed up before they could have the conversation. Later on, though, after you and I went off to the Chinees, she came back by herself and rang the bell, and Mrs. Moen let her in with the—what's it called, again?"

"The *trekker*?"

"Right. So first they talk and then they fight, and finally Rietje sees she's not getting anywhere and uses the knife."

Jet shook her head. "That doesn't make sense. If she came over with the idea of killing Mevrouw Moen already in her mind, why didn't she bring a knife from her own house? And if she wasn't thinking about murder, why did she stop in the kitchen and take one of our knives upstairs with her?"

That took a little thinking, but, after a while, I worked it out. "She didn't bring her own knife because she was afraid it could be traced back to her. She figured if she used one of yours, that'd help pin the killing on you."

"Or maybe she wasn't planning on murder," Jet suggested, "but then, when Mevrouw Moen wouldn't agree to stop blackmailing her, she decided to kill her and went down to the kitchen for a knife."

"That fits. And then when Smit realized the medical evidence wouldn't let him lock you up and you and I came snooping around, she knew somebody was bound to put the pieces together sooner or later, so she split."

"We'd better try to reach him, Jack. The quicker he starts looking for her, the better the chances he'll find her."

"No, wait a minute." I peered around the silent courtyard. There were lights on in several of the houses, but not a soul to be seen on the path or behind the gauzy curtains. "She's been gone all day, anyway. Another couple minutes isn't going to hurt anything. Before we call the cops, I think we ought to take a look around ourselves."

"Jack, that's—"

"I know what it is. But Smit's not exactly a sympathetic ear, Jet." I took a breath. "I want to go in there and scout around a little, see if there's anything to see. Are you coming with me?"

For a while there, I was convinced she was going to turn me down, but then she shook her head and sighed and said, "Do you think one of Mr. Rombach's keys will fit?"

"One way to find out." I sandpapered my fingers on my palm and got to work.

My first six tries were failures. Four of the keys wouldn't even fit the keyhole; two went in but wouldn't turn.

"Lucky seven," I said hopefully, and made my next selection.

"Jack!" Jet gripped my arm. "What was that?"

I froze. There was the sound of footsteps approaching, a hollow clicking of heels on tile that grew louder as we listened.

We pressed ourselves flat against Mrs. de Klerk's front door and auditioned for the Invisible Couple. Someone came through the inner door of the time tunnel, a stooped figure muffled in a dark coat. One of the Begijnhof's swingers, back from a hard night at the disco. If she lived in one of the houses along this end of the complex, there was no way she could possibly miss seeing us.

And, for one terrible moment, as whoever it was hesitated inside the entryway and drank in the still of the night, I thought, *what if it's Rietje de Klerk coming home?* But she was a good head too short to be the Prodigal Daughter Returned, and to my immense relief she muttered something I couldn't quite catch and set off past the Wooden House and #33 and out of sight.

"Jack Farmer," Jet whispered fiercely, *"ik ben nog nooit van m'n leven zo bang geweest."* She went on in that vein, sounding madder by the minute, and, by the time she realized that the reason I wasn't answering her was that she was talking in Dutch, I'd slipped lucky seven into the keyhole and was offering up a silent prayer to St. Jimmy Valentine.

I pressed the key between thumb and forefinger and swiveled my wrist.

The key turned, and Jet stopped swearing.

I twisted the doorknob and pushed the door open. Inside, the hallway was completely black.

"Mrs. de Klerk," I called softly.

There was no answer.

"Mrs. de Klerk?"

Silence.

"Come on," I said, and reached for Jet's hand. She pulled away from me, but I pulled harder, and we stumbled across the threshhold like Hansel and Gretel sneaking into the Gingerbread House.

Jet swung the door shut and locked it from the inside, and I hit the lights.

"Jack," she said urgently, and it came out as close to a hiss as a word without any esses in it can get, "don't you think we should leave it dark?"

"Yeah, sure," I said, "that'll be *gezellig*. Come on, you take the upstairs, and I'll take the downstairs, and I'll get to—"

She grabbed my arm and hung on tight. *"Ben je mal?"* she said, a rhetorical question if I ever heard one. "I'm not going one step away from where you are."

"I can deal with that." I lifted her hand from my arm and intertwined my fingers with hers and led her into the living room.

It hadn't changed any from the way we'd seen it yesterday, but this time we picked up on some of the details we'd missed on our initial visit. The current issue of *Elsevier*, which Jet identified as a Dutch equivalent of *Time*, on the ebony Parson's table before the plush apricot sofa. A Dutch translation of one of Ludlum's commandment books, coffee dregs in a mug and a glass ashtray littered with white cigarette butts on the lampstand beside the matching armchair. Two delicate Oriental vases on the mantle, but no flowers.

The kitchen was almost a duplicate of Mrs. Moen's: small and functional, with off-white cabinets and a gray stone countertop that was cool to the touch, a half-sized refrigerator, a gas water heater hung above the tiny sink. In a plastic rack on the counter, a couple dishes and some silverware that had long since dripped dry.

"Nothing down here," I said. "Let's try upstairs."

There was a painted door set into the underside of the staircase leading up to the second floor. "Cupboard," Jet explained. I tried the knob, but it was locked, and the keyhole was one of those giant jobbies that takes a key you haul around in a wheelbarrow. I didn't need to check Gerrit Rombach's ring to know he didn't have a duplicate.

"Mevrouw Moen kept hers here," said Jet, feeling along the top of the doorframe. And, sure enough, she came up with a dusty old flanged iron key.

The lock argued with her for a moment, but finally it gave up and turned. The door was kind of warped, and it too put up a fight. I had to put some downward pressure on the knob while pulling in order to get it open.

Maybe we should have left well enough alone.

You've heard the phrase, to have a skeleton in one's closet? Well, get ready for this, Gentle Readers: there was a fucking *skeleton* on the floor of Rietje de Klerk's fucking *closet*!

I'm not sure whether or not Jet yelled at the sight.

I know I did.

CHAPTER 18

"*Getverdemme!*" said Roelof Smit. He fumbled in his pockets for a handkerchief and wiped his forehead, though the night was pleasantly cool.

It had taken him forty-five minutes to get there. Since we didn't know how to reach him directly, we called the police emergency number and they switched us through to the Marnixstraat station, where a polite desk sergeant told Jet that Smit was off-duty until eight the next morning and no, he couldn't give out the lieutenant's home number but yes, if it was that important he'd ring him up and have him call us back. So we sat there in Mrs. de Klerk's pretty living room, waiting for the phone to ring and pretending there wasn't a cupboardful of bones on the other side of the tightly closed door.

The phone never rang—but the doorbell did, forty-five minutes later, and, when I answered it, Lieutenant Smit was standing there, pissed off about being hauled out of bed. Until I showed him the closet, and he swore and started toweling himself off with his hankie.

"It's her brother Ab," I explained, the words tumbling out in a rush. "She killed him, seven years ago, only Mrs. Moen saw it happen from her bedroom window and started blackmailing her. Mrs. de Klerk went along with it for all this time, but finally she either ran out of money or decided she just didn't want to have to pay any more, so she killed Mrs. Moen. She knew we'd figure it out, sooner or later, though, so she—"

Smit held up his hands and pushed away the flood of verbiage. "*Wacht effe*," he said, and even I could tell he wanted me to shut up.

I shut up.

He tucked away his handkerchief and glared at us. "Mevrouw Moen was blackmailing Mevrouw de Klerk," he said slowly, as if that was all of it he'd managed to catch. "Now, where did you find *that* clever idea?"

"We went to the bank," I said. "Seven years ago, right around the time Ab de Klerk died, Mrs. de Klerk started paying four hundred Euros a month into Mrs. Moen's account."

Smit seemed bewildered. "They told you that on the bank?" he demanded. "What bank?"

"The Algemene Bank Nederland, around the corner in the Nieuwe—whatever it's called. And, no, they didn't specifically tell us it was Mrs. de Klerk who was paying the money in, but who else *could* it have been? The only thing that makes sense is that Mrs. Moen was blackmailing her."

Smit's expression cleared, and he shook his head sadly, like a tolerant papa whose six-year-old has washed the dishes with Janitor in a Drum in an attempt to be useful. "*Zuster, zuster, zuster*," he sighed. "I can understand this from an American, but *you* ought to know better."

"*Hoe—hoe bedoelt U?*" Jet stammered.

"Do you know how old Mevrouw Moen was when she died?" he said, and I have to give the man credit for sticking to English.

"Yes," said Jet, "of course. She was seventy-two."

"*Precies.* So, how old was she seven years ago, when four hundred Euros started coming on her bank account every month?"

Jet's eyes widened. "Ah," she said, "oh vey."

My own peepers aren't in the same league as Jet's when it comes to widening, but I'm highly skilled at narrowing them. I narrowed them now. "Funny," I said, "you don't look Jewish."

"Jewish?" said Jet.

"Jewish?" said Lieutenant Smit.

"Ah, oy vey," I repeated. "Isn't that—?"

"Ah *oh* vey," said Smit, without the comma.

"A.O.W.," Jet translated glumly. "It's money from the government, Jack. You pay it in when you're younger, while you're working. It's a kind of tax. Then the government starts giving it back to you when you get sixty-five."

"Social Security," I winced.

"'Ah Oh Vey,'" Smit nodded. "Four hundred Euros a month, paid directly on her account at the Algemene Bank Nederland."

"I—well, wait a minute. Four hundred a month over seven years works out to around thirty thousand Euros, and that's what's in the account right now. She never even *touched* that money! So what's she been living off, the last seven years, if not blackmail? She could have—"

"She worked for the *gas-en-licht* for twenty-five years, Mr. Farmer. When she retired, they started paying her a pension. The money went on her *giro*, and that's what she lived from. She didn't touch the A.O.W. because she didn't need it."

"Ah," I said. "Oy vey."

"So Mevrouw Moen *wasn't* blackmailing Mevrouw de Klerk," said Jet miserably. "We were wrong about everything."

"Not so fast," I objected. "'Ah Oh Vey' explains the money in the bank account, and her pension paid for groceries, but what about dem bones, dem bones, dem dry bones in dat closet dere? And where *is* Mrs. de Klerk, if she hasn't done a bunk?"

"A bunk?"

"Sorry, Lieutenant. If she hasn't run off, I mean. Listen, just because that one bank account's been, uh, accounted for, that doesn't mean there's not another one we haven't found yet. Maybe that's the one the blackmail money's been going into. Or else maybe Mrs. Moen just recently found out about Mrs. de Klerk killing her brother—I don't know how, after all this time's gone by, but *somehow*—and the blackmail was just getting ready to start. That's why Mrs. de Klerk went to see her on Sunday, to try and talk her out of it. And when that didn't work, she figured she had to get rid of her." I paused for breath. "I mean, look, if she didn't kill him, then what's he *doing* in there, for God's sake?"

A silence fell over us as we tried to come up with a logical reason for the hip bone connected to the cupboard bone.

"Are you quite sure she's done the bunk?" said Roelof Smit at last.

"Huh?"

"Mevrouw de Klerk. Are you certain she's gone?"

I opened my mouth to say soitinly we wuz soitin, but Jet got there foist.

"No," she said, "we're not certain."

"What? Honey, we've been punishing her doorbell all day. If she hasn't taken off for parts unknown, then where *is* she?"

Lieutenant Smit stroked his bushy mustache. "Have you searched the house?" he asked softly.

⁊

And, as things turned out, Rietje de Klerk had *not* done the bunk, after all. She hadn't even done *a* bunk. We found her in *her* bunk, in her bedroom on the second floor, sitting up in bed in a pair of striped men's pajamas with her spectacles askew and not a hair of her snowy-white coiffure out of place.

There was a long plastic handle sticking out of her chest, and a long metal blade sticking into her chest, and she was about as dead as it's possible for a body to get.

Your Amsterdam police take nothing for granted, though, and Roelof Smit felt dutifully for the vein behind her ear, to see if there wasn't maybe something still pumping away in there somewhere.

There wasn't. But, when he touched her, her head tipped over to the side, and her beautiful white hair slid gracefully off her skull, to land beside her on the flowered bottom sheet with a gentle whump.

Beneath the wig, Rietje de Klerk was completely bald.

The three of us stood there blinking for about forty or fifty years, and then Smit coughed uncomfortably and loosened the drawstring of her pajama trousers and looked inside.

His jaw dropped.

"No," I said firmly. "No, come on, get serious."

The lieutenant licked his lips. "See for yourself," he said.

Feeling very much like a robot in need of a lube job, I crossed the room to Mrs. de Klerk's bedside. Jet, a corner of my mind noted clinically, stayed right where she was in the doorway.

I looked down, inside the pj's—and there it was, all right, all right.

Not only was Mrs. de Klerk no longer among the living, she was no longer *Mrs.* de Klerk at all.

She was a man, with all the appropriate equipment.

"Holy *shit*," I said.

CHAPTER 19

"*Tenminste achttien uur,*" said the same medical examiner who'd dealt with Mrs. Moen forty-eight hours earlier. "*Zou best wel vierentwintig kunnen zijn.*" He was chewing gum as he worked on the body, punctuating his sentences with humungous pink bubbles that threatened to explode in Mrs. de Klerk's face.

That is, Mr. de—oh, hell, you know who I mean.

Whoever he was, he'd been dead for at least eighteen hours, according to Jet's whispered translation, maybe as long as twenty-four. The ME never glanced in my direction or spoke a word of English the whole time he was there. I never even found out his name. Far as he was concerned, I was as dead as the corpse laid out in Mrs. de Klerk's bed. Deader: he didn't talk to either of us, but at least he paid *some* attention to the body.

The whole scene was a summer rerun of Sunday night: same cop, same medico, as far as I could tell the same generic photographer and fingerprint men and uniformed patrolmen I'd watched scour Ans Moen's bedroom for clues. The only changes were that we'd moved over seven houses to a different stage set, and there was a new actor appearing in the role of murder victim.

"Do you have any idea who he is?" Roelof Smit demanded.

Jet and I were sitting side by side in a pair of white wooden chairs one of the uniforms had dragged up from the kitchen, holding hands. It was well after midnight, and both of us were whipped, but Smit had insisted we stick around until he could find time to question us.

And now, it seemed, the time had come, to talk of many things. Of shoes, and ships, and—

"Yes," said Jet. "He's—"

"Now, hang on there, we don't know who he is. We *think* we know who he—"

"Who else could he *be*, Jack? Some stranger? There's no way anyone else could have gotten away with it for all these years."

"I'm not arguing with you. It's just, *we've* never actually seen him before, except when he was dressed up as Mrs. de Klerk. If we're right, though, half the ladies in the Begijnhof ought to be able to identify him. All I'm saying is, maybe it'd be better to let one of them do the—"

"I'm not asking for a formal identification, Mr. Farmer. I'm asking you if you have an idea who he is, and apparently you—"

"Fine," I sighed, and waved a gracious hand. "Take it away, Jet."

She got up and went to the bed and looked down at him. "It's her brother Ab," she said.

"*This* is Ab de Klerk?" The lieutenant glanced up from his notepad. "I thought you said the bones in the closet were—?"

"So we made a mistake." I joined Jet by the side of the bed and took her hand again. "Look, Ab was supposed to have died seven years ago, and Rietje was so upset by his death that she practically turned into a hermit. Only it looks like it must have really happened the other way around: *she* must have been the one who died, not him, and he moved in here and took her place, and the hermit stuff was just an act he put on to keep any of his sister's friends from getting close enough to see through the deception."

"*Momentje, graag.* You're telling me this man—disguised himself as a woman, as his own sister, for seven years, and got away with it? But—but why, Mr. Farmer? *Why?*"

I turned up empty palms. "I haven't got the slightest idea."

"*Zuster? Weet jij d'r iets van?*"

Jet shook her head. "*Nee, ik*—I don't know. I don't understand it. But that must be what happened, otherwise—otherwise...."

She let the sentence trail away unfinished.

"Then the bones downstairs," Smit worked it out slowly, "would be the sister, Rietje de Klerk?"

"*Denk ik ook,*" Jet nodded.

And all at once I remembered this totally bizarre old movie I saw on campus, back in my prehistoric days as a liberal-arts undergraduate. "Oh, sis, poor sis," I paraphrased, "brother's stuck you in the closet and there's something amiss."

Smit glared a question at me.

"Don't you get it, Lieutenant? She didn't just *die*. Ab *killed* her. I don't know why, but that's what happened. Say they got in an argument or something—or maybe it was an accident, he got pissed off at her and smacked her one, and she fell back and hit her head on a table, I don't know. Anyway, he saw he'd have to take the rap if he reported it, and if he just ran away, somebody'd find the body sooner or later and come after him, so he stashed her in the closet and took her place."

"For seven *years*, Mr. Farmer?"

"I know it sounds crazy, but you tell *me* what he was doing living here in women's clothing and a wig and bad makeup, if that's not it."

The lieutenant combed his mustache thoughtfully with the end of his pen. The only sound in the room was the regular cracking of the medical examiner's gum.

Smit called over one of the patrolmen who'd been going through the clothing in Rietje de Klerk's closet and snapped at him like a Dutch uncle, and the cop nodded and left the room without a word. Smit watched him go, then bent over the body and arranged the sheets to completely cover the bloody pajamas, leaving only Ab's neck and head visible. He removed the eyeglasses, stashed them and the wig in a dresser drawer, examined the scene carefully and only then returned his attention to Jet and me.

"He hid his sister's body and took her place," he reminded me. "Go on, Mr. Farmer."

I didn't know what he was up to, but I figured I'd find out sooner or later. And meanwhile, I seemed to be accomplishing what I was hoping to accomplish, which was shifting his attention away from Jet. So what the hell?

"So the problem," I said, "is that Mrs. Moen was a major busybody, see, who spent most of her spare time sitting in her bedroom window spying on her neighbors. She was watching, the day that Rietje de Klerk died, and she saw the murder—or the accident, or whatever it was—she saw it happen. She got in touch with Ab and threatened to turn him in, and he started paying her off to keep her quiet. Only—"

"*Nee, nee, nee,*" Smit scowled. "We have gone over Mevrouw Moen's financial situation very carefully, Mr. Farmer, and there is absolutely no evidence to indicate that she was blackmailing your Mr. de Klerk—or anyone else, for that matter."

"Okay," I said, "so maybe she didn't actually see it happen at the time. But what if she saw something, seven years ago or some time since then, and she finally figured out the truth—this week, a few days ago—and confronted him with it? Either she tried to *start* blackmailing him, or else she threatened to turn him in. Either way, he'd have to kill *her*, too, to keep his secret safe."

The patrolman Smit had sent away ten minutes earlier reappeared in the doorway, and jerked his head back at an invisible someone standing behind him in the hall. Roelof Smit excused himself and went to join them, and, while he was thusly engaged, Jet pulled my ear down to lip level and whispered, "That all sounds wonderful, Jack, except it doesn't make any *sense*. How could Mevrouw Moen have 'figured out' that Ab de Klerk killed his sister, seven years after it happened? What could she have seen that would—?"

"I couldn't begin to tell you," I whispered back. "I'm just makin' noise here."

"Making noise?"

"Just making up a story as I go along."

"But—why?"

"Because Dr. Frankenstein over there figures Ab was killed like between eighteen and twenty-four hours ago, which means real late last night or real early this morning, and those are about the only times in the last thirty-six hours that you and I can't alibi each other for." I squeezed her hand. "We have a saying in America: if you can't fascinate 'em with facts, you better baffle 'em with bullshit."

She smiled wanly. "And you, Jack Farmer," she said, "are the best bullshitter I ever met."

For some reason, I took it as a compliment.

The lieutenant and his flunky came back into the room, bookending one of the old ladies Jet and I had interviewed yesterday afternoon while we were waiting for Rietje de Klerk to show up. Mrs. de Ridder, I think her name was, from #41 next door—although we'd talked to so many of the old souls I wouldn't swear to either the name or the address.

She'd thrown on a ratty chenille robe and slipped her tootsies into a pair of fuzzy pink mules, and, from the absence of cosmetic aids and the state of her hair, it seemed obvious the cop had awakened her from her beauty sleep.

Just as obviously, Smit had gone out into the hall to prime her for the sight of the body, and, when he brought her into the room, she looked as white and frightened as if she'd already seen one. She seemed not to notice Jet and me as they led her past us, and then she was staring down at the man beneath the sheets and blinking in sudden confusion.

She spoke some English, I remembered, but the dialogue that followed was all in Dutch. From what Jet told me later on, when the cop woke her up and asked her to go next door and take a look at a body, Mrs. de Ridder had assumed it was Rietje de Klerk who was dead. The sight of a bald male corpse threw her completely, and at first she insisted she'd never seen the guy before. But Smit told her to think back a few years, that maybe it was someone she hadn't seen in quite some time, and she got control of herself and studied the face carefully.

And gasped.

It's impossible, she said. *It—it can't be true.*

Do you know who he is, Mrs. de Ridder? Do you recognize him now? Can you tell me his name?

"Ab," she said, and I understood that part just fine, both the name and the emotion behind it. "Ab de Klerk."

"I don't want to say we told you so," I began smugly, but Jet cut me off with an elbow to the ribs and a muttered, "Then don't." She's a lovely lady, Jet, but she's got elbows like Swiss Army knives.

I took the hint and shet mah mouf.

Smit and Mrs. de Ridder went back and forth for a while, and, after a couple minutes' chitchat, she glanced over at us and told him something that clearly rubbed him the wrong way. He came over like a lion ready to rip a jackal's throat out and shoved his face a good half-meter closer to mine than etiquette allows.

"You haven't told me what you were doing inside this house tonight in the first place," he growled.

Oops.

"Ah, we'd been trying to locate Mrs. de Klerk all day," I explained. "We thought she might have been involved in Mrs. Moen's murder, and we were afraid she'd run away, so we—"

"So you entered this house illegally."

"We found you another murder victim, Lieutenant."

"You broke into this house, Mr. Farmer. And now Mevrouw de Ridder tells me that you and the *zuster* subjected her to a completely unauthorized interrogation yesterday afternoon."

"Yeah, well, we didn't exactly 'subject' her, and it wasn't exactly an 'interrogation.' We asked her a couple of questions about—"

"She tells me that you also interrogated most of the other women who live in this corner of the Begijnhof about the events of Sunday night."

"We were trying to find out if anybody—"

"Mr. Farmer," he said dangerously, and I'll tell you what, he could have given old Dexter Harriman elocution lessons, "I told you this once already: Mevrouw Moen's murder is a matter for the police to investigate, and you are not an officer of the police. You have no business trying to find out *anything* about—"

"I have no business?" I exploded. "Now you listen to me for a second, Lieutenant. You haven't said one word to indicate that you're not still thinking of my friend as a suspect in this case, and I—"

"Jack!" Jet tugged at my sleeve urgently, but I was thoroughly steamed by then, and I shook her off.

"—and I have got no intention whatsoever of sitting around here twiddling my thumbs while you're off investigating forty-seven other 'police matters.' If there's anything I can do to help prove my friend's innocence, I goddamn well intend to get out there and do it."

Smit opened his mouth to fire another salvo, then seemed to think better of it. Instead, he glared at me for almost a minute, his lips a pair of inflexible parallel lines, then turned to Jet and spoke calmly and at length in Dutch.

When he finished, the room was very quiet for an awfully long time.

Finally, Jet broke the silence. "He's going to arrest us both for illegal entry," she said, "unless we agree to stop—"

She fumbled for a word.

"Interfering," Smit supplied.

"—stop interfering with his investigation." Her voice had gone absolutely flat, the brilliance had left her eyes. "Jack, I—"

"Hearts and minds," I said.

"Hearts and—?"

"Never mind." My academic interest is mainly in seventeenth- and eighteenth-century European history, but the quote I was thinking of was American and much more recent, dating back only as far as the Vietnam Conflict: *If you've got them by the balls, their hearts and minds will follow.*

I grabbed a fistful of the coarse brown hairs between my right wrist and elbow and pulled them hard enough to hurt.

"Okay," I said. "No more interference."

Smit appraised me carefully, and finally he nodded and sighed and checked his watch.

"We're just about finished here for tonight," he said. "I'm going to release the body to the doctor, and I'll have Quispel walk Mevrouw de Ridder home. There will be an autopsy in the morning, and I'll have our forensics lab go over the bones from the closet and see if it's possible to determine how long they've been there. And with *two* murders here in the Begijnhof, Mr. Farmer, you'll be happy to know that I think I can convince the commissaris to put me on this case full-time."

"Be still, my heart," I said. "But what about *us*, Lieutenant? If Ab de Klerk killed Mrs. Moen to keep her from exposing him, at least that lets Jet off the hook, doesn't it?"

"It certainly would," he agreed, pleasantly enough. "I do have one question, though. If Ab de Klerk killed Mevrouw Moen to keep her from exposing him—?"

"*Wie heeft dan Ab de Klerk gedood?*" Mrs. de Ridder asked plaintively from behind him.

"Exactly," said Roelof Smit. "Then who killed Ab de Klerk?"

CHAPTER 20

"With mayonnaise? What are you, kidding?"

"It's not mayonnaise, it's *mayonnaise*." She pronounced it right the first time, *mah-yo-NEZZ-uh* the second. "And, no, I'm not kidding. It's *lekker*."

"*Mah-yo-NEZZ-uh*, then. I still say it's spinach, and I say the hell with it."

"Spinach?"

"Listen, honey, can't we just go across the street and get some Chicken McNuggets or something? I'm serious, did you ever try them?"

Jet made a face. "Once. They tasted like *zaagsel*."

"*Zaagsel?*"

"How do you say it in English? It's like a kind of powder—it comes when you saw a piece of wood."

"Sawdust." I frowned. "Maybe you're right." I perked up again. "They got good burgers, though, and their Filet-O-Fish is—"

"Jack Farmer, you came all the way from America to Holland, you've been here for three days, and already you have to have lunch at McDonald's?"

"All right, fine, forget it, I know when I'm whipped. I just don't think I can eat French fries with mayonnaise, that's all. I don't care how *lekker* it is."

"It's not mayonnaise, I told you. It's—"

"Sorry, *mah-yo-NEZZ-uh*. Don't they have ketchup?"

"Of course they have ketchup. But you can have French fries with ketchup at McDonald's. *Patat met mayonnaise* is real Dutch. Don't you want to—?"

"French fries and mayonnaise," I muttered. "Jeez, I'd rather eat 'em with that peanut sauce from the Chinees."

She looked at me, surprised. "Now that's *real* Dutch," she said, and turned to the kid in the greasy apron behind the counter. "*Eentje met pindasaus en eentje met mayonnaise, graag. En te drinken twee blikjes bier.*"

The kid got busy, and a minute later we each had a can of Amstel in one hand and an oversized paper cone filled with steaming fries in the other, Jet's drenched in creamy white mayonnaise—sorry, *mayonnaise*—and mine slathered with peanut sauce.

Potatoes and peanuts and beers, oh my!

"*Smakelijk eten,*" said Jet, and dug right in.

"Yeah, whatever." I took a slug of *bier* to fortify myself, set down my can and poked around with the little plastic trident they'd given me and found a fry that wasn't completely drowning in sauce. I swallowed nervously, grimaced, and took a bite.

It was *lekker*.

"Here, try this," said Jet, and, when I opened my big mouth to protest, she stuffed it full of *patat met mayonnaise*.

And she was right: it wasn't mayonnaise. It was a lot thicker, richer, with a combination of seasonings I couldn't quite put names to.

"*Lekker,*" I admitted.

"*Heerlijk, zelfs.*"

"What, is *heerlijk* better than *lekker*?"

"'*Tuurlijk.* First comes *lekker*, then *heerlijk*, and then *verrukkelijk.*"

Only in Holland, right? I mean, the Eskimos have got like twenty-five different words for snow, you know? Leave it to the Dutch to come up with three different levels of deliciousness.

"Yours are *heerlijk,*" I agreed, spearing another sample for comparison purposes. "Mine are *verrukkelijk.*"

"And McDonald's?"

"*Zaagsel,* pure *zaagsel.*"

❧

We were in the Leidsestraat, just off Leidseplein, not far from the Café de Klos, where we'd gorged ourselves on lamb chops last—God, was it only *last* night? The snack bar was nothing more than a shallow storefront with an assortment of sandwich meats and strangely shaped breaded objects and cans of pop and beer arrayed behind a glass-topped counter, flanked on either side by walls of coin-operated slots housing eggrolls and chicken drumsticks and a couple of vile items I was doing my damnedest not to look at. Just like the Automat, really, except it was standing room only—no tables littered with drunks and bag ladies nursing cups of long-cold coffee.

The place was open to the street, and crowds of shoppers surged past us and trams rumbled by at regular intervals as we ate our fries and sipped our Amstels.

Despite my arguments of late last night, Lieutenant Smit still seemed three-quarters convinced that at least Jet and probably both of us had been somehow involved in the killings. Fortunately, we'd managed to convince him we had no intention of doing the bunk, so the arrangement we'd settled on was that we were free to come and go as we pleased, as long as we kept our noses the hell out of his investigation.

This morning, in fact, the lieutenant had encouraged us to get out from underfoot while he and his men poked around the Begijnhof. We tried to tell him about the light Ellen Antonie and several of the other women had seen in the English Reformed Church on Sunday and Monday nights, two hours after Reverend Bill insisted he'd locked up and left, but Smit had shooed us out of his sight without paying a lick of attention. The heck with him, we said, and spent a couple happy hours taking in the sights of the city.

I know, I know, I ought to have buckled down and done my homework, but I felt that Jet needed company, and although D.S. Harriman would have made three of her in pure poundage, I decided that she weighed considerably more than he did on my own personal scales.

It was a beautiful summer day for a change, the sun bright and the sky clear and the air warm and clean. Jet was looking like a million Euros in a pale peach skirt that reached just below her knees over a skin-tight yellow leotard, and I was looking like— well, like Mrs. Farmer's boy Jack, in white painter's pants with a deep pocket down the right leg for my shades and a short-sleeved rugby shirt with wide red and white stripes. After *uitsmijters* and coffee at the sidewalk café in the Spui, just outside the entrance to the Begijnhof, we—

What's that? *Uitsmijters?* Oh, yeah, sorry. They're sort of open-faced ham-and-egg sandwiches, with the eggs sunny side up and laid on top of the ham. Maybe halfway between *lekker* and *heerlijk*, if you want to get technical about it. The name, Jet explained, means "bouncer"—as in the urban gorilla who tosses you out of a bar when you've had eleven or twelved too many and are starting to come on to the stuffed moose head on the wall—and neither one of us could figure out what that had to do with ham and eggs.

—so anyway, after *uitsmijters* and coffee in the sun, we strolled across town to the red-light district and checked out the *Onze Lieve Heer op Zolder*, Our Dear Lord in the Attic, one of the spiffiest little museums I've ever seen. Back in the seventeenth century, when the Protestants took over Holland and made it definitely uncool to be a Catholic, the people who *were* Catholic had to either give up their religion or else practice it in hiding. In Amsterdam, about a dozen wealthy burghers had the top floors of their houses converted into secret churches, for the use of their families and friends. *Onze Lieve Heer op Zolder* is the only one left standing today, smack in the middle of the whores; the lower floors have been maintained exactly the way they were three hundred years ago, so you can see how the other half lived, and upstairs is a small but lovely little tucked-away church, complete with pews and altar and even a miniature organ with a full set of pipes—though God knows how they thought they could *play* the sucker without the Protestant neighbors getting just a wee bit suspicious.

From the *ouwehoerenbuurt*, we doubled back to Damrak and boarded a long, flat, glassed-in tour boat called the Koningin Beatrix, which took us along the canals and out into the harbor behind the Centraal Station for an hour and a quarter or so, a synchronized cassette giving us the "On your left, the scenic blahblah" spiel in Dutch, English, French, and German as Jet and I held hands and soaked up rays.

My favorite part was Mr. Tripp's coachman's house, at #7 Singel. The tape didn't go into a lot of detail, but Jet knew the story and filled in the missing pieces in Dutch, French and German before I tickled her back to English. Mr. Tripp's coachman, see, lived in servant's quarters in his employer's beautiful canalside mansion, and one day Mr. Tripp overheard him sighing, "Oh, oh, oh, how I wish I had a house of my own! I wouldn't care if it were no wider than Mr. Tripp's front door!" (A strange thing to sigh, I grant you, but don't shoot the historian.) Anyway, Mr. Tripp, eccentric old bugger that he was, made his coachman's dream come true, and the house is still lived in today, three stories high and less than six feet wide. Jeez, I'd've loved to have seen *that* place from the inside!

The Koningin Beatrix let us off back at Damrak, and we cut through a narrow, dark alley—Buttermilk Alley, Jet translated—to Nieuwezijds Voorburgwal and caught a #2 tram past the Nieuwe Kerk and the Royal Palace and the immense red-brick PTT building and the Nova Hotel.

I got up as we rattled past the Amsterdam Historical Museum and approached our stop, grabbed an overhead strap and turned around to offer Jet a hand.

"Hungry?" she said.

"Mmmm."

So she pulled me back down beside her, and we rode on to the Leidseplein and had French fries and beer.

And then I figured it was time to get serious.

"You're stalling, aren't you?" I said, crumpling up my empty paper cone and tossing it in the trash.

She wiped a dot of *mayonnaise* from the corner of her mouth, and didn't answer me.

"Jet?"

She took a deep breath and let it out slowly.

"I mean, the sightseeing is terrific," I said, "but we can't just hang around museums and take boat rides until this thing gets resolved."

She picked an invisible bit of thread from my shoulder and stood there smoothing the fabric of my shirt with her fingertips and avoiding my eye.

"Jet?"

"We broke into Mevrouw de Klerk's house," she said softly. A tram was going by as she said it, and I could hardly hear her. "Lieutenant Smit will arrest us, if we don't stay out of it. He could send you back to America, if he wanted to."

"And what do *you* want? Do you *want* to stay out of it?"

She didn't answer me for a while.

"Jet?" I said again.

"It doesn't matter what I want," she said. "If we don't leave it alone, Jack, Lieutenant Smit will—"

"*Fuck* Lieutenant Smit. Right now, he's going from door to door in the Begijnhof asking, 'Duh, excuse me, ma'am, you didn't by any chance happen to murder Ans Moen and Ab de Klerk, did you?'—and what are *we* supposed to do, stroll around town admiring the pretty Rembrandts and Van Goghs until one of them breaks down and says, '*Ja, ja*, I cannot tell a lie'?"

She looked at me then, the sapphires glittering in the sun.

And then the gems melted, and the tears came.

✁

"Questions," I said, a while later. We'd resisted the mating call of the adult male Big Mac and settled on ice-cream cones from Cyprian, instead. Jet went straight for strawberry, while I, after giving the matter considerable thought, opted for *stracciatella*, which had the most exotic name. Turned out to be chocolate chip, which wasn't that exotic after all but tasted jes' fine, thanks. "When I have a research project," I said, as we headed up the busy Leidsestraat alongside the tram tracks, "the way I handle it is I break the overall problem down into a bunch of smaller questions. It's a lot easier to handle a stack of little issues than to—"

"*Ietsje pietsje spinnetje*," Jet nodded.

"Eat your what?"

"*Ietsje pietsje spinnetje.* The—*hoe zeg je 't nou?*—the teeny-weeny spider. He wants to get to the top of the drain, but it's much too far to go all that way in one jump, so he—here, hold this." She handed me her cone and touched her left thumb to her right forefinger and her right thumb to her left forefinger, then broke the bottom of the diamond apart and swivelled that thumb and forefinger upwards to rejoin them at the top. And did the same thing again, and again, and—

"The eensy-beensy spider! You have that, too?" I took a lick of strawberry that was about to drip all over my fingers and gave her back her cone.

"*Ja, hoor.* And if the rain comes down and washes him away, he just starts climbing again, one step at a time."

"Like us," I gurgled around my last gob of *stracciatella,* "featuring Roelof Smit as the rainstorm."

Jet linked her free arm through mine. "So we don't worry so much about the big question, right now—"

"Like, who killed your boss and Ab de Klerk?"

"—but instead we start to look at all the little questions."

"Like, why did Reverend Bill say he was gone by seven on Sunday when there was a light still burning in the church several hours later?"

"And what does Henk Kleijwegt know about Mrs. Moen?"

"If anything. And what was Ab doing at your house on Sunday afternoon in the first place?"

"Well, I told you that: Mevrouw Moen called him up and asked him."

"There's another question: asked *him,* or asked *her?*"

Jet pursed her lips. "I don't know. I don't think she knew that he was a man, but I'm not sure."

"Okay, but, either way, had she ever done that before? Invited Ab *or* Rietje over, I mean."

"I don't think so. Not since I've been there, anyway. Not ever, that I know of."

"Then why did she do it on Sunday? What happened all of a sudden to make her invite him? Or her?"

"And why did Ab agree to *go*, after keeping so much to himself for all those years?"

"Excellent! And why did Ellen Antonie and Mrs. Boonstra show up on Sunday, when they usually came visiting during the week?"

"And did either of *them* know Rietje was really Ab?"

"And how come Ans and Rietje were killed twenty-four hours apart? Why didn't the murderer just do them both on Sunday night?"

"And did the same person do both of the murders, or did Ab kill Mevrouw Moen and someone else kill him?"

We zipped across the Spui, dodging traffic, and—

"Hold it," I said, a step from the time-tunnel door. "Mrs. Moen and Ab de Klerk saw each other up close on Sunday, Jet, for the first time in four months, anyway, maybe for the first time in seven years. And then, that same night, she got herself killed."

Jet saw what I was driving at immediately. "And then Ab got murdered, the very next night! Jack, do you think the murders could be related to the time they spent together on Sunday?"

"It's a hell of a question," I said. "Because, listen, Sunday was the first time Ans and Ab saw each other in months or maybe years. But they weren't the only people in your house that afternoon."

Jet's eyes widened. "*Nee*," she said. "*Nee, het kan gewoon niet.*"

No, I heard. *No, it can't be.*

"I don't see why not," I said, proud of myself for understanding my first complete sentence of Dutch. "Your boss and Ab de Klerk are dead. What if Ellen Antonie and Mrs. Boonstra are on the killer's hit list, too?"

Except it turned out that, once again, I hadn't understood her at all. Sure, I had the words right, but—

"That's not what frightens me," said Jet. "Don't you see it? Yes, if Mevrouw Moen and Ab de Klerk were killed because of something that happened on Sunday, it's possible that Ellen Antonie and Mevrouw Boonstra could be the next victims. But, Jack, isn't it just as possible that one of *them* is doing the killings?"

CHAPTER 21

Ridiculous is not a strong enough word to describe it.

Sitting across from Ellen Antonie in her immaculate living room, it was impossible to imagine that anyone could want to kill her, let alone that she herself could be a murderer.

Ans Moen, okay, that was a different story. She'd been a meddling old evil-tempered bitch—not to put too fine a point on it—and it was easy to imagine somebody wanting her permanently out of the way.

Ab de Klerk? Sure, I could buy him in either role.

But the bicycle lady? This sweet little woman, the only one of the Begijnhof's spinsters who'd seen me—not just as an American, a foreigner, an intruder, a man—but as an actual living human being?

Ridiculous. Absurd. Ludicrous. Impossible. You must be joshing.

And yet....

And yet Ans Moen and Ab de Klerk were dead, and *somebody* had to have killed them.

And the murderer had to have been someone who had access to the Begijnhof during the hours when the time-tunnel door and the Begijnsteeg door and the Historical Museum gate were all locked, which pointed pretty directly at one of the residents.

And two of the four residents who'd been present at the Sunday afternoon tea party in Mrs. Moen's bedroom were dead, which made the two still living logical candidates for future victims— and equally logical suspects.

And, the more I tried not to think about it, the more I found myself remembering that fourteen-year-old Turkish girl Lieutenant Smit had told us about.

Only... *Ellen Antonie*, for God's sake?

Or, even weirder, the innocuous Mevrouw Boonstra?

Ridiculous.

And yet....

☙

"That policeman," Ellen said. "*Luitenant* Smit. He was here this morning."

"Yes," said Jet quietly.

"He said me that Rietje is—like Ans, she also is dead."

We waited.

"He said me that she has been dead for seven years, and her brother was living in her house and pretending to be her." She shuddered. "Ab, her brother Ab."

She twisted a white lace handkerchief in her hands. She'd been holding it in her fist when she came to the door, dressed plainly in a long black skirt and a gray blouse with pearl buttons down the front. She had not offered us tea this time, had simply led us to the living room and let us sit. The fabric of her skirt rustled sadly as she wrung the handkerchief between her weathered hands. Its lacy edge seemed damp, and I wondered if she'd been crying.

"He was her *twin* brother, wasn't he, Ellen?"

She looked up at me blankly.

"*Haar tweeling broer*," Jet translated. "*Waren Ab en Rietje de Klerk tweelingen?*"

Ellen Antonie shook her head. Her black-and-gray hair shivered in the sunlight that streamed through the front windows.

"*Nee*," she said. "*Dat niet. Maar ze leken sprekend op elkaar. Heb ik dat niet eerder gezegd?*"

"No, they weren't twins," said Jet. "But they looked very much alike."

"What—? I—?" You could see Ellen struggling with a language gone suddenly unfamiliar. And this was supposed to be a *suspect*?

Humbug.

Was it possible, though, that she was scheduled to be the next one to die?

"We don't understand it, either," Jet said. "We're trying to understand it. We're trying to find out what happened, and to stop anything else bad from happening."

"Sunday afternoon, Ellen." I said it as gently as I could, but I was referring back to a time when Ans and Ab were still alive, and she took it like a slap in the face. "You and Mrs. Boonstra went to visit Mrs. Moen."

"*Ja, da's waar.*"

"You didn't usually go there on Sundays, though, did you?"

"*Nee.* No, we went on—*hoe zegt man diensdag in 't Engels?*"

"Tuesday," Jet murmured.

"On Tuesdays."

"Then why did you go on Sunday this week?"

"Lien and I wanted to have a—"

"Lien?"

The old woman looked confused. "Mevrouw Boonstra," she said—and that, I realized, was the first time I'd heard anyone mention Mrs. Boonstra's given name. "We wanted to have a walk in the city, but it wasn't very good weather, so we decided to see Ans instead."

"Whose idea was it to visit Mevrouw Moen," asked Jet. "Yours or Lien's?"

"*Ik weet niet meer.* Lien's, I think. *Toch wel.* We were walking past the house, and we saw Ans in the window, and Lien said me we should stop and see her."

"Can you remember what time you got there, Ellen?"

She thought back. "*Nee. Ik weet 't echt niet meer.*"

"Jet?"

She turned up her palms. "She's not sure. Neither am I. It must have been somewhere around four thirty, but I don't know the exact time."

"And was—the man you all thought was Rietje de Klerk—was he already there?"

"*Nee, nee.*" Ellen seemed to be pleased to have a question she could answer. "Rietje didn't come until ten minutes or a quarter later."

"Ten or fifteen minutes. And how long were the four of you together before I turned up?"

"Another quarter, I think."

Jet nodded a confirmation of the times.

Chewing absently on a thumbnail, I worked out the math: I'd gotten there about a quarter to five, so Ellen Antonie and Lien Boonstra must have arrived around four fifteen, four twenty, with Ab de Klerk following them at roughly half past. I couldn't for the life of me see what difference the numbers made, but like the bicycle lady I was happy to have something I could feel confident about.

"When you and Mevrouw Boonstra first saw her on Sunday," said Jet, "before Mevrouw de Klerk came, what was Mevrouw Moen like? Did she seem the same as usual?"

Ellen considered the question carefully. "No," she said. "She was always—*ja, een beetje kortaf.*"

"Abrupt. A little abrupt."

"*Precies.* But it wasn't only that, on Sunday. She was—*elders met d'r gedachten.*"

"Distracted?"

"*Ja*, distracted. I was feeling like she didn't really want us to be there."

"What did you talk about?"

"Before Rietje came? *Ik bedoel—ach, wat is 't moeilijk, zeg, met al dit geRietje en geAb!*"

Jet smiled encouragingly. "You didn't know he was Ab at the time, did you?"

"No, no, not until *Luitenant* Smit said me it this morning."

"Just say Rietje then, if that's easier. What did you talk about before Rietje came?"

"*Niets.* I was trying to make some conversations with her, but she almost said nothing. Lien—*nou*, Lien doesn't say very much, but even *she* tried, and Ans almost didn't say 'n word."

I stood up and jammed my hands in my pockets and paced over to the windows, gazed out across the bleaching green, through the tall chestnuts and past the blank concrete north wall of the church to the houses that lined the far side of the courtyard.

"And then," Jet went on, "after I brought Rietje up to you?"

"It—it was terrible." She sniffled, and touched her handkerchief to the corner of her eye. "I was so happy to see her, I hadn't seen her in so long time, I wanted to say her so many things—but she only looked very surprised Lien and I was there, and then she was not so nice to us. *Onbeleefd, bedoel ik. Grof.*"

"She was rude to you? How?"

"She said, 'Why are they here?'" The imitation of Ab de Klerk's mannish Rietje voice was uncanny. "And Ans said her, 'I don't know. I didn't ask them to come.' *Ik voelde me zo—beledigd.* After that, we only sat there and looked at each other."

Jet joined me at the window. "When I brought the tea things up," she whispered, "about five minutes after Ab got there, the room was like a morgue."

"I'm not surprised. Ab and your boss are all set for their big confrontation scene, and suddenly they've got an audience neither one of them wants. Then I come along and make the crowd even bigger. They must have been going berserk on the inside. Why didn't Ab stay on for the showdown when Ellen and Mrs. Boonstra left, though?"

I started to ask that question aloud, but Jet touched my arm and shook her head. Across the room, Ellen Antonie was crying softly into her handkerchief. She wasn't crying about the way Moen and Ab had treated her, I knew. For whatever they'd been worth, she was mourning the loss of two friendships.

We got out of there quietly and left her to her grief.

ꞔꞝ

"Reverend Bill," I said, "you told us you went home around seven on Sunday night."

"Ye-es," the rev said cautiously. "That's right."

"That's right that's when you left, or that's right that's what you told us?"

He stared at me woodenly for a moment, then chewed his lower lip and looked away.

"Ellen Antonie saw a light on after nine," said Jet, "on Sunday and again on Monday. So did several of the other ladies. You *didn't* leave at seven, Reverend, did you?"

He raised his head again, and ran his fingers distractedly through his thin sandy hair. His pale face was agonized. "No," he said hoarsely. "No, you're quite right. I was here until a quarter past nine or nine-thirty, both nights. It was foolish of me not to realize that someone was bound to see the lights."

I wasn't sure how to handle this. I mean, it ain't often I hear a man of the holy cloth admit to having told a story that was made out of whole cloth.

"So why did you lie about it?" I asked.

Tactful, right? Well, excuuuuuse me. But how else was I supposed to phrase it?

Reverend Bill got up from behind his desk and paced restlessly to the bookshelves that lined one wall of his small paneled office. The top shelf was just below eye level, and he raised a hand to stroke the spine of a fat leatherbound volume with a thin forefinger. From my chair on the other side of his desk, I was too far away to make out its title, but I had a solid hunch we were talking Bible here.

"I can't tell you," he said, more to the book than to us.

"You can't *what*? Jesus, Reverend, there've been two *murders* here in the last three days, and there's a good chance you were on the scene when they happened. You damn well *better*—"

"I don't know if you realize how important this is," said Jet. "The police still think I may have been involved in the—in the killings. If you were—"

"I'm sorry, Miss Schilders. I *do* understand how frightful all this must be for you. The investigation, the uncertainty, the doubt." He was forcing the words out, and each syllable seemed to cost him a terrible price. "I wish I *could* tell you about Sunday and Monday, but I simply can't. My being here had nothing to do with the murders, you must believe me. I—"

"Why?" I banged my knee with an angry fist. "Why *should* we believe you? You already lied to us once, why should we believe you now?"

A long minute went by, and when he finally let his hand drop limply to his side and turned back to us, his face was a tortured mask.

"I'm sorry," he said again, his voice thick and strangled. "I *am* sorry. I can't say any more."

I glanced at Jet, and I'll be damned if she didn't have sympathetic concern written all over her.

"Come on," I said, disgusted. "Let's get out of here before I puke."

〜

"*Ja, ja, ja,*" Henk Kleijwegt said gruffly, "I already told that policeman." He struck a match and held the flame just above the bowl of his pipe and sucked in half a dozen quick breaths. "Smit." A cloud of blue smoke filled the air. "On Monday night, I locked the gate at five o'clock and the Begijnsteeg door at seven o'clock and the main door at nine o'clock. The same as Sunday night, the same as last night, the same as every night."

We'd found him in a little cul de sac between the back of the church and the front of #47, standing on a stepladder to replace the light bulb in the ornate iron-and-glass fixture bolted to the red brick wall. The bulb in place and his pipe alight, he folded up his ladder and hoisted a wicker basket filled with new and old bulbs.

"Here, let me get that for you," I said, taking the basket.

He muttered something I took for grudging thanks, and the three of us walked around the church to the fixture on the other side, next to the Begijnsteeg door.

"How well did you know Mevrouw Moen and Mevrouw de Klerk?" asked Jet, as he set his stepladder in place.

"Mevrouw de Klerk," he repeated sarcastically. "Tscha." He gave us that look of his that said he knew more than he was telling.

"Did you know he was really a man all along, then?"

"I have eyes, don't I? I'm not a blind man, am I?"

I handed him a new bulb and laid the old one carefully in the basket. "Then why didn't you do anything about it? Why didn't you tell Mr. Rombach?"

"Tell Rombach?" The pipe jiggled irritably. "Ha! Why should I tell him? You don't think he tells *me* anything, do you?" He spat smoke at us. "No, no, no, I'm only the caretaker; no one tells *me*." Suddenly, he smiled. "But I see things," he said. "I see more than anyone knows."

Jet said, "Can you think of anyone who had a reason to murder Mevrouw Moen or Ab de Klerk?"

He chuckled slyly and folded up his ladder. I bent down for the wicker basket, but he got his callused hands on it before me.

"Have you noticed any strangers hanging around here the last few days?" I tried, just in case.

"*You're* a stranger," he observed drily.

"Ah, yeah, well, I mean anyone else."

"Ha! This is a tourist attraction, Mr. American. Every guidebook of the city brags about it. We get more strangers visiting here than there are old women living here!"

He got a better grip on his ladder and basket, and stormed off in a cloud of smoke.

ↄ

"Anyway," said Jet, "it couldn't have been a stranger, we already know that. The doors were locked, so it had to be a resident."

"Or someone with a key."

"But the only people who have keys are the residents."

"*He* has keys," I pointed out.

"Henk?" Jet frowned. "Well, yes, of course. And Reverend Bill has a key to the Spui door, but...."

We climbed the steps of #19—Mrs. Boonstra's house—and rang the bell.

"Do you really think he knew about Ab?" I wondered.

Jet shook her head. "I don't know. Maybe he *is* just trying to make himself look important."

"He might have, though. He's around here all the time, maybe he really did see something. But if he did, why didn't he do anything about it? Maybe he was—"

The door swung open.

"Well, well, well," said Roelof Smit, "Mr. Farmer and the *zuster*. Come to pay a little social call, have you?"

"We, ah, we—"

He stroked his mustache thoughtfully. "I told you to stay out of this," he said at last. "I told you more than once."

"But, Lieutenant, we—"

"*Geen gebut!*" he exploded. "I want you *out* of here, Mr. Farmer. You can have the rest of Amsterdam to play Sherlock Holmes in— you can have all of Holland, for what I care—but, from now on, the Begijnhof is off-limits!"

CHAPTER 22

"You can't throw me out," I spluttered. "I have Gerrit Rombach's permission to stay here until Friday."

"That's *your* story. But I understand Mr. Rombach is away for the week. Did he leave you a written authorization to—?"

"He didn't write anything down. But he—"

"Mr. Rombach told me that Mr. Farmer had his permission to stay here," Jet put in quietly. "I'm a witness."

"You're a *suspect*," said Smit. "Excuse me for saying it, *zuster*, but your word on this matter doesn't mean very much."

Behind him, Mrs. Boonstra appeared in the hallway, fluttering like a moth at a lightbulb. "*Wat is er?*" she twittered. "*Wat is er?*"

No one paid any attention to her.

"Look, Lieutenant," I tried, "we can get Mr. Rombach on the phone, and he'll tell you it's—"

"I don't care what Mr. Rombach says. The Begijnhof is a homicide scene, Mr. Farmer, and that means *I* get to decide who

can come in here and who can not. I asked you over and over to
stay away from my investigation, but you insist on sticking your
nose into it. And now it's enough."

"I just—"

"*Ophouden!* I want you out of here, Mr. Farmer. You may have
until noon tomorrow to get yourself organized and find another
place to stay, but if I find you talking to anyone about these
murders between now and then, or if I catch you with one foot in
the Begijnhof after twelve o'clock tomorrow, you are going to jail
for obstruction of justice. Do you understand me?"

"Lieutenant, I—"

"Do you *understand* me, Mr. Farmer?"

I swallowed and nodded, and the dirty bastard closed the door
in my face.

෬

There was a patch of sunlight sandwiched between the shade
of two chestnuts on the low brick bleaching-green wall, and Jet
plopped herself glumly onto the warm spot and pulled me down
beside her.

It was a magnificent day, the Begijnhof was an oasis of beauty
and peace, the delicate scent of narcissus perfumed the air.

"Shit," I said. "Motherfuck. Goddamn cocksucking son of
a—"

Jet pressed a finger to my lips. "Does that help?"

I pushed her hand away. "Damn straight it helps. I hope the
shit-eating son of a bitch bastard winds up with a knife in *his*
chest."

Jet sighed. "If it helps," she said, "I hope the *driedubbel
vervloekte choleralaaier direkt naar de hel gaat.*"

"Yeah, that'd serve him right. I hope a fourteen-year-old
Turkish girl throws him in a canal and the fish eat him."

"There aren't any fish in the canals," Jet giggled. "The water's too dirty."

"Fine. I hope the *dirt* eats him. I hope his fucking mustache grows so big it wraps around his neck and chokes him to death."

And then Jet was laughing and trying not to laugh, and then *I* was laughing and trying not to laugh, and we laughed and hugged each other and I buried my face in her long blond hair and before very long there were tears between us, and I couldn't tell for sure if they were Jet's tears or my own.

At last she broke away from me, wiping her eyes with the heel of her hand.

And froze.

"Jack," she said. "Look."

"I'm looking," I said. "I promise you, I'm looking."

"Not at me, you *oen*, behind you."

"Oh, no, I'm not falling for *that* old—"

"Jack Farmer, don't be such a *drol*. Turn around and look behind you."

I turned around and looked behind me. There was no use arguing with a Dutch girl, I'd learned that lesson fast enough.

"*Goed zo*," said Jet. "Now, tell me what you see."

"Grass," I recited obediently. "Trees. Flowers. Houses. An old lady in a lawn chair. A Japanese guy in a suit taking a picture. The Begijnsteeg door. The church. The Wooden—"

"The church," she pounced. "The *church*, Jack! Look at the church!"

"I'm *looking*! What am I supposed to see?"

She snuggled up close and asked, "Which window did Mevrouw Antonie see the light in, Sunday and Monday nights?"

And I stared.

The north wall of the church, the only wall visible from this side of the courtyard, was a blank expanse of dull gray concrete, same as always. No doors, no windows, no nothing.

"I can't believe it," I said. "We've gone past that wall a hundred times since she told us. I can't believe we never noticed."

"There aren't any windows on the front, either. If Mevrouw Antonie saw a light, it had to have been shining through the stained glass on the other side."

"Jeezus. So, somewhere around the time your boss was killed on Sunday night, and somewhere around the time Ab was killed on Monday night, Ellen was over at that end of the courtyard!"

The more I thought about it, the less I liked it. And Jet didn't seem any happier than I was.

"What are we going to do?" she said.

I jumped to my feet. "We've got to go ask her about it."

"We *can't!*" She grabbed my arm and held me back. "You heard the lieutenant, Jack, he'll put you in prison."

"No, he won't. I'm an American citizen, he wouldn't dare."

"*No,* Jack. Listen to me." She pulled me back down beside her and held on tightly, as if she was afraid I'd break loose from my moorings and float away with the tide. "I got you into this—this mess," she said, "and I can't even start to tell you how much I appreciate everything you've done. But it's over now, Jack. It's time to stop. I want you to leave it alone."

"But we're finally starting to *get* somewhere! We got the reverend lying through his teeth, we got Ellen lying through her dentures, we got—"

"Jack." She massaged the back of my hand with her thumbs, not realizing she was rubbing hard enough to hurt. "Please."

I looked at her closely.

She was very serious.

"Okay," I said. "All right. We'll leave it alone. Can we at least tell that prick Smit about Ellen and Reverend Bill?"

She nodded. "I think we should."

"Fine. And then what do we do?"

"I don't know," she said. "I—I don't know."

We sat there on the low brick wall, hand in hand, and I studied the façades of the houses across the path from us, as if they might hold the answer to my question.

And—wouldn't you know it?—they did.

℘

Carved into the stone lintel between the second- and third-story windows of #25, directly opposite us and two doors down from Ellen Antonie's place, was the phrase I'd noticed when I first came to the Begijnhof on Sunday morning: *INIVRIA VLCISENDA OBLIVIONE.*

"What the hell does that mean?" I demanded, not caring, not expecting a reply, just filling in an uncomfortable silence.

Jet looked up and read the inscription.

Her lips parted slightly.

"*Gossie*," she said. "It's just like the church wall: I've seen it a thousand times, but I never really noticed it before."

"Can you read it? It's Latin, isn't it?"

"Latin, yes. I had it at school. And Greek, and English and French and German."

"And you actually *learned* them? I mean, I had like five years of Spanish, but all I can remember is *dos cervezas, por favor*. What does it say?"

"What?"

"The inscription. *Inivria* blah-blah. What's it say?"

"*Iniuria*," she corrected me. "*Iniuria ulcisenda oblivione*. I don't know why, but every time there's a U in a Latin word, they carved a V instead."

"How nice for them. Now read my lips: what does it say? I'll give you a hint, it's something about oblivion, right?"

She blushed. "Sorry. It says, 'Oblivion avenges all injuries.'"

"Yuh-huh. And what exactly does that *mean*?"

She pulled my hand toward her, pressed the back of it tightly to the warm skin just below her throat. A soft breeze whispered playfully to her hair.

Finally, she looked up at me. "It means maybe we shouldn't be cursing Lieutenant Smit, after all. Maybe we shouldn't even worry about who killed Mevrouw Moen and Ab de Klerk."

"Three lousy words mean all of that?"

"Yes. They mean two people who care about each other shouldn't waste the little bit of time they have together trying to get revenge on other people, because sooner or later the other people are going to die anyway, and death is the ultimate revenge."

"Death is the ultimate revenge," I repeated slowly. "Huh. In America, we say living well is the best revenge, but I guess it boils down to pretty much the same thing, doesn't it?"

I got up from the wall. "Come on," I said. "We've got a couple quick errands to run, and then—well, hell, the last stage don't leave Dodge City till high noon tomorrow, so let's see how well we can live between now and then. *That'll* fix 'em!"

☙

First thing we did was mosey on back to Mrs. Boonstra's to tell that swell feller Smit about the rev and the bicycle lady. He couldn't even spare us a thank-you, the pri—uh, the prince, so we bade him adios and vamoosed. Then, while Jet went up to change into her glad rags, I ducked into *het houten huys* to exchange long-overdue pleasantries with Dropje and bring Gerrit Rombach up to date on the latest developments.

Turned out he'd been asked to participate in a panel discussion that was just getting started, though, so I left a message for him to ring me back, cradled the phone, sniffed my pits, and climbed the stairs to get a clean shirt out of my backpack and run a blade over my five-o'clock shadow.

Who knows what evil lurks in the hearts of men?

The Five O'Clock Shadow do!

Fifteen minutes, Jet had said, so I figured that gave me half an hour at least—and, when the doorbell rang fifteen minutes after I'd left her, my first thought was that Roelof Smit had finally seen the error of his ways and was here to beg for my forgiveness, pin a deputy's badge on me and put me in charge of the investigation.

So I clumped downstairs and threw open the door, snarling, "Badges? We don' need your esteenkeen'—"

She was wearing a knee-length pale-blue cotton dress with short sleeves and a modest neckline, cinched at the waist with a cord of the same material. Her golden hair floated loose to her shoulders, there was a touch of violet on her eyelids, a hint of rose on her lips.

Lemme tell ya somethin', Bunkie: if the Begijnhof was a magical place, a Wonderland, an Oz, then Jet Schilders was its Circe, its Alice, its Dorothy.

"Hi," she said.

"Hi," said I. "Uh, listen, come in and read the cat a story or something for a minute, would you? I gotta go upstairs and talk to Wardrobe."

≈

The bar was dimly lit and crowded, alive with the murmur of hushed conversations and an endless succession of sixties tunes from the old Wurlitzer jukebox and the clatter of dishes from an invisible kitchen. A green-and-white pennant from Slippery Rock State College hung over the filthy bar to the left of the ancient cash register, above the shelves of dusty bottles. The bartender, a bald geezer in horn-rimmed specs, was reading a yellowed *Herald-Examiner* with the headline CHILDREN KILL CHILDREN IN VIETNAM RIOTS and ignoring his customers. In the cramped back room, next to the booth where Jet and I were sitting pretending to sip from pretended bottles of pretend beer, a drunk lay sprawled across a table beneath a sign that read, "Minimum charge for table service 25 cents." Someone had taped a coin to the sign and scrawled "This here quarter is so Dwayne can sleep" beside it.

Dwayne was not breathing, but not because he was dead. He was made out of papier maché, like the waitress serving shots and beers to the couple at the other booth, like the couple themselves and the rest of the customers, like the baldheaded bartender. All the background sounds were taped, and Jet and I were the only living souls in the place.

The place was "Barney's Beanery," a lifesized reproduction of a sleazy LA bar by California sculptor Edward Kienholz. I don't know *what* it was doing in the Stedelijk Museum, Amsterdam's modern-art gallery, but it was a little slice of home and I was in love with it.

"This is just like some of the joints I hang out in back in Ann Arbor," I sighed happily. "The Del Rio, the Old Town, the Star Bar. Hey, Barney, can we get a couple more beers back here?"

Barney didn't look up from his paper, the dummy, never even indicated he'd heard me. Actually, he was the only one of the figures with eyes to see and ears to hear. All the rest of them perched realistically on bar stools, hunched authentically over their drinks, leaning casually against a wall, dressed in real clothes and surrounded by the buzz of perfectly ordinary conversations— all the rest of them had clocks instead of heads, their hands all stopped at ten minutes after ten.

"Although on the whole," I said, "this crowd's a lot better-looking than the scum that hangs around the Star Bar."

Jet forced a smile. "Are you—?" She looked away for a second, then came back to me and tried again. "If Lieutenant Smit won't let you back into the Begijnhof after noon tomorrow, you won't be able to do that work for your professor."

Damn. This was a subject I'd been hoping we'd be able to avoid for at least a little while longer.

Scratch that pipedream.

"Yeah," I said. "I know. And if I can't do the work, he's not going to pay my expenses."

I took her hands across the scarred wooden table. On the jukebox, the Penguins were crooning "Earth Angel."

"I have a couple hundred dollars saved up," I said. "I don't know how long I can make it last. There's no way I can afford the Nova for very long. Unless this thing gets settled pretty quick and the lieutenant gets out of our hair, Jet, I'm afraid I may have to go home."

Someone dropped a plate in the kitchen, and a woman's voice yelled angrily.

Jet's eyes were very round and very bright and very blue. "I have an apartment," she said, "in the Wibautstraat, on the other side of the river. It's tiny, it doesn't even have a shower, and it's not such a nice neighborhood, but it's on the ground floor and there's a little garden in the back. You could stay there."

There was something in my throat, and I had to swallow hard to get rid of it. "Thank you," I said. "That's really sweet. But I can't—"

"I have a housing permit, Jack, so the rent's almost nothing, it isn't even a hundred and fifty Euros a month. You could—"

"That's not it, honey. What am I going to *do* if I stay on? I'm here on a tourist visa, so I can't work—what am I supposed to do for money?"

God, I wished Barney would hurry up with those beers.

"I could only stay for a couple months, anyway," I said. "School starts the first week in September. Maybe it's better if I go back now, before we—before you and I get—"

I couldn't finish the sentence. We sat there and held hands beside the sleeping Dwayne, and neither of us spoke. The hands on the faces of the clocks all around us stood still.

"You don't have to decide this minute," said Jet at last. "Can't you wait at least until you talk with Mr. Rombach? Maybe he can fix things with Lieutenant Smit so you can get your work done."

Her hands were warm in mine, her fingers soft and smooth.

"Okay," I said. "Okay."

જી

We found a little Greek restaurant Jet had never been to before—the Mykonos, deep in the heart of the Jordaan, the oldest section of Amsterdam—and ate *taramasalata* and *tsatsiki* with hot *pita* bread, skewers of *souvlaki* and an enormous *horiatiki* overflowing with tomatoes and cucumbers and marinated black olives and *feta* cheese. Our waiter didn't speak any English, but he must have been an American driving instructor or something: every time he brought food or another shot of *ouzo*, Jet called him *F. Harry Stowe* and he told her to *park it in low*. It was all Greek to me.

I wanted to try Gerrit Rombach again and I'd left the number of his hotel back at the Wooden House, so we made an early evening of it. It was a little before ten and the sky was just settling into full darkness when we got back to the Begijnhof. The time-tunnel door was locked, and I opened it up and locked it tight behind us.

We walked up the stone steps to the green front door of #33. Jet fished her keys from her small black handbag, unlocked the door and turned to look up at me.

She was so damn pretty it hurt, and all I wanted to do was pick her up and carry her upstairs to her room and lay her down on her bed beneath the Sorcerer's Apprentice and—and so on.

I mean, that's how it always works in the movies, doesn't it? Boy Meets Girl, Boy Smooches Girl, Boy Rips Clothes Off Girl— and cut to a dramatic shot of surf pounding on a deserted beach.

I remembered the other poster she had hanging on her wall, the Japanese one. I'd spent enough time staring at it while waiting for her to regain consciousness yesterday morning that the caption was fixed firmly in my mind.

I am moving all day and not moving at all. I am like the moon underneath the waves that ever go rolling.

Which was exactly the way I was feeling at that moment. Mixed up, confused, my brain spinning around at twice the speed of light—but underneath all that, down below the turmoil and desire, I was strangely calm.

I knew what I wanted, but I also knew that it still wasn't right, not with so much hanging over our heads, with a killer at large and our relationship nowhere near resolved.

"What is it?" said Jet, smiling quizzically.

"Nothing," I said. "I'll see you in the morning. *Slaap lekker.*"

The kiss was long and warm and wrapped in silk. There were no words attached to it, yet it answered a lot of questions for me.

"*Slaap lekker, lieverd,*" she said, and then she was gone.

I took a breath and let it out, leaned back against the door and surveyed the empty courtyard. Televisions flickered narcotically behind second-story windows. Henk Kleijwegt's new bulbs cast just enough light to navigate the path around the bleaching green.

A single bird chuckled at some private joke, and outside in the city a car horn criticized a careless pedestrian.

I stood there on the doorstep, listening, and suddenly I realized what I was waiting for.

Jet's scream.

It didn't come, of course, and, after a while, I went next door to use the phone.

CHAPTER 23

Gerrit Rombach was off painting the town with a couple of his fellow delegates, but he'd left a message for me with the hotel's switchboard operator. He'd gotten *my* message and returned my call and found me out, and he'd try me again when he came in. If I was going to bed and didn't want to be awakened, I should unplug the phone and call him back in the morning.

It was thoughtful of him to make the suggestion, but there was no way I'd be able to sleep until I talked with him, so I opened a beer and settled down for a cozy tête-à-tête with my good friend Dropje.

"If I could figure out who killed Mrs. Moen and Ab de Klerk," I told her, "Lieutenant Smit'd have to pack up his fingerprint kit and his dirty looks and get the hell out of here. And then I wouldn't have to leave, so I could get Old Glitterdome's research done for him and... and have a little more time to figure out where things with Jet are going."

She jumped up from the floor and paced around on my stomach, looking for a comfy place to settle. "*Mmmhow?*" she said.

"How? Yeah, that's the problem. I've got a box full of jigsaw pieces, but it's like they're all to different puzzles, and I can't see how any of them fit together." I ticked the points off on my fingers. "Seven years ago, Ab de Klerk kills his sister and takes her place, but no one knows why he did it. Then all of a sudden, seven years later, Ans Moen calls up her old friend Rietje and asks her over, and Ab goes, and Ellen Antonie and Lien Boonstra happen to turn up at the same time, and no one knows why any of *that* happened, either."

Dropje's belly shivered happily against mine, maybe about an 0.2 on the Richter scale.

"So then Mrs. Moen gets herself murdered," I went on, stroking her soft black fur from the back of her neck down to the base of her tail. "And then Ab gets murdered, and both times all the entrances to the Begijnhof are locked up tight, so the killer has to be somebody on the inside or somebody with a key, which means one of the old ladies or Henk Kleijwegt or Reverend Bill or Jet or me. And both nights the rev was on the scene hours later than he was supposed to be, and both nights the bicycle lady was out and about at the time of the killings. And maybe Mrs. Moen saw something she wasn't supposed to see, and that's why she got stuck—only why the second murder, then, and did the killer know she was killing Ab, or did she think she was killing Rietje?"

I noticed the pronoun I'd used, and realized I'd pretty much decided the murderer had to have been a murderess. I mean, I knew *I* hadn't done it, and I just couldn't see Henk Kleijwegt in the role. And Reverend Bill? Not bloody likely.

But *who* then? Sweet Ellen Antonie? Fluttery Lien Boonstra? Innocuous Mrs. de Ridder? One of the others?

It didn't make sense, it didn't make sense, it didn't make sense.

I dropped Dropje to the wooden floor and went back to the kitchen for another beer.

☙

The phone rang a little after eleven, and I scooped it up almost before the sound began.

"Mr. Rombach?"

"Yes, hello, Mr. Farmer. I'm sorry I didn't call you before, but I made a late night with some of my colleagues, and I am only now back to my hotel."

"That's okay, sir, I—"

"Is somesing wrong, Mr. Farmer? You sound—"

"Yes, sir, it's terrible. I haven't even really had a chance to *start* Professor Harriman's work yet, and now Smit says I have to be out of the Begijnhof by noon tomorrow and I can't come back."

"Smit?"

"Yes, sir, Lieutenant Smit. He's the police officer investigating the murders."

There was a silence at the other end of the line. "The murders, Mr. Farmer? Murders, with an 's' on the end?"

Oh, shit, that's right, he didn't know about the second killing yet. Unbelievable.

So I told him.

I told him about Rietje de Klerk's bones in the closet, about Ab not dead after all but masquerading as his sister for seven years— but dead *now*, himself a murder victim, with a blade in his chest and his wig askew. I told him about Jet and me investigating, and Smit getting pissed and ordering me off the premises. It was all so awful, I wasn't sure *how* to tell him, so I followed the King's advice to Alice and began at the beginning, went on until I reached the end, then stopped.

The silence that followed my recitation was a long one.

"I have worked in the Begijnhof for fifteen years," Rombach said at last, his voice wooden, "wissout ever a murder happening there. Now I am away for half a week and there are *two* murders?" A tired sigh drifted down the long-distance wires from the north of Holland. "It is too late for me to drive to Amsterdam tonight," he said. "Tomorrow morning I will come."

"Uh, yeah, I think it's time, sir. And, listen, I hate to ask, but maybe you can talk with the lieutenant and explain to him about my research?"

Another pause.

"I will have to sink about it, Mr. Farmer. You didn't tell me about the second murder until now, two days after it happened. I am not happy about that. I don't sink you have acted very— *verantwoordelijk, hoe zeg je 't in 't Engels?* Responsibly, yes. Perhaps the policeman is right, and you should plan on moving back to your hotel."

"But he won't even let me—"

"*No*, Mr. Farmer, I don't want to discuss it now. I will be back late tomorrow morning, we can talk then. Goodbye."

He hung up. He was so dazed by the news, he hadn't even remembered to ask after Dropje.

I hung up, too, and went upstairs to pack my pack.

❧

That took all of five minutes, and when I had my odds and ends all stashed away I stripped and crawled into bed.

I still couldn't sleep, though. There was too much rattling around between my ears. So I dragged myself out of my cot and pulled on my jeans and leaned against the window frame, staring out across the quiet Begijnhof.

Such a peaceful place. It was hard to believe that the tranquil surface spread out before me could cover undercurrents strong enough to have led to a pair of murders.

I'd seen the bodies, though, seen them myself. That poor old woman, that poor old troubled man. Stabbed, bloody, dead.

Mrs. Moen had left her money to Jet, giving her a crystal-clear motive for murder—except Jet hadn't known about the will. I'd found her standing over the first body with the knife in her hand, which gave her means and opportunity, too—except she hadn't done it, I knew that as surely as I—no, *more* surely than I knew my own damn name.

But if Jet wasn't guilty, then someone else was—and despite all the questions we'd asked, all the brainstorming we'd done, we hadn't come up with a single answer that made the slightest bit of sense.

I stood there at the window, and the word "Why?" beat on my brain like a sledgehammer in an Anacin commercial.

Why had Ab de Klerk taken his sister's place seven years ago?

Why had Ans Moen asked him to come see her Sunday afternoon, and *why* had Ab agreed to go?

Why had Reverend Bill lied about the time he left the Begijnhof?

Why had Ellen Antonie been on the south side of the church on Sunday and Monday nights?

Why was Henk Kleijwegt acting so mysteriously?

Why had Ans been killed?

Why had Ab been killed?

I stood there peering through the night at the dark curtained windows of #40 across the empty courtyard, filled with questions, not an answer in sight.

Maybe Roelof Smit was right, I thought. With all our messing around, Jet and I hadn't accomplished a thing except to get in the way of a police investigation. Maybe all we'd been doing was muddying the waters. Maybe I was too—

And then I saw it.

Not all of it, not by a long shot—but one of the pieces I hadn't previously considered was staring me in the face, and I had a horrible feeling it was going to turn out to be the key piece around which the entire puzzle revolved.

"Oh, no," I said aloud, and Dropje roused herself and purred at the sound of my voice.

I turned it upside-down and inside-out and examined it from every angle I could think of. Sure, it answered some of the questions, like who had murdered Mrs. Moen and Ab de Klerk— but it still didn't tell me *why*, and it sure as hell didn't tell me how. In fact, if I was right about the identity of the killer, then the crimes all at once became impossible, like something out of John Dickson Carr.

Jet, I thought.

I had to talk it out with Jet.

I fumbled a T-shirt out of my pack and pulled it over my head, pounded down the stairs and flung open the front door of the Wooden House and zipped across to lean on the bell of #33.

And nothing happened.

No sounds of someone stirring, no lights going on in upstairs windows.

Nothing.

I rang the bell and beat on the door, but the silence of the Begijnhof and the distant murmur of city traffic were my only response.

Suddenly my throat was very dry.

I grabbed the doorknob and rattled it, and it turned in my hand.

Which was wrong, because Lieutenant Smit had had the broken lock repaired, and Jet, I knew, was always very careful about locking up at night.

An eensy-beensy spider of fear crawled up my spine and wrapped its eight cold legs around my neck. And grew.

I threw open the door and yelled her name, but the house was black and still. I took the stairs two at a time, ran down the hall to her bedroom at the back of the house.

The overhead light was on. Jet lay sprawled across her bed, and the sheet twisted crazily around her was streaked with blood.

"Oh, Jesus," I whispered. "Oh, God, no."

I stood there in the doorway, and my eyes began to itch, to blur—

—and, through the tears that fogged my vision, I saw that there was something missing from the scene.

The knife.

There was no knife, and the front of her nightgown was a clean, beautiful, unblemished satiny pink!

An instant later, I was on my knees beside her, my palm pressed flat to her heart.

And it was beating, it was beating strong and alive beneath my hand!

She was unconscious, with a nasty lump on the side of her head that was almost as big as the ones my mother used to put in my oatmeal when I was a kid, but the skin wasn't broken and she was breathing and alive. I took a deep, gasping breath and touched her pale cheek gently with my lips.

And a loose board creaked in the hallway, the loudest single sound I have ever heard in my life.

I jumped to my feet and looked around wildly for something I could use as a weapon, but Jet's reading lamp was on a nightstand on the far side of the bed and there was nothing within reach.

I knew who was out there, who it had to be—I'd figured it out in Gerrit Rombach's bedroom upstairs in *het houten huys* next door.

But I also knew that I was wrong. I *had* to be wrong. What I was thinking, as much sense as it made, as many questions as it answered, just wasn't possible.

A shadow detached itself from the shadows of the darkened hall and stepped forward into the glare of the overhead light.

I wasn't wrong.

There in the doorway—a long, wicked blade clutched tightly in his right hand—stood Gerrit Rombach himself.

CHAPTER 24

Four thin lines flared bright-red down his cheek. Jet had fought with him, had scratched his face, and it was *his* blood that had stained her sheets, not hers.

"Mr. Farmer," he said, with a mocking little bow that scared me worse than the knife in his hand. If he wasn't already crazy, he wasn't far from the edge—and you put a madman and a blade together, I don't like what that spells in any language.

"But—Mr. Rombach, you can't be here. I just talked to you, twenty minutes ago. You were—"

"*I* called *you*, Mr. Farmer, from my—how do you say it?—from my mobile phone, yes, in the Spui. And, as soon as I hung the phone up, I came directly here."

"But how did you get in? Everything's locked up tight, and I've got your keys."

He smiled and shifted the knife to his left hand and pulled something from his trouser pocket. He held it up before his twisted face and jingled it like Christmas bells.

Duplicates. Of course. I mean, *obviously* he'd have a spare set of keys, why the hell hadn't we thought of that earlier?

"So it *was* blackmail, after all," I said, but to tell you the truth I didn't really give a damn. What I was thinking was, if I could just get him talking and keep him talking until Jet regained consciousness, at least then there'd be two of us available to deal with him.

The thing was to get him talking.

"We figured Mrs. Moen must have seen Ab de Klerk kill his sister seven years back," I said, "but a few minutes ago I was upstairs next door looking out across the Begijnhof, and it finally hit me that, if *she* could have witnessed the murder from *her* window, then *you* could have seen it just as easily from *yours*."

His cold gray eyes twinkled merrily, evilly. "It wasn't murder," he said, "but you're right, I did see it happen. They were in her bedroom, moving a heavy wooden dresser away from the wall, and *de gordijnen*, the curtains, were open. It was foolish: she was an old woman, she had no business doing heavy work like that. For a few Euros, she could have had a boy from the university come and move it for her. But not Rietje. She was very—*zuinig*, how do you say it?"

His brow furrowed and his knife hand wavered as he searched for the *mot juste*. I took a half-step towards him, but he saw me coming and raised the blade again. I backed away.

"Economical," he said. "She was very economical, yes."

I licked my lips. "So what happened?"

He grinned, as if he understood what I was up to but wasn't the least bit worried about it. "Suddenly," he said, "she clapped a hand to her heart and fell to the floor. Her brother knelt beside her and tried to help her, but it was already too late. I couldn't see her anymore, she was below the bottom of the window frame, but I could see him very clearly. It was like a program on the television. There was a phone in her bedroom, I kept waiting for him to get up and call a doctor, an ambulance, someone—but he didn't move. A quarter of an hour went by, and he just sat there. He didn't seem to be grieving. It was more like he was sinking."

"Thinking?"

"Yes."

I was getting interested in spite of myself. "So why didn't *you* call the cops?"

"I don't know. I should have, sings would be very different right now if I had. But I was—how do you say it?—transfixed. Yes, transfixed. After a while, he got up and dragged her body out of the bedroom. He had her by the legs, I remember I saw one of her slippers drop from her foot as he pulled her out of sight. I didn't see him again for almost an hour, but I stayed by my window, watching, and finally he came out of the house and left the Begijnhof. I went to the telephone then, and picked it up and dialed for the police, but when it started ringing I hung up and went back to the window."

I risked a glance down at the bed. Jet was still out cold.

"He came back in another hour with a big plastic shopping bag," Rombach continued, "let himself into the house and closed all the curtains so I couldn't see any more. I tried to do my business, but I couldn't stop sinking about it. That night, after dark, I finally had to know what was happening. I went over there and rang the doorbell. He didn't answer, of course, so I let myself in with my passkey. I found him in her bedroom. He was wearing one of his sister's dresses, his legs were shaved, and his face was clumsily made up; the wig he had bought that afternoon was on his head. He was trembling with terror: he was afraid I was a policeman, come to arrest him for not reporting his sister's death."

"But why did he do it, dammit? What in the hell was the *point*?"

And then at last I realized what the point must have been. "The house," I said dully. "It was the goddamn *house*, wasn't it?"

Gerrit Rombach laughed, a chilling sound. "The house, yes," he said. "What else?"

He told me the rest of it then, but except for the minor details I could just as easily have told it to him.

Ab de Klerk was a tired old man, living on a fixed income in a tiny third-floor walkup in a dismal neighborhood in Amsterdam-North; with the housing crunch that plagued the city even then, the odds were he'd be stuck where he was for the rest of his days. And there, on the other hand, was his sister Rietje with comparatively palatial quarters smack in the heart of town—quarters which, now that she was dead, would automatically revert to the Begjinhof's housing authority and automatically be turned over to the next old woman on the waiting list.

Unless, of course, brother Ab hid the body and passed himself off as sister Rietje and installed himself in her house.

That was what he'd been thinking about, there in her bedroom, for the hour he sat hunched over her lifeless form. His first inclination had in fact been to call for help, but he could see that it was too late for anyone to help her—and the scheme exploded full-blown into his mind within a few moments of her death.

Could he carry it off? Could he successfully take her place? His initial reaction was that it would be impossible to make it work, but he couldn't put it out of his head, and the more he considered it....

He was long retired from his job. He had few friends in Amsterdam-North, and no other family left alive. And he and Rietje had always been remarkably alike in appearance. He had little to lose by the masquerade, and much to gain.

Those were the things he considered, as he sat there by her side. And eventually he decided that, yes, what he stood to gain was worth the risk, and yes, there was a chance he might even get away with it.

The plan was outlandish, crazy, absurd. Back where I come from, you want a big apartment, you rent a big apartment—no muss, no fuss, no bother. But here in Amsterdam, where space was at such a premium the government spent billions to reclaim a few hundred lousy acres of farmland from the sea, it all made a sad, perverted kind of sense.

"So you soaked him," I said, disgusted with the seediness of it.

Rombach looked at me, confused.

"Blackmail," I translated. "You threatened to turn him in if he didn't pay you off."

The confusion disappeared, and offended righteousness took its place. "It was *his* idea," he insisted. "I only wanted to understand what was happening, but he offered me money to keep quiet."

"What money? I thought he didn't have any money."

"If I allowed him to take over his sister's life, he did. He had his own A.O.W., and hers, and her savings, and he wouldn't have to pay rent on his *woning* in Amsterdam-Noord any more."

"How could he keep collecting his own A.O.W. if he told everyone he was dead?"

"He wasn't going to tell everyone, only the women here in 't Begijnhof, so they would sink Rietje de Klerk was in—how do you say it?—in mourning, yes, and leave 'her' alone. He had everysing planned out already, and he promised me sree hundred Euros a month if I would let him live in the house. He begged me not to say anysing to the *woningbouw-vereniging*, he went almost down on his knees to me, and I—finally I agreed."

Once again he shifted the knife to his free hand, his left hand. He was right-handed, I knew—I remembered him writing down his phone number in the north of Holland for me before he left the Wooden House on Sunday—and I tensed, hoping for a chance to get close to him. He fished a handkerchief from his pocket and mopped his forehead, tucked it away again and passed the knife back to his right hand.

Shit.

"He kept his end of the bargain," he said. "Every month, sree hundred Euros. And he was very careful. He wouldn't see any of his sister's friends, and for the first few months he never even left the house except once a week to do shoppings for food."

"He was a prisoner," I marvelled.

"It was what he wanted. He kept his curtains closed and lived a comfortable life in a beautiful big house, and on the times when he had to go out, he put on his disguise and pretended to be his sister."

"So how does Mrs. Moen come into it?"

Rombach frowned. "After seven years of getting away with the—how do you say it?—with the deception, yes, he became careless. Only one time, but that was enough. Last Sunday morning, he left the curtains open, and Ans Moen saw him wissout his wig."

"Oh, no."

"*Ach, ja.* She didn't realize that he was a man—if she had guessed that, she would have screamed right away for the police. But she sought"—and he shook his head condescendingly at the stupidity of it—"she sought maybe the shock of her brother's death had made Rietje de Klerk lose her hair, and that was why she had stayed 'n hermit for so many years. If Ans wasn't such a meddling old fool, nussing would have happened. But she couldn't leave well enough alone, so she called him on the—maybe I should say *her*—she called 'her' on the telephone and told 'her' what she had seen."

"But not what she figured it meant?"

"*Juist.* Poor Ab sought she'd found out his secret, and he was petrified that she was going to expose him. He needed time to sink sings over, to come up wiss a story that would satisfy her, so he promised to come and see her that afternoon, and asked her not to tell anyone else about it until after he'd had a chance to talk wiss her."

"Only, by the time he got there, Ellen Antonie and Mrs. Boonstra had dropped in for an unexpected little social call."

"Yes, yes, yes." If he hadn't been holding the knife, I think he would have rubbed his hands with glee. "But you see, Mr. Farmer, after Ans hung up the telephone that morning, she didn't want to have to wait for Rietje to come in the afternoon before she could talk about the sing she had seen. The *zuster* was out, so she telephoned to me and asked me to come over and see her, and when I went to her, she told me about the wig."

There was the faintest rustling of sheets, but Rombach seemed not to notice.

Keep him talking, half my mind ordered, while the other half was praying that Jet would wake up quietly, if she was waking up at all. *Keep him distracted from the bed.*

"You were afraid she'd figure it out, sooner or later," I said, "so you decided to kill her. For three hundred lousy Euros a month."

"Not for the money, no! Don't you understand it, Mr. Farmer? If the truth came out, I would go to prison for seven years of blackmail. I *had* to kill her, to keep her from exposing me."

"But you were way the hell up in the north of Holland by Sunday night! That's been driving me crazy since I realized it had to be you that killed them. Unless—unless that conference of yours was a fake, and you were really right here in Amsterdam all the time!"

"No, no, Mr. Farmer, the conference was real, and I was indeed 'way the hell up in the north of Holland,' as you say it." He chuckled. "Dexter said me you are a talented historian, but your geography is—how do you say it?—deplorable. Yes, deplorable. Holland is a very small country, Mr. Farmer, just a little larger than your state of Maryland, I sink. From Amsterdam to Groningen, where I had my conference, is less than two hundred kilometers— perhaps one hundred and twenty or one hundred and sirty miles. I drove up there on Sunday afternoon—the roads are very good, and it takes only about two hours. After I checked into my room, I had a very nice dinner in the hotel restaurant where everyone could see me, and then I made a big yawn and told the woman at the reception I was going to bed to rest before my speech in the morning, and please don't let anyone disturb me."

And that was when I spotted her in the hallway, her head cocked prettily to one side and a question shining in her eyes. Gerrit Rombach, inside the doorway with his back to her, went right on talking, but I was too busy figuring out what the hell she was doing there to pay him no nevermind.

In my hurry to tell Jet about the view from Rombach's window, I must have forgotten to shut the door of *het houten huys*. I'd left the front door of #33 open, too, and she must have gotten tired of waiting for me and followed her nose on over to check things out.

If she'd been Lassie or Black Beauty or even Flipper, for God's sake, I'd have yelled at her to fetch the sheriff, and she would have bounded right off and brought him back in the nick of time. But I don't think cats are quite that talented. I mean, that's why they stuck Morris in commercials instead of giving him his own series, isn't it?

"I had to do it," Gerrit Rombach said. "Don't you see, Mr. Farmer? I didn't have any choice. And, now, I'm afraid, *you* have left me without a choice."

His knife was pointing right at my heart, as threatening as any gun could have been. Rombach was maybe six feet away from me, but it would take only a second to cover that distance.

One second to close the gap between us, two seconds to raise the knife and plunge it into my chest, perhaps another half a minute for the blade to do its damage.

Which left me, I figured, with about thirty-three seconds left to live.

Right then, though, Dropje came through for me.

Recognizing her master's scent and voice, she padded joyously into the room and rubbed up against his leg and purred.

And, at the feel and sound of her, Rombach glanced down for the one infinitesimal moment I'd been waiting for.

I am not very fast on my feet, as a rule. I don't think I've been in a fist fight since I was twelve years old and Eric Shapiro down the street gypped me out of a worthless stamp collection that'd meant a lot to me.

But I made it across that bedroom in about an eighth of a nanosecond and hit Gerrit Rombach upside the head with everything I had in me.

And the rest, as Dexter S. Harriman might have put it, was history.

CHAPTER 25

"So he convinced her to let *him* handle it," I said, "and went back to the Wooden House to try and figure out what the hell to do. He had to be up in Groningen the next morning, he was hyper about his speech, and now all of a sudden Mrs. Moen is getting together with Ab de Klerk in a couple of hours, and between the two of them they're going to send him to jail."

It was a little after seven the next morning, and Jet was in bed with three thick feather pillows propped behind her and a steaming pot of tea on the spindly nightstand at her side. Lieutenant Smit and I had been up all night; he was on his forty-thousandth cup of strong black coffee, and I was maybe a pot and half ahead of him.

Gerrit Rombach was in a holding cell at the Bijlmer Bajes, the immense white prison complex several kilometers outside of town, awaiting a ten-thirty arraignment on two counts of homicide and assorted additional counts of attempted murder and aggravated assault.

"He had to kill her, he decided. It was the only way to make sure she didn't find out the truth about Ab. If he did it right away, though, Sunday morning, when everyone knew he was on the scene, he'd be a suspect; it'd be much safer if he went up to Groningen as scheduled, snuck back later on that evening and took care of her while he was supposed to be half a country away.

"And then, smack in the middle of all that weirdness, *I* showed up. So he talked me into catsitting and sent me back to the Nova to pick up my stuff, and while I was gone he went over to see Ab de Klerk."

Jet pressed the side of her head gingerly and winced.

"Hey, are you—?"

"I'm fine." She forced a smile. "I am, really. Go on."

I drained my cup, and Smit immediately refilled it. "Ab was scared to death your boss was about to blow his cover," I said, "but Rombach was able to get him calmed down. He'd made up a story to pacify Mrs. Moen, he told him—and then he just repeated the garbage *she'd* come up with, that Rietje de Klerk had lost her hair, and that's all there was to it. And the upshot was he told Ab there was nothing to worry about anymore, it was all taken care of, Mrs. Moen understood the situation, and Ab didn't even have to bother keeping his appointment with her that afternoon."

"But wasn't Mr. Rombach afraid that, after he killed Mrs. Moen, Ab would realize who must have done it and go to the police?"

"And have to admit to his own deception, and wind up tossed out in the street, and maybe even do time for fraud—after all he'd done to protect his secret for seven years? No way! Rombach knew *that* wasn't going to happen. Anyway, he had his talk with Ab and went back to the Wooden House, and once I got back from the hotel and settled myself in, he brought me over here to introduce me to Mrs. Moen. See, he figured that, given the opportunity, he might as well place me inside your house—I mean, I was a stranger in the Begijnhof, a *man*, no less—maybe he'd be able to set me up as a suspect."

Smit squirmed in his chair.

"Only Mrs. Moen was napping when we got here, so he made me promise I'd come back and see her later on, and then he showed me how to use the archives in *het houten huys* and took off for the north of Holland."

"But Ab decided to keep his appointment, after all."

"Yeah. We're not sure why—Rombach doesn't know, and it's a little late to ask Ab—but apparently he decided to go through with it in spite of Rombach's assurances. Except when he got there—"

"—Ellen Antonie and Mevrouw Boonstra were ahead of him."

"Right. They'd dropped in unexpectedly, so whatever Ab was planning was going to have to wait until after they'd left. As the four of them sat there drinking tea and exchanging unpleasantries, though, it dawned on him that Rombach had been right, that your boss didn't know the truth about him, that he was still getting away with the masquerade—I mean, he was right there in the same room with three of his sister's closest friends, and they didn't have the vaguest idea he was anyone other than Rietje de Klerk. So when Ellen and Mrs. Boonstra finally gave up trying to be sociable, he left the house with them instead of sticking around for his little chat with Ans.

"And that night Gerrit Rombach set up an alibi for himself in Groningen, slipped out of his hotel and drove back down to Amsterdam, let himself into the Begijnhof and this house with his duplicate keys, stabbed Mrs. Moen with a knife from your kitchen and took right off again. He was back in his room, sound asleep, by one, and the hotel receptionist would have sworn that he'd been there all night."

"And Ellen and Reverend Bill?" said Jet, the teacup in her hands completely forgotten. "How do *they* fit in?"

Roelof Smit picked up the story. "I spoke with them both yesterday afternoon, after you told me what you'd found out about the light in the church. Mevrouw Antonie wasn't hiding anything; the only reason she didn't tell you what she was doing on the south side of the Begijnhof Sunday and Monday nights was that you never asked her."

"She was excited about seeing Rietje again," I said, "after seven years of practically no contact." I wasn't guessing; Smit had filled me in on this part of it during the course of the night. "That's all there was to it. She wanted to try to revive the friendship, so she went over there on Sunday night. Only Ab wouldn't let her in, and she went home disappointed. She tried again on Monday, but that time Ab wouldn't even come to the door. Either he was ignoring her, or he may have already been dead by then."

"That's something that's been bothering me," said Jet. "I see why Mr. Rombach thought he had to get rid of Mevrouw Moen, to keep her from finding out about the blackmailing. But why *in hemels naam* did he murder Ab? That's like killing the—*hoe zeg je 't in 't Engels?*—something about a duck?"

It took me a minute to get it, and Smit was totally bewildered.

"Not a duck, you goose, a *goose*. The goose that lays the golden eggs. And you're right, that didn't make any sense to us, either. But Rombach explained it. When he called me at the Wooden House Monday night, after we got back from the Pacifico, I told him you and I were looking into Mrs. Moen's murder, and I told him I had a couple of promising ideas and had made some notes on the case." I drank coffee and set down my empty cup. "No, thanks, Lieutenant—one more and I'll float out into the canals. Anyway, so Rombach got worried. What if he'd slipped up somewhere, and we were on to something important? He figured he'd better get a look at my notes, so he came back down to town again, got here like around two and let himself into the Wooden House while

I was sound asleep upstairs. Well, a lot of what I'd written was about Rietje de Klerk—like that I thought we ought to grill her on Tuesday—and Rombach knew Ab was liable to crack under pressure and spill the whole story."

Jet's expression cleared. "And if *that* happened, he wouldn't only go to jail for blackmail. They'd have him for Mevrouw Moen's murder, too."

"Exactly. He was getting in deeper and deeper, and the only way out of it now was to get rid of Ab—so he ducked across to #40, used his key, borrowed a knife and—used that, too."

"And he told you all this? He confessed to both murders?"

"Yeah. It was really weird: once he realized it was all over, the only thing he seemed to care about was what was going to happen to Dropje."

A long strand of gold fell forward across Jet's eyes as she shifted position and rearranged her pillows. "What *is* going to happen to Dropje?" she asked.

"I don't know. I'd kind of like to keep her. I mean, she pretty much saved your life."

She brushed the strand of hair back where it belonged. "I'd kind of like to keep her, too," she said. "I mean, she pretty much saved *both* our lives." She smiled up at me prettily—and then the smile wilted into a puzzled frown. "That's another thing I don't understand. Why did Mr. Rombach want to kill *me*, of all people? I didn't—"

Smit made an embarrassed noise and set down his cup and saucer. "Someone still had to take the blame for the two murders," he said, "and from Rombach's talks on the telephone with Mr. Farmer, he knew that we had suspicions of you, *zuster*. He decided to sneak back to Amsterdam one last time, to—take care of you in such a way that it would appear to be a suicide. I would then—"

"You'd think I must have killed Mevrouw Moen for her money, and Ab de Klerk because—well, maybe because I was afraid he'd found out about it, somehow, and was about to tell you what he knew." She put the back of her hand to her forehead dramatically. "And then at last I realized the horror of what I had done and chose to end it all, rather than wait around for you to catch me and put me away in a dark and rat-infested dungeon."

"Something like that," the lieutenant admitted.

"And it might have worked, except for my bedroom door."

"Your excuse me?" I said.

"My door. Close it and see what happens."

I squinted at her. "Are you—?"

She folded her arms across her chest and gave me a Look. Not just a look, mind you, a Look. "Close the door, *oen*. Go ahead."

I got up and went to the door and swung it closed.

It creaked.

Loudly.

"I've been meaning to put some oil on that hinge," Jet smiled. "I suppose it's a good thing I didn't. The noise woke me up when Mr. Rombach came in, and I fought with him in the dark. Then— I'm not sure—it seemed like somebody turned all the lights on, and that's the last thing I remember until this morning."

"He knocked you out," I said. "Then he *did* turn on the light, so he could set up your suicide—and he realized he hadn't brought anything for you to kill yourself with."

"You're joking!"

"Thank God I'm not. He went downstairs for a knife, and while he was in the kitchen I started banging on the front door. So he snapped off the light in there and waited to see what would happen, hoping I'd give up and go away."

"Only you didn't," said Jet softly. "You broke down the door and—"

"It wasn't locked," I said. "Rombach didn't bother to—"

"Never mind that. You came and rescued me."

"Well, sort of." I turned up my palms and shrugged. "Jack be nimble, Jack be quick, that's all there—"

"Don't you dare be flip with me again, Jack Farmer. You march right over here and kiss me before I knock you unconscious."

Well, hey, you don't argue with a direct order like that.

I marched right over there and kissed her.

From behind me came the sound of one Smit coughing, and then the bedroom door creaked open and shut, and he was gone.

℘

"Wait a minute," Jet gasped, coming up for air. "What about Reverend Bill?"

I blinked. "Say what?"

"Reverend Bill. Why did he lie about being here Sunday and Monday nights?"

"Oh, right." I snuggled in a little closer beside her. "Smit wormed it out of him yesterday afternoon. Remember that big black ledger he was reading when we went over to ask him about Henk Kleijwegt?"

She nodded.

"The English Reformed Church's financial records," I told her. "Apparently nobody's bothered to go over them within human memory, and about a week ago the rev decided it was time to run an audit. He couldn't get the figures to add up right, though, and it was driving him crazy. So that's what he was doing those nights, working late, trying to get the damn books to balance."

Jet scowled, unsatisfied. "But why did he lie about it? Why not just—"

"If he admitted he was there that late on the night of the murder, the cops'd've wanted to know why, and he'd've had to tell them about the missing money. He was afraid people would think he'd been mismanaging the church funds, so he didn't want to let anyone know what was going on until he had it all figured out."

"*Nou en?* Did he figure it out?"

"He sure did," I grinned. "It seems your friendly neighborhood handyman's been dipping his friendly neighborhood hands into the church's petty cash for nigh onto the last twenty years, and—"

"*Henk?*"

"The one and only. Looks like he really *did* have a line on a couple things going on around here that nobody else was aware of. The reverend figures he's been getting away with a good twenty or thirty Euros a month."

"Twenty or—Jack, that's *nothing.*"

"It's stealing from a church," I pointed out. "I think the lieutenant's going to try and get Henk and Rombach adjoining cells. I'm sure they'll be very happy together. Anything else, *zuster?*"

"Well," she said, "there *is* one more thing."

She put her arms around me and pulled me closer.

"Oh," I said. "Oh, yeah."

And cut to a shot of the Japanese poster on her wall: a yellow sea, and the moon underneath the waves that ever go rolling.

It must have been after ten before I realized that I ought to give D.S. Harriman a ring, but the six-hour time difference meant it was still the middle of the night in Michigan, so I waited till midafternoon Amsterdam time before placing the collect call.

"Ah, Mr. Farmer," his familiar baritone rumbled, "it's good to hear from you. How are you getting on over there?"

"Just fine, sir," I said loudly. "Just great."

A couple seconds went by as my words swam across the Atlantic and the prof's swam back. "Excellent, Mr. Farmer, I am delighted to hear it. The research progresses, then?"

I cleared my throat—which, at six dollars and forty cents for the first three minutes, must have set old Dexter back about a nickel. "Well, uh, actually it's been pretty strange around here the last few days, sir. There've been, uh, well, there've been two murders in the Begijnhof, and it took a while to get it all straightened out."

Either the professor growled or there was a burst of static, I'm not sure which. "There is something amiss with this connection, Mr. Farmer. It sounded as if you said—"

"—murders, sir. Two of them. It was really awful, Professor. They were stabbed to—"

"You are not making a bit of sense, young man. Perhaps I should speak with Mr. Rombach. Is he there with you?"

"Ah, no, sir. He—Jesus, I'm sorry, Professor, but he turned out to be the one who did it. He killed two old ladies, sir, it was terrible. He's in jail."

Silence.

More silence.

Expensive silence.

"If this is your idea of a joke," said Harriman at last, "I am not at all amused."

"It's no joke, sir. I wish it was. He murdered two women—well, actually, one of them turned out to be a man—and came damn close to making it… well, it's a long story, sir. I'll write it all up for you, as soon as I get a chance. But first I've got your research to take care of."

I could hear the ruffled feathers smoothing back into place. "And when," he cooed, "may I expect to see you and the fruits of your labors back on campus?"

"I ought to be able to get a package of fruit off to you within the next week or two, sir. But I don't think you'll be seeing me again. Not in the foreseeable future, anyway."

"What on Earth are you babbling about now?" A crackling on the line made him sound even more exasperated than usual. "You are taking History 644 with me in the fall semester, are you not?"

"Uh, no, sir, 'fraid not. I'm gonna be staying on here in Amsterdam."

"Staying *on*? But—but what about your degree?"

I smiled. "I think the world'll manage to get along with one less historian in it, sir. I hope so, anyway."

"Mr. Farmer, have you been drinking?" he demanded. "What do you intend to do with yourself?"

"Dunno, sir. I'll find something, I'm sure."

"You are courting disaster, young man. What have you found there in Holland that could possibly be more important than your career?"

I squeezed Jet's hand and looked deep within the brilliant sapphires of her eyes.

"Everything," I said, but there was something amiss with the connection, and I don't think the old glitterdome heard me.

THE MILKY WAY

It was raining in Amsterdam, but that was nothing new. It was usually raining in Amsterdam, and I was used to it by now. The chill drizzle stung my skin like tattoo needles as I held the door for Jet and followed her into the smoky *gezelligheid* of the Zwarte Zwaan. The warm air misted my glasses, and I latched onto Jet's elbow and let her do the steering.

"*Ha, die Jack en Jet,*" a couple of the regulars greeted us as we wound through the maze of wooden tables toward the back. Doesn't look much like a greeting when you see it written out on paper, but in Dutch the *die* is pronounced *dee,* and all the sentence means is, "Well, if it ain't Jack and Jet."

We stopped a couple of times to trade friendly insults with Nico d'Angelo and the other derelicts, and by the time we reached our usual nesting place I could see again.

What I saw was a middle-aged couple straight off the farm— her a dowdy matron with ruddy cheeks in a flowered housedress that'd seen a lot of wear and him a hundred kilos of well-muscled hayseed—sitting ramrod straight with their meaty hands clamped around his-and-hers shots of *jonge jenever*, the potent Dutch gin that tastes like all they did was run the juniper berries through a press and let 'em ferment.

Clients, obviously. Unless Gijs had specifically told them where to sit, the *Gereserveerd* sign on the table would have scared them off. One thing about the Dutch, they don't claim-jump.

"Meneer Farmer?" the hayseed asked dubiously. Our pictures have been in the papers often enough since we cleared up those murders in the Begijnhof last year, but we're a lot better looking in full color than we come across in black-and-white. Well, Jet is, anyway. With a schnoz like mine, color's probably not much of an improvement, after all.

Anyway, I admitted I was Jack Farmer and introduced Jet as my associate. The hayseed turned out to be Wiebe Boorsma from Sneek, and the pumpkin with the cheeks was his wife Engelien. Some angel. We shook hands all around, and I pulled up two chairs for myself and my lady love.

"The barman thought you'd be here an hour ago," Boorsma complained. After almost a year in The Netherlands, my Dutch was fair to middling, but this character's Frisian accent was so thick I leaned back and let Jet cut it into bite-sized pieces for me. "Were you—working on a case?"

Actually, we'd been working on a six-pack, but the gag wouldn't have translated so I let it lie. "Just a little something we had to clear up for the Heineken family," I improvised, and Jet, who'd put away a quantity of the foaming gold herself, kicked me under the table and said my name like she didn't much care for the way it tasted.

Gijs materialized out of the cigarette smoke, dropped coasters in front of us, and balanced a beer on each of the cardboard circles.

The way he raised an eyebrow told me the Boorsmas were still on their original gins, and anything we could do to encourage them to stop nursing and start drinking would be much appreciated.

"*Proost,*" said Jet cheerfully and raised her glass. I took the hint and clinked with her, and Old MacBoorsma and his hefty soulmate reluctantly followed suit. We set down our empties, and I smiled at Gijs for another round. E-I-E-I-O.

"So, what brings you all to Amsterdam?" I asked. It was nice and dry inside the *kroeg* and I didn't relish the thought of going back out into the wet, but our exchequer was even drier than the Zwarte Zwaan and we hadn't had a client in almost a month. Whatever Meneer and Mevrouw Boorsma had in mind for us, we were interested.

Engelien rummaged around in her capacious shoulder bag and handed me a small rectangular photograph of herself at seventeen. It might have been her high-school graduation picture, except as I examined it I saw that the print was thirty years too new and the style of the graduate's clothing was current.

"*Jullie dochter?*" said Jet, and Wiebe confirmed that it was in fact their daughter Geja we were looking at.

"Terrific," I scowled, as Gijs came back and juggled glasses. "This isn't one of those deals where your sweet little girlie's disappeared and you want us to track her down for you, is it? I hate those. Ross Macdonald's already *done* all of those."

Jet prettied that up for them, then settled back and nodded sympathetically as the Boorsmas took turns unburdening themselves of their tale of woe.

Last June, Jet translated, Geja had completed her fourth year of *atheneum*, which is the highest level of the multi-tiered Dutch public-school system. She'd finished third in her class and, after helping her parents on the farm all summer, had come down to the big city to study medicine at the Vrije Universiteit. She'd been in Amsterdam for seven months now, and she'd rung them every weekend to let them know that all was well. She didn't have a cell phone or a landline in her dorm room, but she lived close to the student union and would duck in there and use one of the antique pay phones in the lobby.

Saturday night in Sneek: Maw crochetin' an afghan for Cousin Wiske's first-born and Paw smokin' his corncob in front of the TV whilst waitin' for Little Geja's call.

Only Little Geja hadn't called this past weekend, and here it was Wednesday. Wiebe and Engelien had lasted until this morning, when they left the farm in their oldest son Jaap's capable hands and took the train down to Am*dam to see Eke Capel, Geja's roommate, who told them she hadn't seen their daughter in several days and had been trying to convince herself it was time to stop wondering about it and get in touch with *them*.

Lew Archer would have loved it.

಄

The next morning, a yellow 171/172 bus took us out through a furry rain past the Olympic Stadium to the borderline between Amsterdam and Amstelveen, where the Free University's medical faculty occupied a concrete Mondrian painting with blue reflective windows where old Piet had daubed his squares of color. The porter inside the main entrance looked up Geja's schedule on a fancy laptop at his station and directed us to the *aula*, where eighty stringbeans in white lab coats were watching a PowerPoint presentation on the wonderful world of myocardial infarctions.

We fed Euros into an *automaat* and hung around chugging chocolate milk until class let out, then eyed the stream of escapees as it passed through the double doors.

No Geja, no one looking even remotely like her.

The last one left in the auditorium was the guy who'd been running the slide show, a rumpled couch potato in his thirties who had reached and was apparently settled into his level of incompetence. He was packing his class materials into a backpack and looking distracted as we climbed down to the stage and approached him.

"Good morning," I served. "My name's Jack Farmer, and this is Jet Schilders." With Holland's Wiebe and Engelien Boorsmas, I let Jet do most of the talking, but with a college professor I figure I can take a turn myself.

Mr. Wizard glanced up from his labors. "Piet de Jong," he said, and seemed about to offer me a hand when he changed his mind and narrowed his hazel eyes. "Yes?"

I gave him Smile #17: Ingratiating Foreigner in Need of Assistance. "We're private investigators," I said, reaching for Geja's photo. "We're looking for this girl. Do you know her?"

He hooked a pair of wire rims around his ears and took the picture and studied it. "Yes," he nodded, "she's in this class." He looked out at the ocean of theater seats and seemed for the first time to notice that they were empty. "My class," he amended, "twice a week. She's been absent for the last few meetings, though. Is something wrong?"

"She's missing," Jet explained. "Her parents have hired us to find her. We were hoping you might be able to—"

"I'm sorry," he interrupted, "but I don't even know her name. There are more than a hundred students in the class, and I can't be expected to"—this time he cut *himself* off—"I'm afraid I'm in a bit of a rush today. My mother is ill, and I have to get back to her. I really shouldn't have come in at all today, but—"

The rest of the sentence was lost as he slung his backpack over his shoulder and hurried up the steps to the wide exit doors.

We watched him go, then faced each other and laughed.

"Nice man," I said.

Jet arched an eyebrow. "Helpful, too."

❧

We located three more of Geja's instructors in the building and got basically the same story from each of them: she was a first-year student, it was early in the semester, the classes were large. Like Piet de Jong, her physiology and chemistry professors recognized her picture but couldn't match it with a name. The frowzy redhead who taught medical ethics wasn't sure Geja'd ever attended her class at all.

We had slightly better luck in the canteen, where we dug up several kids who'd shared a cup of coffee and a *broodje* with her between classes. A pleasant enough girl, they agreed, though she seemed a bit out of her element in the big city. No, they hadn't seen her lately—not for the last couple of days, anyway. No, they had no idea what might have happened to her. No, none of them knew if she had any particular friends in town, anyone she was especially close to. Of course, her roommate would know. She was sharing a *kot* with someone, wasn't she?

❧

Geja's apartment was on the sixth floor of a tall drab block of student flats set in the middle of the university complex. Its official name was *Uilenstede,* or "Owl Town," but the residents called it, not entirely affectionately, *Betondorp.*

Concreteville.

A tall brunette with a sunlamp tan and a nice shape on her bones opened the door to our knock. She had a thick blue textbook in her hand, her index finger tucked between the pages to mark her place.

"Eke Capel?" said Jet.

"*Ja?*"

"*Sorry dat we je storen. We zoeken Geja Boomstra.*"

A frown settled across her lips. "*Ze is er op 't ogenblik niet. Ik weet eigenlijk niet waar ze—*"

"Yeah, we know," I said. "Her parents hired us to find her. My name's Jack Farmer, and this is Jet Schilders."

"Ah." The frown gave way to a neutral expression, and she shifted the book to her left hand and shook with us solemnly and ushered us in.

The apartment was about what you'd expect. Institutional furniture, books and papers everywhere, Madonna and Prince and—incongruously—Mickey Mouse as the Sorcerer's Apprentice doing their damnedest to brighten up the dreary walls. A kitchenette with a single plate and teacup dripping dry beside the miniature sink. Two rain-smeared windows looking out at the back of the student union. The Capel girl cleared a term paper in progress off the sofa for us, and we sat.

"When was the last time you saw her?" I asked.

"*Vorige week vrijdag,*" she replied promptly. "Last Friday."

"Friday the thirteenth," mused Jet. "An unlucky day."

"I'm sure it was Friday. We had lunch in the canteen just before my practicum. They were taking us to the morgue for the first time, and I was nervous about it."

"Geja isn't in that class with you?"

"Oh, no, she's *eerste jaars* and I'm *tweede.*"

Nice of them to spare the first-year students the dead bodies, I thought.

"The practicum was over at four," Eke continued, "and it went much better than I was afraid it would. I came right home to tell Geja about it, but she wasn't here." She looked down and clasped her hands in her lap and swallowed. "I haven't seen her since then."

Jet leaned forward. "You didn't worry when she stayed away all night? Has she ever done that before?"

"No, never. But, well, it was the weekend. I thought maybe she'd decided on the last minute to go to her parents."

"Wouldn't she have left you a note if she was going to do something like that?"

Eke looked up. "I don't know. We're roommates, but we're not really *friends*." She seemed on the edge of tears.

"Suitcases," I said softly.

"Suitcases?"

"Suitcases. How many suitcases does she have?"

"I—two, I think. Yes, two, a big one and an overnight bag."

"And if she was going to her parents for the weekend, would she have taken one of them with her?"

She gazed up at me like I'd just announced a cure for cancer. "*Ja,*" she said. "*Natuurlijk!*"

The girls shared a single bedroom with matching beds and study desks and dressers and closets. All that was missing was a red line down the center of the room to divide it into My Side and Your Side. I don't want to suggest that Wiebe and Engelien had spoiled their little *honneponnetje,* but Geja's closet was stuffed with enough clothing to stock a warehouse. Way at the back, behind a collection of shoes that would have made the late Imelda Marcos ask for her autograph, were the suitcases: two of them, a big one and an overnight bag.

"Hmm," I said. "So we scratch that idea. Mind if we take a look around?"

Jet found Geja's agenda in the top drawer of her desk. We don't have anything quite like the *academische agenda* in America, but no self-respecting Dutch student from the *kleuterschool* on up would be without one. It's a compact but thick little number, bound in imitation leather and with absolutely *everything* in it, from a place to record the names of the people who owe you money and a train schedule and an atlas and an illustrated guide to the world's traffic signs and a table showing how far it is from anywhere worth being in Europe to anywhere worth going in the front to an address book and a notepad and a five-year calendar in the back.

The bulk of the agenda is its center section, the diary: two days per page, with plenty of room for recording class meetings, homework assignments, and other appointments, and a funny or thoughtful one-liner at the bottom of every sheet.

"Look at this," Jet said, and held it out to me.

For Thursday, March 12, Geja had several classes and a practicum listed. Friday the thirteenth showed classes all morning and afternoon, and underneath her schedule she'd written "21 *uur*" and a big capital M with an exclamation point.

"M," I said. "What did she have, a date with Peter Lorre?"

"Peter—?"

"*Let maar niet op hem,*" said Jet, which certainly put me in *my* place. "Geja's parents didn't tell us anything about a boyfriend. Was there someone she was likely to be going out with at nine o'clock on a Friday evening?"

Eke thought it over. "She didn't do much dating. She was very serious about her study. But before Christmas there was a boy she saw a few times. They had a fight, I think. I don't remember what it was about."

"*En hoe heet die jongen?*"

"Visser. Maarten Visser."

Maarten Visser.

I read the printed saying at the bottom of the page: "*Het leven is hetgene wat gebeurt met je terwijl je bezig bent met het maken van andere plannen.*"

Life is what happens to you while you're busy making other plans.

ↂ

With his fresh good looks and his blond hair worn in the traditional little-Dutch-boy cut and—so help me!—a pair of wooden *klompen* on his feet, I was half-surprised we didn't find Maarten Visser with his finger in a dike.

It took us close to two hours to track him down. We finally located him in a carrel in the VU medical library, making notes on the human arm. Not *his* arm. *The* arm, for a lecture he was preparing for the next day's classes. He tried to brush us off at first, but when Jet whipped out Geja's picture and shoved it in his face, his antagonism dissolved like a dose of salts in a glass of water.

"Geja," he said.

I pursed my lips and let the name hang in the dry air between us.

"What do you want?" he said.

"We want to know where she is."

The question seemed to confuse him. "I don't know where she is," he said. "I haven't seen her in months."

"I thought you were the lab assistant in one of her practicums."

"Yes, well, that was last semester. Since Christmas, I have a new group of students."

We waited.

"What's this all about?" he demanded. "Why are you looking for her?"

"She's disappeared," said Jet. "Her parents hired us to find her."

"Disappeared? What—? How—?"

"That's what we'd like to know—what and how. What did you and she have planned for last Friday night, and how come she never went home afterwards?"

"Last Friday night?" he echoed, apparently mystified. "I didn't see Geja last Friday night. I told you: I haven't seen her for—"

"Come on, Maarten," I cut him off, putting some tough guy in my voice and stretching the truth maybe just a couple hundred meters. "She had your name written in her agenda: nine o'clock Friday night, Maarten, with a big exclamation point after it."

He slammed his book shut and got to his feet. He was tall for a little Dutch boy, and his thick wooden shoes made him even bigger. "I don't care *what* she had in her agenda," he insisted. "I didn't see her on Friday, and I didn't have any *plans* to see her on Friday."

"*Ach, ja, dat was ik vergeten,*" Jet nodded wisely. "You had a fight with her, didn't you?"

"A fight?"

"Yes, her roommate told us you went out for a while, and then you fought and split up."

"*Getverdemme.* We went into Amsterdam a few times. She's a very nice person and I would have liked to go on seeing her, but she wasn't really interested in me. I asked her out a few more times, but she always had something else planned—at least that's what she kept telling me. After a while I took the hint and stopped asking. That's all. We didn't fight. We didn't spend enough time together to fight."

"But you resented her turning you down," I tried.

Maarten glared at me. "*Rare jongens, die Amerikanen,*" he said.

It was not a kind remark.

❧

"… and two minutes later, she says it *again.*"

"'Mister,'" Jet supplied impatiently, "'give him some chicken soup. Give him some *chicken* soup.'"

"Yeah, right. Well, by this time the rabbi's getting really annoyed. So he pulls himself up to his full height and gives her this *withering* look and says, 'Madam, Mr. Feldman is *dead*. Believe me, chicken soup wouldn't help.' And she says, 'Maybe not, *rebbe*. But it wouldn't *hoit*.'"

Jet stopped walking. "It wouldn't hurt?"

"*Hoit*. It wouldn't *hoit*."

"*Nou en?*"

"That's all. That's the punch line."

She put her hands on her hips. "And that's supposed to be a *joke?*"

"A Jewish joke, yeah. Don't you get it?"

"I get it," she said. "I just don't think it's funny."

"Yeah, well, it's a lot funnier than your lame Belgian jokes. *Er lopen twee Belgen in de Kalverstraat—*"

She giggled. "*Zegt die ene tegen die andere, 'Mag ik in 't midden lopen?'* Oh, oh, oh!" Still chuckling, she lowered her umbrella and opened the door.

Two Belgians are walking along the Kalverstraat, and one of them says to the other one, "Do you mind if I walk in the middle?"

That was her idea of a joke? No wonder Holland's no longer a major world power.

I shook my head and followed her in.

It was only eight o'clock, but the Zwaan was already full. Behind the bar, Gijs was on the phone, and when he spotted us he waved and pointed at the receiver. Jet went over to take the call, and I stopped by Nico d'Angelo and Frank Kuypers' table to say hello.

"*Neem maar wat,*" Frank offered, pushing a plate of *bitterballen* toward me.

I held my stomach and groaned. "*Nee, alsjeblieft,* we just ate. We went to—"

"*Wacht effe,*" Nico cut me off. He slapped a blue banknote on the table and grinned at his buddy. "*Mexicaans,*" he said.

Frank looked me up and down and sucked in a breath and let it out again. "*Chinees,*" he decided, laying a pair of pink ten-Euro bills beside Nico's twenty.

I swear, those two would bet on anything.

"It's Thursday," Nico grinned. "They always go to the Pacifico on Thursdays. Jack had enchiladas suizas and Jet had a combination plate, and they drank a pitcher of margaritas." He laid a hairy hand on the money and looked up at me expectantly.

"Sorry, Frank." I shrugged. "But it *is* Thursday."

When I left them, poor Frank was muttering into his *jenever.* You'd think by now he'd have learned.

Jet joined me at our table a couple minutes later with a pair of beers and a furrowed brow. "That was Eke Capel," she said.

"Hey, hey, good thing we mentioned this place. We really ought to have some cards printed with our cell numbers. She remember something?"

"Yes, but I don't know how important it is. When they had lunch together on Friday, Eke was so nervous about her trip to the morgue that she didn't pay much attention to Geja's mood. Now she says she thinks she was excited about something."

"She remember what it was?"

"She's not sure. Geja told her she was going to do some exploring, and Eke has the impression she was talking about Friday night."

"Exploring? Exploring where?"

"That's the part that doesn't make sense. What Eke remembers is she said something about new worlds and outer space."

"Outer *space?*"

"That's all she could remember."

We drank beer and chewed it over. New worlds, outer space, 21 *uur*, a capital M, and—

"The Melkweg!" Jet exclaimed.

"The what?"

"The Melkweg, *lummel*."

I struggled with the Dutch. "The milk road?"

"Not bad." She smiled her patented Mona Lisa smile. "Not right, but not bad."

"The milk street? The milk lane? The milk *run*?"

"Outer space, Jack. Think outer space."

"The Milky Way," I gaped. "Of course."

Jet downed the rest of her beer. "*Zullen we*?"

I checked my watch. Twenty to nine. "But it's Thursday," I argued. "She had it in her agenda for last Friday."

"Maybe so," said Jet. "But it wouldn't *hoit*."

☙

The #5 tram dropped us off at Leidseplein, smack in the heart of Amsterdam's entertainment district. The rain had tapered off some, but it was still wet and chilly, and the square was far less crowded than usual. A juggler with a bushy black beard and harlequin makeup did amazing things with four Indian clubs next to the tram stop, but no one was paying attention to him. The few people who were out were much too busy getting themselves into one of the area's dozens of brown cafés, where the moisture has a frothy head and comes in a glass. Jet dropped a coin in Pierrot's hat and raised her umbrella and led me around the side of the Stadsschouwburg—the National Theater—and into the Lijnbaansgracht.

Halfway down the rain-slick alley, a skinny drawbridge offered passage across a miniature green canal to a hulking old red-brick building with the word "Melkweg" in blue neon above its gaudily painted doors.

"So this is the Milky Way," I said, then noticed the blue-and-white glow of a *Politie* sign farther down the street and added, "Here?"

Jet followed my gaze. "Why not here?"

"Honey, I've heard about this place—a couple of my hipper friends back in America told me this was one of Amsterdam's main attractions. But, well, I know dope's supposed to be more or less legal here, but still— practically next door to a police station?"

She looked puzzled. "Dope? The only dope I know is—"

"Don't go there, girlfriend. I mean drugs. Soft drugs. Weed. Marijuana and hash."

Her expression cleared. "Oh, *zo bedoel je*. No, it's not legal, but it's tolerated. The government figures people who want it will get it one way or another. If they set aside places where it's okay to have it—like the coffee shops and the Bulldog and the Melkweg—then they won't have to worry about it taking over the city. They've done the same thing with prostitution in the *ouwehoerenbuurt*."

"The *ouwe* what now?

"The *ouwehoerenbuurt*. You know, the *walletjes*."

"The wallets?"

She rolled her eyes. "The Red-Light District, Jack."

"Oh, right, the *ouwe*hoeren*buurt*. Why didn't you say so?"

It cost us twelve and a half Euros apiece to get in. A ghoul with orange hair and a hint of green eyeshadow took our tickets and rubber-stamped the backs of our left hands so we could leave and return until closing time without having to pay again. On closer inspection, the stamp looked like a faucet with water running out of it.

"What's tomorrow night's design?" I asked, just making conversation.

The boy regarded me with interest. "I'm not supposed to tell," he said primly, then leaned forward and whispered, "but maybe we can work something out."

"Ah, right, we'll talk later, okay?"

I grabbed Jet's hand and pulled her past the barrier.

છ

Inside the Grote Zaal, the place was packed, with hundreds of people our age and younger crammed together in a space that didn't seem big enough to hold half its current population. It was a mostly white crowd, but the other colors were also represented, and on stage a dozen dreadlocked Rastafarians were covering, ironically enough, Jimmy Cliff's "I'm No Immigrant." They were playing loud. *Really* loud. The air was thick with smoke—not all of it tobacco—and a revolving mirror ball hanging from the high ceiling threw flecks of colored light around the room like darts.

There's no way we're going to find Geja Boorsma in this chaos, I thought, *even if she* does *happen to be here.*

I wormed around to see what Jet had to scream-to-be-heard for herself, but she was gone.

Wonderful, I thought. *That's* two *of them missing.*

I began shoving my way through the sardines, hoping for a glimpse of my sweet babboo or at least our client's vanished teenager.

The reggae band finished its number to enthusiastic applause. I didn't think they were all that good, but the volume they were putting out made it hard to be sure. I was concerned about Jet, so I wasn't focusing much attention on the music anyway.

I should have known better than to worry.

As the lead singer started in on "The Harder They Come," Jet popped up out of nowhere with a couple of beers, handed me a glass, and moved her lips.

"Huh?" I said, and I couldn't even hear *myself* over the din.

She scowled, got up on her tiptoes, and put her mouth to my ear.

"Huh?" I said.

She huffed out a sigh and took my free hand. No one seemed especially interested in letting us pass, but Jet hacked a path through the mob and I followed along like a good little doggie. Next to the bar I hadn't noticed was a doorway I hadn't noticed, which opened onto a passageway with a flight of steps at the far end. It was quieter there.

"We'll never find her in this chaos," said Jet, "even if she *does* happen to be here. Let's try upstairs."

"Huh?" I said.

The look she gave me practically made me spill my beer. "Come on, *oen*," she commanded.

She can be so sweet sometimes.

∞

At the head of the stairs was a cramped landing with doors marked Fonteinzaal and Cinema. We decided to try the movie theater first and found a film in progress and about a hundred people filling most of the seats. On screen, a gray-haired gentleman in a dark suit and a crimson cravat was looking out over the audience. "There are those who say that life is an illusion," he remarked, "and that reality is simply a figment of the imagination. If this is so, then Brad and Janet are quite safe."

I squinted through the dimness at the rows of spectators, but after about half a minute of that my squint rounded off into a stare. Mixed in with the blue jeans and T-shirts, at least half a dozen of the females were clad in nothing but white bras and knee-length white slips. And that was just the ladies. I swear to God I saw three different guys wearing black net stockings and black leather corsets they could only have purchased across town in the *ouwehoerenbuurt*.

"Uh, Jet," I said quietly, "do you see her?"

She shook her head. "I don't see her," she said. "Do you see her?"

"No," I said, "I don't see her. So, uh, do you think we could get out of here before the *rest* of them start changing into their underwear?"

But Jet was already heading for the door.

"What was *that*?" I said, when we were back on planet Earth.

"That," she explained, "was Amsterdam."

❧

The Fonteinzaal turned out to be a smoky tearoom dripping with ferns. There was a piano up front and a sort of bar with several waitresses brewing tea and slicing cheesecake, a pair of million-gallon aquariums teeming with brightly colored tropical fish, and ten or twelve plain wooden tables scattered amidst the vegetation, each fully occupied. An Australian with hair that hadn't seen a barber or a comb since the turn of the millennium sat on the piano bench with an acoustic guitar, strumming unrelated chords and haranguing his audience in broad-voweled Strine.

They didn't much seem to care. They were a pretty laid-back crowd. Hell, if they'd laid back any further they would have fallen off their chairs. One whiff of the sweet-smelling atmosphere told me how they'd got to be that way: I wasn't sure what exactly they were smoking, but I'd lay long odds it had been grown a lot closer to Afghanistan than North Carolina.

Geja wasn't there. We showed her picture around, but no one recognized it. Not that that meant much: half of them were so wasted they wouldn't have recognized their *own* pictures. The waitstaff seemed pretty grounded—disproving once and for all, as far as I was concerned, the myth of the contact high—and none of *them* could remember having seen Geja before, either. But they agreed we should try the Gallery, back downstairs behind the Grote Zaal.

"You bleedin' bahstuds 'aven't 'eard a note a *music* in yer entire bloody *loives*," the Aussie was ranting as we left.

A teacup rattled in response, but that was the only argument he got.

ↄ

The Gallery was a brightly lit hall with an exhibition of framed computer graphics displayed on its whitewashed walls. There were fifty-odd people in the room, but none of them were there to look at the pictures.

I mean, they were fifty *odd* people, gathered in twos and threes and fours on folding chairs around a dozen white metal tables, each table with a hole for an umbrella in the middle in case the roof started leaking. They were mostly in their early to mid-twenties, mostly males, quite a few of them with single gold earrings glittering in their left lobes. It was stuffy in the room, but most of them had their coats on, as if they hadn't made up their minds whether or not they were staying for more than a few minutes.

The joints, meanwhile, were jumping. There was a plastic Ziploc baggie on every table, and lazy plumes of smoke drifted toward the ceiling as chillums and small brass pipes and spliffs and roach clips were passed from hand to hand.

We poked around for a while, looking for Geja, listening to the gentle buzz of gently buzzed conversations about life, the universe, and everything, trying not to breathe in too much of the wacky tobaccy. The language of choice seemed to be English— both the American and British versions thereof—but there was also some French and Italian and a smattering of Dutch. An older woman in a baggy green sweater that looked like she'd knitted it herself roamed the tables collecting empty beer glasses, stacking them twenty high in a tower that leaned precariously against her shoulder, before going off and dumping them and coming back empty-handed to start all over again. It was a chore that seemed never-ending, like painting the Golden Gate Bridge.

You could buy juice and yogurt from a snack bar along one wall, underground comix and an assortment of paperbacks and postcards from the Labyrinth Bookshop at the rear, or penny candy and mixed nuts from the left half of a long wooden table in the center of the room.

The other half of the table was where they dealt the dope, and it was set up like a Mickey D's for potheads: you strolled up to the counter and ordered off the chalkboard menu, and they'd either wrap your purchase up for takeout or you could find a seat and dine in. They had hash from Nepal, Kashmir, Lebanon, and Morocco in twenty- and supersized fifty-Euro portions, plus grass from Thailand and Nigeria and a cheaper variety called *Nederwiet* I figured had to be homegrown.

I am very down on crack, smack, coke, and the rest of the hard-core pharmacopoeia, but I have to admit that I smoked my share of weed when I was back at the good ol' U of M. I might have been interested in checking out the quality of the Melkweg's merch, but Jet seemed disapproving and there was a line… and anyway, we were on a case.

Some other time, I promised myself.

An older man with a heavy white beard and drooping eyelids pushed to his feet and shambled off, and we were able to snag his table before anyone else got to it.

"Peter Pan," said Jet with a sigh.

"Looks like it," I nodded.

I have a theory about investigative work—I call it the Peter Pan Theory. In a detective story, see, your PI gets a lead and follows it doggedly through its intricate twists and turns. He may get beat up a time or two. He might get knocked over the head with a blunt metaphor. But sooner or later that lead will always carry him through to the solution he's after. (Or she, and God bless V.I. Warshawski and Kinsey Millhone.)

In real life, though, nine leads out of ten peter out instead of panning out, and the Milky Way was apparently one of the nine.

"Or not," Jet said, a minute later.

"Not?"

She turned her head away and hid her face behind her hand. "Don't be too obvious about it," she said, "but look what the cat just dragged in."

I did a yawn and stretch and snuck a casual glance over my shoulder. Piet de Jong was standing in the doorway, chewing nervously on his lower lip. His sandy hair and long tan trench coat were damp from the drizzle outside. The distinctive shape of the paper bag he was holding indicated he'd stopped at an *avondwinkel* for a bottle of wine on his way over.

"What's *he* doing here?" said Jet.

"He's got a sick mother, remember? He must've asked somebody how to get to the nearest drugstore, and this is where they sent him."

She gave me that look she gives me. "Ha ha," she said, "another funny joke."

When I risked a second peek, de Jong was stuffing his bag into a pocket and unbuttoning his coat. Underneath it he was wearing an open-necked white shirt, blue slacks, and a tweed sport jacket. I bet myself ten Euros there were leather patches on the elbows. He fumbled his wire rims from a shirt pocket and peered around the room, spotted the line at Candyland and took his place at the rear.

I skootched my chair around to keep my back to him. "Nudge nudge, wink wink," I whispered. "What'd I tell you?"

"Maybe his mother likes licorice."

"Yeah, right. And it's so reasonable here, if you don't count the twelve-fifty to get in." I got up. "Sit tight for a minute and try not to look so much like Jet Schilders."

The room was busy enough that it wasn't any problem to swing around behind him without being spotted. When he reached the head of the line, I watched him pay a hundred Euros in cash for four baggies, two each of *Nederwiet* and Lebanese Red.

Licorice, indeed.

"What now?" said Jet, as I slipped back into my seat.

De Jong stashed his stash in an inside breast pocket, belted his coat, and headed for the door.

I pointed my chin at his back. "That bottle of wine he's got?"

Jet's brow furrowed. God, I love it when she does that.

"Yes?" she said. "What about it?"

"Don't let it out of your sight."

"Don't let it—? Jack, what are you—?"

"C'mon," I said, getting up again. "Don't you Dutchies know how to play Follow the Liter?"

❧

The tail job was a snap. It was bucketing down hard again and the prof had come out without an umbrella, so he held his shoulders hunched and the collar of his trench coat pulled up around his face like blinders. Even if he saw us, there was little chance he'd recognize us through the rain.

He got on the front end of a #2 tram heading away from the city center and bought a ticket from the driver. We boarded from the rear and tapped in with our handy OV chip cards.

As it turned out, we weren't going far.

Most people when they think of The Netherlands picture springtime tulips and heavy wheels of *Edammer kaas* in their waxy red rinds. Me, I conjure up the sour steamy smell and droning clatter of an Amsterdam streetcar in the rain. I mean, they have flowers and cheese in Detroit, but those Dutch trams are unique.

On the aisle, Jet pulled off her cap and shook out her lovely golden mane. She says she does that to keep it from frizzing, but I think she's just showing off. I had the window seat, and I sleeved condensation from the glass so I could see where we were going.

We swung into the Constantijn Huygensstraat and past the narrow entrance to the Vondelpark, stopped at the corner of the Stedelijk Museum to pick up a punk with a spiky green coiffure.

"The thing I like about leather and chains," I murmured, "is they never go out of style."

Jet parted with a courtesy laugh and tucked her arm through mine, leaned over and kissed me on the cheek. "Shut up," she said.

We made a rattling turn into Willemsparkweg, and Piet de Jong reached up and pressed the red button saying he wanted out at the next stop. When he tripped up the three stone steps at number 142 and let himself in, we were twenty yards—no, excuse me, make that nearly twenty meters—behind him.

We crossed the street and ducked into a doorway to get out of the rain and watch. Number 142 was a tall brick house with a squat white step gable, one of the thousands of patrician homes that had sprung up outside the Singelgracht during the eighteenth century. The ground-floor windows were dark. Upstairs—on what the Europeans have for reasons I have never been able to understand call the first floor—flickering lights and shadows told us someone was watching television.

On the second floor, a reddish glow filtered through gauzy white curtains. Suddenly a dim yellow light snapped on, and Jet clutched my elbow.

"That's him," she said.

A taxi hissed past on its way downtown, and when its wake settled we nipped back across the street. There were three buzzers beside the door, and the white paper rectangle next to the top one read "P. de Jong."

Jet hunkered down and wriggled her hand through the mail slot.

The older houses in Amsterdam have this neat little gimmick called a *trekker*, which is a wire that runs from a latch inside your front door up along your staircase wall and into your apartment. When a caller rings your bell, instead of having to trudge all the way downstairs to let them in, you just tug on your *trekker* and the street door below clicks open. It's a clever system, but more often than not it's been laid in sort of carelessly, and there's extra wire dangling down from the latch.

"Can you reach it, hon?"

Her mouth was scrinched up with the strain of making her fingers as flat as a panhandler's wallet. "It's all the *patats met mayonnaise* you eat," I said helpfully. "Goes straight to your fingers, makes 'em fat."

She unscrinched her mouth long enough to stick out her tongue at me before replying. "Me? You're the one who wants to stop at the snack bar every five minutes. Ah, *hebbes!*"

She worked the tail end of the wire through the mail slot and gave it a yank. "Fat fingers," she muttered, and pushed me ahead of her into the building.

We took the stairs in slow motion, hugging the outside wall to keep them from creaking. There was only one apartment to a floor and, sure enough, two flights up we found another card with de Jong's name on it in a little brass holder.

I laid an ear against the door and listened. Soft jazz, a mellow combination of tenor sax and vibes that had to be Stanley

Turrentine and Milt Jackson. I tickled the knob experimentally, but it wouldn't turn.

"*Verdikkemus,*" Jet whispered, coming as close as she ever gets to swearing. She shrugged her slender shoulders and reached for the doorbell, but I caught her hand in time.

"Wait a second," I said.

My Wells Fargo debit card expired not long after I landed in Amsterdam, but the plastic's still good. The lock on de Jong's apartment door was a joke, and it took me all of four seconds to spring it.

"I never leave home without it," I grinned, returning the card to my wallet.

☙

Piet de Jong's living room was what the Dutch call *klein maar fijn*, which the nearest you can get to in English is "good things come in small packages." There wasn't much space, but what there *was* was nicely furnished, with a plush sofa and a comfy leather armchair in front of the windows and hand-tinted reproductions from *Gray's Anatomy* on the walls. That's Gray's with an *a* as in the medical textbook, by the way, not Grey's with an *e* as in the TV show.

A half-open door to our right offered a glimpse of a bedroom. To the left, a closed door probably led to the kitchen. Tall shelves overflowed with books and knickknacks and an expensive stereo system and an impressive collection of record albums and CDs. A walnut stand across from the couch held a television, a DVD player, and a line of keep cases.

The professor was nowhere to be seen, but sitting cross-legged on the thick shag carpeting that stretched from wall to wall was Geja Boorsma, wearing nothing but her creamy white skin and a dreamy expression as she puffed happily on a bubbling hookah and rocked gently back and forth in time with the music.

The air was sweet with strawberry incense and hash. We stood in the doorway, watching her, but her eyes were closed and she obviously had no idea we were there.

So, I thought, so *this* was the new world she was so excited about exploring. Her prof took her off to the Milky Way and got her stoned and brought her home, and all he's had to do since then was *keep* her stoned and he's got himself a live-in model for his anatomical research.

I looked at Jet. In the apartment's dim light, tears had turned her eyes to star sapphires.

"I hate these," I said softly. "I told you, I really *hate* these."

The kitchen door opened, and Piet de Jong backed into the room. He turned around, a pair of crystal glasses in one hand, the bottle of wine in the other. He was still wearing the tweed jacket, but there weren't any leather patches on the elbows, after all. I made a mental note to pay myself the ten Euros I owed me.

He saw us, and the bottle slipped from his fingers. It hit the floor with a *chunk* and tipped over on its side. Wine gurgled, painting the carpet with a bloody stain the next tenant was going to have a hell of a time getting out.

The record ended. The tone arm lifted and swung back to its home position, and the turntable clicked itself off.

"I," the prof explained. "I—"

Jet pulled her fingertips from her eyebrows down across her high cheekbones and sniffed and sighed.

"Dr. de Jong," she said grimly. "Aren't you going to introduce us to your mother?"

OTHER BOOKS BY THIS AUTHOR

First Week Free at the Roomy Toilet
(coming from Level Best Books in February 2024)

The Man Who Wrote Mysteries: The Rest of Brittain
(coming from Crippen & Landru in January 2024)

*Happiness Is a Warm Gun:
Crime Fiction Inspired by the Songs of the Beatles*
(Down and Out Books)

Paranoia Blues: Crime Fiction Inspired by the Songs of Paul Simon
(Down and Out Books)

The Adventures of the Puzzle Club and Other Stories
(Crippen & Landru)

*The Man Who Solved Mysteries:
More Short Fiction by William Brittain*
(Crippen & Landru)

*Monkey Business: Crime Fiction Inspired by the Films of the Marx
Brothers*
(Untreed Reads)

*Only the Good Die Young:
Crime Fiction Inspired by the Songs of Billy Joel*
(Untreed Reads)

*The Great Filling Station Holdup:
Crime Fiction Inspired by the Songs of Jimmy Buffett*
(Down and Out Books)

The Further Misadventures of Ellery Queen
(Wildside Press)

The Misadventures of Nero Wolfe
(Mysterious Press)

The Beat of Black Wings:
Crime Fiction Inspired by the Songs of Joni Mitchell
(Untreed Reads)

Amsterdam Noir
(Akashic Books)

The Man Who Read Mysteries:
The Short Fiction of William Brittain
(Crippen & Landru)

The Misadventures of Ellery Queen
(Wildside Press)

The Tree of Life: The Mahboob Chaudri Stories
(Wildside Press)